DEATH AND BOULES

A FOLLET VALLEY MYSTERY

IAN MOORE

Farrago

First published in 2025 by Farrago, an imprint of Duckworth Books Ltd
1 Golden Court, Richmond, TW9 1EU, United Kingdom

www.farragobooks.com

A catalogue record for this book is available from the British Library

Printed and bound in Great Britain by CPI Ltd, Croydon, CR0 4YY

The authorised representative in the EEA is Easy Access System
Europe, Mustamäe tee 50, 10621 Tallinn, Estonia.

Hardback ISBN: 9781788425155
Trade paperback ISBN: 9781788425179
Ebook ISBN: 9781788425162

Cover design and illustration by Patrick Knowles

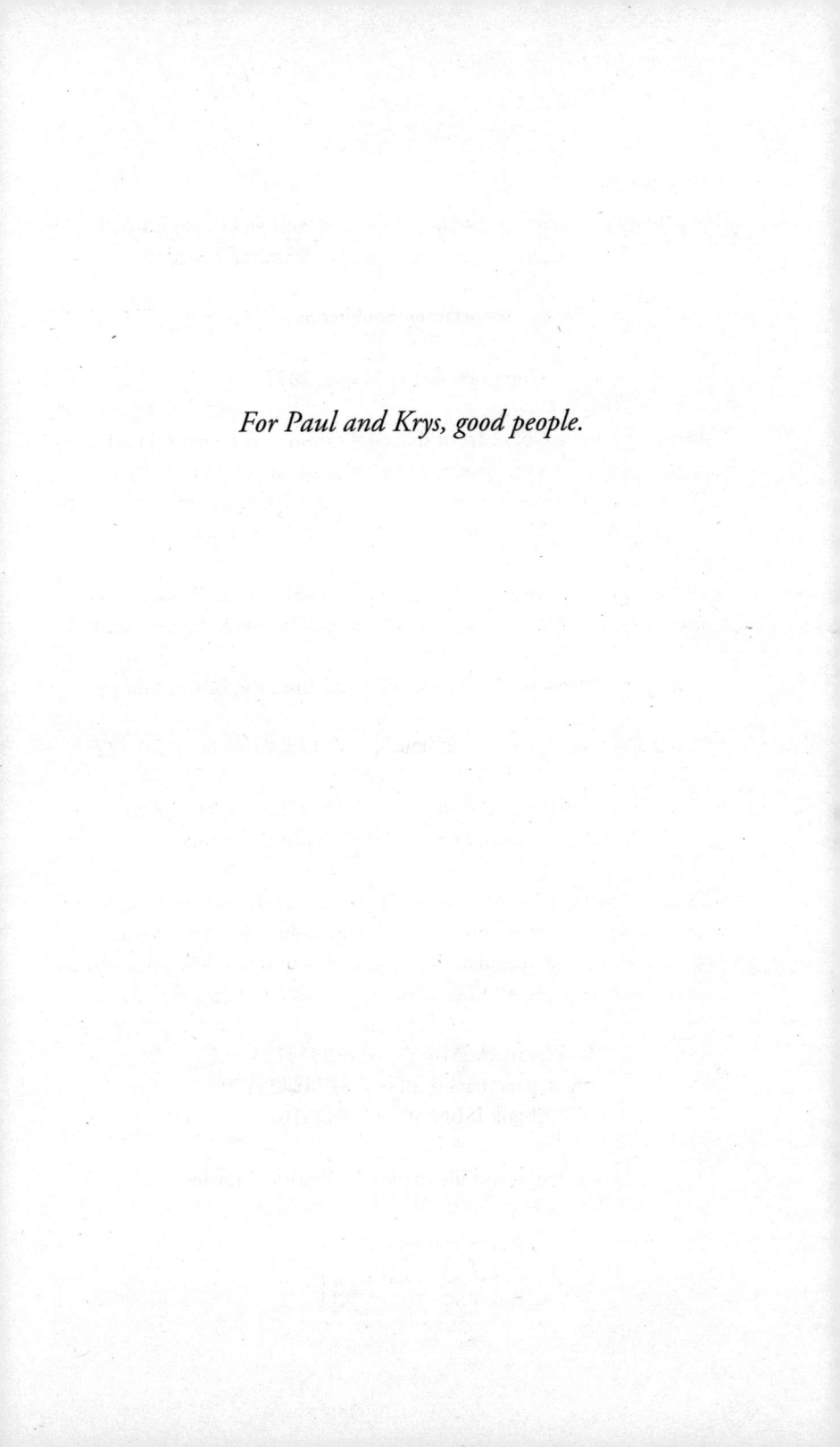

For Paul and Krys, good people.

Chapter One

The excited chatter of the large crowds competed with unbroken birdsong, under the hottest sun anyone could remember for the first of May. It felt almost like a party atmosphere, and the French love a party. The small town of Saint-Sauver in the Follet Valley liked to take the first bank holiday in May seriously and had closed off its centre to road traffic. A large *brocante*, the French version of a car boot sale, had stalls winding through its narrow streets, all under large shade-giving parasols. Accordion music was being piped through discreetly placed speakers hung from lampposts and the mass throng of locals and visitors were treating this as, finally, the day they could safely emerge from a long winter's hibernation. Wine flowed, joy abounded and there wasn't a cloud in the sky.

There was, however, Richard Ainsworth, a localised storm of disgruntlement, who leant moodily on an antique dresser on the one stall without decent shade. In front of him was a trestle table showcasing a low-rent assortment of, in his opinion, whatever the French is for the word 'tat'. It was the usual *brocante* collection, including old plates, mismatched cutlery, beer glasses celebrating the 2014 Tour de France, which had passed close by, some old copies of *Paris Match* from an inelegant era, a selection of vinyl records which Richard had covered before they melted, and some empty tobacco tins. It was hardly the Harrods' sale and Richard resented having been left with it. As a result, in his hand was a plastic goblet of rosé and on his face a look designed to repel any potential price hagglers.

'*C'est combien?*' A tiny old woman wearing a hairnet and with a prominent bouquet of lily of the valley tucked into her housecoat as is May the first tradition, stood on the other side of the stall and picked up a chipped porcelain candlestick holder, thrusting it at Richard in menacing fashion.

'Fifty centimes,' Richard replied, eliciting a sharp intake of breath from the woman.

'For that?' she spat. 'I'll give you thirty centimes and not a *sous* more!'

Richard sighed heavily, trying to avoid the temptation to just smash the thing on the floor and nip this absurd trade in the bud. 'It's not my stall,' he said for about the four hundredth time that morning. 'I'm looking after it for Mayor Planchet… if he ever turns up.'

The old woman turned the thing over in her hand and gave Richard a look suggesting he was attempting to rob her blind. 'Thirty-five centimes,' she said eventually. 'That's my final offer.'

'Oh just bloody have it!' he whined and the old woman, not needing to be told twice, pocketed the candlestick holder and skipped off without a word. 'No, *merci* to you!' he called after her, before taking a sip of his wine.

'You cannot just give things away, Monsieur Ainsworth.' The voice came from somewhere under Richard's chin.

'That is fifty centimes less for our charity collection.' Without taking his eyes off the much smaller Noel Mabit, the town's bullying senior bureaucrat, Richard silently fished out a fifty-centime piece from his trouser pocket and threw it into the virtually empty ice cream tub that was doubling as a cash till.

'There,' he said quietly, trying to hold his temper together, 'we wouldn't want the Veterans of Viticulture to go hungry now, would we?'

Noel, his slicked-back grey hair glinting in the sun, put his glasses on and peered into the ice cream tub, making obvious signs of mental arithmetic. Then he fished out two coins and gave them to Richard, a look of prissy one-up-manship on his face. 'Here is fifteen centimes. I believe the final price was thirty-five.'

'How kind. I'll go and buy a tenth of a croissant.'

If Noel was aware of the sarcasm, he didn't show it. 'There is now a cash float of twenty-seven euros and thirty-five centimes.' He arched an eyebrow at Richard. 'We started with ten. I made a sale of seventeen euros and you have contributed just thirty-five centimes in revenue.'

'You sold something for seventeen euros?' Looking at the wares on offer, Richard was astonished.

'It pays to arrive early at a *brocante*, Monsieur Ainsworth.' With that Mabit strolled off into the crowds, looking right and left, his hands behind his back, like an army colonel inspecting his troops.

'When's the mayor going to get here?' Richard called after him. 'I've got things to do, you know?' Noel Mabit ignored him and was swallowed into the crowd.

'What have you got to do, Richard? Are you not enjoying yourself?' Richard spilled his wine as Valérie d'Orçay, as she so often did, sneaked up on him when he least expected it, and when any semblance of dignity was draining away from him, like dishwater around a plughole. The woman had a habit of just appearing and no matter how often it happened, it still unnerved him. He knew it was part of her training, from her beginnings in the French secret service to her current role as one of Europe's leading bounty hunters and, if the rumours were true, assassin, but he could never get used to it. How could someone who, dressed as she was in a tight black T-shirt, red capri pants, expensive shoulder bag and with throwback glamorous good looks suddenly spring from nowhere like that? She stood out a country mile in these rural surroundings even before you noticed her chihuahua, Passepartout, asleep in a bejewelled dog carrier.

'I haven't got anything to do, have I?' he moaned. 'As well you know. Our business is flatlining.' They kissed in the traditional cheek-to-cheek manner, and did so warmly, though not as warmly as Richard would have liked.

'Something will turn up, I am sure.' She smiled her perfect smile and swished her hair out of her face. 'It is only a couple of weeks since our last investigation, remember; even our Les Vignes Detective Agency needs a holiday, no? And today is a holiday in France.'

Richard understood that, but he was thinking more long term, which he knew Valérie never did, as she was hard-wired to concentrate only on the now. He had explained the significance of the day to some English guests at his bed and breakfast that morning when they heard that there would likely be no vineyards open for a wine-tasting. 'May the first is a double celebration,' he had patiently begun, warming up into his tourist *spiel*. 'It's a day off for International Workers' Day and it's the Lily of the Valley Day, when men present women with a small bunch of *muguet* to wish them luck. Not only that, this year the bank holiday has fallen on a Thursday which means everyone will take Friday off as well.'

The look of horror on his guests' faces suggested that they couldn't possibly go more than a day without getting sloshed at a vineyard, and Richard had had to reassure them that the Friday would be unofficial and, really, only the bureaucrats wouldn't be at work, much to the benefit of France as a whole.

Valérie had been referring of course to their recent case of murder in nearby La Chapelle-sur-Follet, something they had resolved successfully but which Richard now preferred not to dwell on. One of the initial suspects, the famous singer and self-described 'activist', Oriane Moulin, had actively and mischievously found one of Valérie's numerous ex-husbands. 'Found' being the important word for Richard, as he wasn't sure anyone had actually been looking. A beleaguered and war-torn Edmond Masson had duly arrived, and where this placed the fate of subsequent ex-husbands of Valérie, Richard didn't know. If Edmond Masson was, for example, husband number four, he wasn't sure of the actual figures. Where did that leave five and six, or seven and eight for that matter, not just in their order of appearance, but legally? What he did know was that it put him very much on his business partner's romantic back burner, just as he'd begun to think that he was finally getting somewhere.

'You have your *chambre d'hôte* to occupy you, Richard; that's good, yes?' He had noticed in the last couple of weeks and since her husband had re-emerged her frequent attempts to bolster his confidence. Much as he appreciated the effort, it made no difference whatsoever, only serving as a reminder that his fragile ego had taken an absolute battering. A reminder that even if she and Edmond were married, the stone cold truth of the matter was that in a romantic duel – that was how he saw it – he had lost out to an eyepatch-wearing, limping shell of a man, albeit a war hero. Also, Valérie just wasn't very good at ego boosting. For the most part, she had a cold, clinical mind and usually said the first thing that came into it. She would work hard to give with one hand, then instinct could very rapidly take it back.

'I do have my *chambre d'hôte*, yes.' He was trying to sound stoic.

'For now anyway,' she said. There it was, the brutal honesty of the emotional *idiot savant*.

'Yes. For now.'

'I mean once the divorce with your wife comes through and Madame Tablier buys her out…'

'Yes, yes, yes,' Richard interrupted irritably. It was his estranged wife Clare who was now stalling on the divorce; not that Richard was in any hurry himself for financial reasons, but her solicitor – and former boyfriend – had just been arrested for fraud with menaces and that had put a stop to the paperwork. Madame Tablier, Richard's housekeeper at the *chambre d'hôte*, had offered to buy her out, but Clare turned out not to be very keen on the idea, realising that she still had an asset and some leverage. It all left Richard feeling that there were three women in control of his life and that he was just wheeled out ceremonially from time to time like a constitutional monarch. He decided to change the subject.

'How's your business doing? Snatched any good dictators lately?'

If she heard the question, she ignored it. 'There is Edmond!' she said, waving to her husband across the narrow street. This woke Passepartout, who opened his eyes and, upon seeing Richard, closed them again. The small dog responded to Edmond Masson's back-scratching stroke though when he drew closer to them. *Fickle*, thought Richard. *Even the dog's knocked me back.* He tried not to look as Valérie and Edmond kissed a greeting, but he couldn't help but search for any indications that things weren't going as they should. Surely, if your supposedly dead husband turns up alive after twenty years, it's going to put something of a strain on the relationship. It was noticeable that they weren't living together anyway. Not yet at least. Edmond was staying at another bed and breakfast, this one owned by Richard's friends – though he preferred the term 'acquaintances' – Martin and Gennie Thompson. He didn't mind that at all; if Martin and Gennie's shameless sideline in erotic tourism didn't cause awkward marital moments, Richard didn't know what could. He certainly hoped it would.

'Good morning, Richard.' Edmond held out a gloved hand, the visible sign of yet another injury the man was carrying, but his smile was warm. He had forsaken the eyepatch for a pair of large, dark sunglasses, making his face look like that of a bee but – and this in particular upset Richard – his charm was genuine and Richard liked him. Not the thought of him, obviously, not the fact of him, but as a person he was very likeable. Also, he was yet another secret service trained killer, and it didn't do to upset secret service trained killers.

'*Bonjour*, Edmond, how are you today? Can I interest you in someone else's old rubbish?'

Edmond smiled; unlike his wife, he had a sense of humour. 'You never know, Richard, someone may uncover a gem today. It happens.' He wagged a gloved finger at Richard in mock admonishment.

'Maybe they did once,' Richard replied, 'but I can't see it happening nowadays. Not unless bottle tops, rusty spanners and scratched Johnny Hallyday LPs are taking the antiques world by storm.'

'*C'est combien?*' They were interrupted by an elderly man in blue dungarees who held up a faded insurance company keyring and a ten-centimes coin.

'You can have it.' Richard shrugged. The man gave a toothless grin and moved off. 'Don't let me keep you two here in the world of high finance,' he said, immediately castigating himself for making their life together easier. A proper man, or at least a good old-fashioned cad would be throwing his rusty little spanners into the marital works, but Richard knew that he just wasn't like that. He would just have to accept defeat the only way he knew how. Internally.

'Are you coming to watch the *boules* match after lunch?' Valérie asked. 'There is a team from England I am told.'

He smiled. Again, she was trying to look after him, almost mother him and it didn't really suit her. 'If I can get away from this stall, I will. The mayor is supposed to be running it, it's his stuff after all. No one's seen him though. I know the man falls asleep at the drop of a hat, but you'd think he'd make an effort on the town's big day.'

'I am sure he will turn up, Richard,' Valérie said softly, before she and Edmond walked off. *Was there a slight gap between them as they walked?* he asked himself. *And wasn't Edmond Masson limping on the other leg last week?*

'*C'est combien?*'

Richard reluctantly turned back to the stall.

Chapter Two

Richard looked at his watch again, a show of very-English petulance if anyone had been taking notice but also a futile gesture as time in rural France, like time on a deserted island, means very little. The pace of life was what had attracted him to Follet Valley in the first place, and he knew that to complain about its charms now would fall on deaf ears, or, as was more likely the case, no ears at all as no one would be listening. The crowds had thinned out as lunchtime approached, as French crowds do, but Richard had remained at his post. The so far unexplained absence of Mayor Narcisse Planchet would not dim Richard's civic duty, only heighten his blood pressure. He knew the mayor would need to show his face at some point, if only in a ceremonial manner just like Richard at his bed and breakfast – everybody in the town knew that it was really Noel Mabit who ran things.

Many years ago it had been Noel, a fledgling bureaucrat looking to make his name, who had come up with the idea of Saint-Sauver's May the first celebrations. And the crowds this year were testament to how successful the whole idea had been. Hundreds of *brocante* pitches were booked well in advance and thousands of punters

– somehow desperate for what might ordinarily, and in Richard's view with good reason, be thrown into a landfill site – came from miles around. René's bar and restaurant, the Café des Tasses Cassées, was booked up weeks ahead; Jeanine's *boulangerie* took on extra staff and the Sharifi brothers, Taz and Shilal, whose first year this was, had been pre-warned and had doubled the stock in their mini-market. Richard, though he wouldn't openly admit it, was proud to be involved. He liked to make a show of hanging around on the edges of life, but this life, this rural French existence suited him. As an 'outsider' he could dip in and out as he chose, and the addition of Valérie in the last couple of years had given him a certain cachet too. He liked to think that it left people wondering if there wasn't actually a lot more to Richard Ainsworth than first met the eye. He secretly revelled in this potential exoticism even if, in truth, there really wasn't more to Richard Ainsworth than first met the eye at all and that suited him just as well. The appearance of Edmond Masson, however, had tarnished that fragile image, and Richard now felt that he struck a slightly tragic figure. Lonely, sad and cuckolded. He was actually none of those things, but that's how he felt he was being perceived. He had even given thought to moving on. He stood tall and proud as the thought took hold again, holding his stomach in and lifting his chin. He fancied himself as the hero cowboy; he had run the rustlers out of town and handed Valérie back to her man, where he knew she belonged. He'd now ride off into the sunset, like Alan Ladd at the end of the classic Western *Shane*...

Who am I kidding? he thought. *I don't even like horses. Or Westerns. And even Alan Ladd was only about five foot three. They had to dig trenches for his leading ladies to stand in opposite him.*

The thought inevitably led to him pondering his film viewing options for later that evening. As a former film historian, whose knowledge had been superseded by the internet, they were obviously plentiful but he liked his viewing choice to reflect his mood. A man on his own clearly suggested a Humphrey Bogart classic, *Casablanca* where he gives up the 'dame' for instance. But he was feeling more wistful than that; he had reached a crossroads in his life, another one, so he needed a character closer to his state of mind and background. Trevor Howard, the doomed lover in *Brief Encounter*; James Mason, the flawed former great in *A Star is Born*. Yes, he definitely felt more English stiff upper lip right now, less American private eye. His daydreaming was interrupted by a loud cough that projected itself through the town speakers. Noel Mabit cleared his throat. '*Mesdames et messieurs,*' he began. 'No, don't touch that,' he said quietly and presumably to a colleague. 'Welcome to the Saint-Sauver Fête de Printemps. We have once again been blessed with beautiful weather – I said don't touch that – I hope you will enjoy yourself today. This is just a quick reminder that on Sunday we will have our twentieth Saint-Sauver *boules* tournament in the er, well in the *boules piste* naturally. We have an all-star professional team up from Avignon in Provence this year, an English team from our twin-town of Anglethorp Spa and our very own Saint-Sauver stars.' He coughed again.

'Er, we hope to see you there. Right, now you can touch it. Oh, no, one more thing. Could Mayor Planchet report to the town hall, please?'

The Saint-Sauver *boules* tournament had quickly become a tradition, and like all traditions, old or young, was strictly observed. This year was particularly special in that it marked the twenty-fifth anniversary of the town-twinning between Saint-Sauver and the English seaside town of Anglethorp Spa in Lincolnshire. The team, like Edmond Masson, were staying at Martin and Gennie's bed and breakfast as they already had a *boules piste* installed in their garden. Why you needed to practise at *boules*, Richard wasn't sure. Whenever he'd played the game he was usually a good way into a bottle of pastis and just threw the balls in the general direction of the jack. Martin and Gennie took the game very seriously, however, and had even decided to dampen down some of their more flamboyant pastimes for the duration of the team's stay.

'Just in case they're not, you know...' Martin had explained glumly, like a little boy who's had his football confiscated.

'Perverts?' Valérie had helpfully suggested.

Richard smiled at the memory. He hadn't yet met the English team. He hadn't for that matter met the local Saint-Sauver team either as it usually just consisted of whoever was still upright after a long lunch, but he assumed that Noel had that all under control. He had seen some of the team from Avignon, the Avignon Arrivistes, staying at René's place and apparently they were the Harlem Globetrotters of the *boules* world. They had arrived in a sponsored team minibus, occasionally wore matching tracksuits and took themselves very seriously indeed, even ostentatiously practising some form of Tai Chi in the market square. He couldn't for the life of him believe that fitness would be an issue in the matter, but live and let live was his new way of thinking; let it be. He wasn't either, if he were honest, aware that *boules* would warrant an all-star team but the names had caused some animated discussion already in the *boulangerie* queue, where gossip was principally spread.

'I brought you some lunch, Richard.' He turned to see a smiling Valérie with a *saucisse* baguette in one hand and a small tray of chips in the other. She made an incongruous sight holding the food at arm's length, looking like an advert for a 1950s American diner.

'Thank you,' he said, a little too stiffly. He hadn't meant to sound like that, but the stiff upper lip had taken hold and there was no denying that their relationship was more awkward than before her husband had turned up and sometimes he just couldn't help himself.

'I put a lot of tomato ketchup in,' she said, showing her disdain at the thought. 'I know that you like it like that.'

'Thank you,' he repeated. And took the food from her, placing both hot dog and chips on the dresser.

'Is that thing for sale?' She looked dubiously at the ugly piece of furniture.

'Yes, apparently. The mayor must have been having a right old clear-out.'

'Before he ran away, you mean?' She looked at him with deadly seriousness.

He leant in closely and kept his voice down. 'Do you really think he's run away?'

'No!' She laughed. 'I do not even think the silly man exists! I am not sure that I have ever actually seen him.'

'Shame. We really could do with the business. Chip?'

Her face creased into disgust.

'Monsieur Ainsworth, please do not put food on that antique *buffet*!' Noel Mabit's admonishment rang through the town speakers like the voice of God. Richard looked guiltily into the clear blue sky wondering if the little man had reached uber-bureaucrat status and gone into pen-pushing omnipresence, before finally noticing Noel at his side, holding a wireless microphone at his chin, his face flushed with outrage.

'I thought you were supposed to put food on a *buffet*!' Valérie sprang sharply to Richard's defence, taking the wind out of Noel's sails. 'If you call that food, which I do not.'

'Yes, well…' he began, before remembering the microphone, which he now lowered. 'I'm merely protecting the mayor's property.'

'Where is old Planchet anyway?' Richard asked. 'Has he fallen asleep somewhere? That's normally the case.'

'I am sure he is doing his job.' Noel stiffened at the suggestion that Mayor Planchet wasn't up to scratch as an official.

'You don't know where he is, do you?' Valérie pounced.

'No,' the defeated factotum admitted, before returning the microphone to his chin and turning sharply on his heels. The speakers blurted into action. 'Ladies and gentlemen, as a special treat there will be a short exhibition *boules* match starting in five minutes. Avignon Arrivistes will play Anglethorp Spartans. Five minutes everyone!'

'I should go and find Edmond,' Valérie said, leaving Richard to wonder if there was a trace of guilt in her voice. 'He likes *boules*...'

'Who doesn't?' interrupted Martin Thompson, a salacious edge to his question. He had a talent, if that's the right word, for double-entendre that bordered on the heroic. Yet to look at him and his wife Gennie, you wouldn't guess their deviant proclivities at all. Valérie tutted at Martin as she left and gave Gennie a sympathetic look. The Thompsons were wearing matching baseball caps with Saint-Sauver stitched into the front and a rather dubious image of a pair of *boules* alongside a baguette. Martin preened his tidy military-esque moustache, trying to force Richard to make a comment while Gennie smiled sweetly at him, a look suggesting butter wouldn't even think of melting in her mouth.

'Have you seen the English team, Richard?' she asked anxiously. 'We seem to have lost them.'

Richard shook his head as he bit into his sandwich. 'Sorry,' he said through a mouthful of barbecued sausage. 'I don't actually know what they look like.'

'Oh you can't miss them,' Martin said with a look of distaste, 'they stand out rather.' Richard considered this a bit rich coming from a man sporting Martin's headgear but he let it go.

'There's four of them,' Gennie offered helpfully. 'Two men and two women, the older one looks like that actress.' She gave no other information than that and even Richard, with his encyclopaedic knowledge of film, was struggling.

'Which actress?' he asked eventually, realising that Gennie considered she had already given sufficient data.

'You know, she was in that thing!'

Martin rolled his eyes apologetically at Richard.

'What thing?'

'You know!'

'Probably, yes.'

'She means Angela Lansbury. She looks like the *Murder, She Wrote* woman.'

'And she's even called Angela! Which is a lovely coincidence.'

Not enough of a coincidence to actually jog your memory, Richard thought. Out loud he rattled off Angela Lansbury's screen credits, which kept Martin and Gennie out of the conversation for a good couple of minutes.

'She's here with her niece, Olivia.'

'She doesn't look like anyone,' Gennie offered with a touch of disappointment.

'One of the men is called Roddy,' Martin said. 'Very tall chap, very long arms. Posh, wears a lot of tweed. Has ginger hair too, looks like a tree in autumn.' Richard had an image in his head of an aristocratic orangutan and he felt sure he would have seen this Roddy.

'And the other is Derek.' This time it was Gennie who couldn't hide her distaste. Martin made a low rumbling sound, indicating his agreement on the subject.

'You don't like him?' Richard asked, surprised. He'd never known Martin and Gennie to have a bad word to say about anyone.

'He gives me the creeps,' Gennie said, conspiratorially.

Again, Richard was surprised. For someone whose life partner was Martin he'd have thought that the bar on Gennie's creep level would be set pretty high.

17

They were interrupted again by the loudspeaker system. 'Ladies and gentlemen,' – it was Noel still in microphone control – 'we have our two teams here.'

'Oh, they must have found where to go then,' Gennie said, her beaming smile returning. 'Let's go, Martin, I want to watch. Are you coming, Richard?'

Richard took another mouthful of hot dog and shook his head. 'I can't really leave this. If you find the mayor, drag him over here, will you?'

'Unfortunately, Mayor Planchet is indisposed.' Noel's voice rang out. 'But we should see him later.' He went on to needlessly explain the rules of *boules* to the mostly French crowd, before introducing the teams. Richard couldn't see anything from his position behind the crowd, except for Noel, who had naturally given himself a raised stage so, as absolutely no one was looking in his direction, he climbed on to the dresser to get a better view of proceedings. The all-star Avignon team were an eclectic bunch, with the tall ladies' world champion from Mali standing out especially as she stood next to another woman so old she might have been there at the birth of the sport, and was sitting on a walking frame with a seat. All four were in their matching outfits too and looked slightly sinister as a result, rather than athletic. The tall Roddy stood out on the English team; Angela did indeed look like Angela Lansbury and the third, who he assumed was Derek, stood slightly apart, a bright tartan tam-o'-shanter covering his head.

The crowd cheered as the *cochonnet*, the jack, was thrown ceremoniously by Noel from his perch to herald the start of the match, and Richard joined in the applause.

Unfortunately, he lost his footing as he did so, slipped on his tray of heavily sauced chips and came crashing down to the ground, bringing a selection of the mayor's cast-offs down with him. The crowd all turned around as one to see what the commotion was, as a red-faced but physically unharmed Richard grabbed a handle on the dresser cupboard door to pull himself up. The door opened halting his progress but freeing its contents. A thin, bare arm flopped out of the now open dresser, an arm attached to a body. Someone screamed and the loudspeakers fuzzed. 'Mayor Planchet!' Noel exclaimed into the microphone.

Chapter Three

A police cordon had been hastily erected around Richard's stall. Until a forensics tent could arrive, however, the dresser, still containing the body of Mayor Planchet, lay under some vintage linen bought for a knockdown price of five euros from a nearby seller. The seller hadn't been happy about the price but the weary officialdom of Commissaire Henri Lapierre had convinced her to take the hit this time for the common good. The Commissaire, looking tanned, nevertheless wore a fatalistic expression as he regarded Richard, who was shakily sipping from a restorative goblet of rosé.

'Do you ever think, monsieur,' – the Commissaire sighed through his bushy moustache that for once didn't contain fragments of food – 'that you are quite simply a magnet for trouble?'

'Just unlucky I guess,' Richard mumbled. He felt guilty that just half an hour earlier he'd been keen to drum up some business for himself and Valérie and all the while he'd been effectively trying to sell off a corpse as he did so. And not just any old corpse either, an officially elected one. These things are not taken lightly in small town France.

'Oh, Henri, it is not Richard's fault!' Valérie was not only defending Richard but attacking the policeman. He was another ex-husband, possibly the original if Richard's chronology was correct, but was treated with no greater respect for that.

'How do you know it was not his fault, Madame d'Orçay? Can you vouch for his movements all day, or even last night?' His eyes narrowed and after Valérie fell silent, there was a brief look of triumph on his face.

'I have been away for two weeks,' he said, strolling in a circle within the cordon and pointing at anything in his eyeline, starting with Richard and Valérie. 'Two weeks of fishing heaven. I am relaxed. I say to myself, I am refreshed, I can go back to work...' He shook his head sadly. 'I did not even get to start my lunchtime meal!' His voice was raised dramatically but the pointing finger finished unfortunately on Passepartout who bared his teeth aggressively.

The loudspeakers coughed into action once more. 'Ladies and gentlemen,' – it was inevitably Noel Mabit – 'this unfortunate turn of events means that the *brocante* is now closed. The police will be in charge of your exit, but we will reconvene for the *brocante* some time in the future! Er, I hope.'

If Commissaire Lapierre was indeed refreshed after a fortnight's fishing, it would be short-lived. Richard could almost see the hope and verve physically leaving the man's body; he seemed to shrivel slightly.

'Doctor!' he snapped at a man approaching carrying a medical bag. 'It is about time!'

'I was finishing my lunch, Commissaire,' the heavyset medic shot back in outrage. The belief that even the untimely death of a local dignitary shouldn't interrupt a French lunch was a strong one. 'I have my own health to think about,' the man added petulantly.

The watching crowd seemed to take a step forward as the doctor approached the dresser, straining the police tape cordon. 'You two!' Lapierre barked at Richard and Valérie. 'I want you each to take the end of the sheet and hold it up as a screen; let's give the mayor some privacy and the doctor some space to digest his lunch.'

'I cannot do that and hold Passepartout, Henri.' Valérie didn't offer it as an excuse, more a verbal brick wall. This time the policeman sighed so heavily through his nose that his moustache rippled.

'Maybe I can help?' Edmond Masson called from the other side of the cordon peering around one of the guarding *gendarmes*.

'Good idea.' Valérie sounded like a schoolteacher.

'And who are you?' The Commissaire's eyes narrowed again. 'Come forward.'

'I am Edmond Masson,' was the reply. He limped towards the official and took Passepartout from Valérie.

'You are Edmond Masson,' repeated Lapierre. 'But who is Edmond Masson?'

'I am Valérie's husband.'

'You are Valérie's husband.'

'I just said that.'

'I know you just said that,' the Commissaire snapped. He then turned his gaze on Valérie, who shrugged a touch guiltily in Richard's eyes, or maybe that was wishful thinking. 'Do not go too far, Monsieur Masson. I don't like strangers who appear at the same time as a dead body.'

It was Edmond's turn to shrug. 'You're the stranger. I've been here the past two weeks.'

It was not the best of starts to what would undoubtedly be an uncomfortable acquaintanceship and Valérie knew it. Silently she handed Richard one end of the large white sheet and they stood apart holding the inadequate screen while the doctor peered into the dresser.

The Commissaire paced up and down on the crowd side of the protective barrier, watched intently by the gathered crowd. He stopped briefly by Valérie and leant in. 'He is your husband?'

'Yes,' she replied, not looking at him.

He turned and walked the other way, towards Richard. 'He is her husband?' he whispered.

'So I'm told.' Richard was fortitude personified.

'You do not believe it?' The policeman immediately latched on to the doubt.

Richard shrugged.

Lapierre went back to Valérie. 'May I ask when…?'

'He was after you, Henri, a long time after you.' Some posture returned to Lapierre at this information and he strode more purposefully back to Richard.

'And where does this leave you, monsieur?' There was no mockery in his voice, no edge, but Richard felt the need to respond impassively, like the still saluting captain of a sinking ship going down with the fleet. Noël

Coward, in *In Which We Serve*, sprung to mind and his reply was clipped and brooked no discussion.

'Currently it leaves me holding antique linen to hide a corpse. There is very little room for other thoughts.' He looked coldly into the distance.

A strange noise came from the other side of the curtain, a throaty, mournful sigh. 'Ah,' – the Commissaire shook his head sadly – '*le râle d'agonie*, the death rattle. When the body is moved…' He shrugged as he tailed off and the three of them looked at the ground as a mark of respect for the late Mayor Planchet.

'No, sorry, that was me,' a bilious doctor apologised. 'Oysters always repeat on me.' He burped again.

Lapierre rolled his eyes and shook his head; Sisyphus himself had nothing on the policeman's toils. 'Will this take much longer, Doctor? I would like to move the body and then the crowds will clear.'

'You may as well get on with it then. But it will take a while for forensics to get here I'd have thought.' The doctor poked his head around the edge of Richard's end of the sheet. 'Either way, I can't very well examine a man in a cupboard, can I?'

'What can you tell us for now?' Lapierre was fighting to control his temper.

'Well,' the doctor pulled off his gloves. 'He's been dead at least twelve hours and stabbed in the neck.'

'And is this knife, the murder weapon, still in the neck?'

'Oh, it wasn't a knife,' the doctor replied. 'It was one of these.' From his jacket pocket he produced a ballpoint pen and needlessly clicked it on and off.

'You have removed the murder weapon?' Lapierre's indignation was clear.

'No, this is mine, we all got one.' He held the pen up higher, so that the Commissaire could get a closer look. Richard immediately recognised it. A commemorative ballpoint pen with Saint-Sauver written on one side of the tubing and *Brocante et Tournoi de Boules – 20 ans* on the other. The doctor clicked his pen again and stood in full view of the crowd. 'Like I said, we all got one.' And to confirm what he said dozens of ballpoint pens were fished out and clicked simultaneously by the numerous and rapt onlookers. Richard thought the Commissaire might wilt at that point, but maybe to save his blushes Valérie let go of her end of the linen sheet, leaving Richard and the two officials momentarily trapped in what looked like a ghost wrestling match.

Eventually, and with little dignity, they managed to disengage themselves, letting the sheet drop to the ground. Valérie was peering in at the dead body of Mayor Planchet.

'Madame d'Orçay!' Lapierre was struggling to regain his composure and the sight of his ex-wife potentially messing with a murdered man and evidence was almost too much for him. 'This is a police investigation, not a place for amateurs. Kindly step away from that dead mayor.'

Valérie slowly rose to her feet and, though Richard couldn't say where she'd got them from, began to remove her own rubber gloves. 'I agree twelve to fifteen hours.' She snapped off the first glove. 'Also, stabbed in the neck with a pen.' She took out her own pen and clicked it, much to the Commissaire's annoyance.

'There you go,' said the doctor. 'You needn't have called me after all!'

'But the pen did not kill Mayor Planchet,' Valérie continued. 'The pen was driven into the mayor's neck well after death.'

'Yes, well I was just coming to that!' The doctor, like all put-upon officials, puffed his chest out at the slightest hint of incompetence. 'You see there…'

'…isn't enough blood.' Richard finished the man's sentence for him, not in any competitive way, he was merely thinking aloud and on to an obvious conclusion.

Valérie snapped her second glove off. 'Brilliant, Richard!' she said, and gave an admonishing glance to both the doctor and to the Commissaire, signalling her thoughts on their competence.

'Well, obviously.' The doctor rolled his eyes. 'But I can't tell you what killed him yet, can I? We need a full examination.' He smirked at Lapierre. 'Honestly.' He tutted and made an odd attempt at a giggle, making a gross error of judgement that the policeman knew better than to play along with.

'You did not notice a smell, Monsieur le Docteur?' The tone in Valérie's voice would have told any sensible person, and certainly a puffed-up official, to pipe down and just keep quiet for a moment. The doctor didn't know Valérie d'Orçay.

'A smell?' he repeated, almost mocking her tone. 'Of course I noticed a smell. The distinct smell of garlic. It is nothing, madame, it was my lunchtime *amuse bouche* of heavily garlicked snail butter. There is no conspiracy there!' Again, he smirked at the Commissaire expecting support against this amateur sleuth.

'No, Doctor, not your distasteful lunch which you have managed to breathe all over a murder scene.' Richard could tell that Valérie was regretting snapping off both rubber gloves as she was moving inexorably towards a stunning indictment of the medical man's working practices, and the whip-crack of a third glove would been a perfect accompaniment. He also noticed Commissaire Henri Lapierre take a couple of steps away from the doctor as a symbolic disassociation from the man, as did most of the crowd including, Richard noticed, Edmond.

'All I can smell is garlic.' The doctor was sullen, sensing an ignominious defeat.

'That is because you are a Frenchman at lunchtime,' Valérie countered. 'And no better than a dog hunting truffles!' There was a murmur in the crowd as dozens of Frenchmen either concurred or took offence, while also remembering that they were indeed hungry.

Richard, tired of standing on the fringes, approached the dresser and the flopped corpse of Mayor Planchet. 'Is that perfume?' he asked. To be honest, he'd been smelling it all morning but assumed it was from the stall next door, which was selling empty perfume bottles.

Valérie beamed at him. 'Brilliant, Richard! And do you know which perfume?'

'I'll leave it to you to tell the Commissaire,' he said, successfully dodging the question.

'Caron Muguet du Bonheur!' she said triumphantly. 'A vintage lily of the valley scent. Our mayor was poisoned with a 1980s perfume.'

The crowd of onlookers looked first at their traditional bouquets of the toxic *muguet* and then at Valérie who stood in triumph with two officials slumped defeatedly in front of her and the dead mayor slumped behind her. Then, as one, they broke into applause, the embarrassment of officialdom far outweighing their horror at the scene.

'Can I go and finish my lunch now?' a contrite doctor asked the red-faced Commissaire.

Chapter Four

As much as he had been able to over the course of the next hour, the Commissaire had made a pretty good fist of things. He had at least been *seen* to have made a pretty good fist of things anyway, which as a public official is ninety per cent of the job. The remaining ten per cent wasn't the point, but satisfying the taxpayer in terms of visible effort certainly was. With just a few officers he had corralled the large crowd out through one exit and had all the names taken with proof of ID and contact details. Each stallholder and their stall had been photographed before then being told to clear away and their IDs were also logged. It was efficiently done. A smattering of the crowd complained, though most were resigned to the inevitability of bureaucracy acting as a self-important emergency service. Some were just enjoying the excitement and the drama of it all, but one, however, was stamping her foot and shaking her head.

'Honestly, Henri, he has been dead for fifteen hours!' Valérie was like a pressure cooker close to bursting. 'The baby has already hit the tiles!'

Richard was a fan of French idioms. It's raining rope, as opposed to cats and dogs; to have mustard up your nose instead of losing your temper and so on, but shutting the stable door after the horse has bolted is a far more agreeable image than a baby hitting tiles. This was certainly not the time to argue the point, however, as Lapierre sighed so long and heavily it was like a desert mistral.

'Presumably, Madame Masson,' he said pointedly, 'you have a better idea at this stage?'

The effect of using Valérie's latest old married name was immediate. Her whole body seemed to wince. There was the pain of hers and Lapierre's shared history coming to this, for sure, but Richard sensed it was far more than that. If Valérie was anything, and to Richard she was a whole lot of things, then above all she was a proudly and fiercely independent woman. She was now being seen as an appendage and Henri had known that would hurt.

'I am Valérie d'Orçay,' she said quietly, though with a low rumble of menace under the words. It was also, Richard felt, a reminder to herself, maybe even a wake-up call. He had never seen her this close to breaking point.

'Madame Ma… Valérie…' The Commissaire perhaps felt he had gone too far and opened his arms wide partly in defence, but partly in a gesture of appeasement. 'Please, I beg you. Wait with the others at René's bar. I will join you all there shortly.' He turned away before she could reply and started giving unnecessary orders to a uniformed policeman.

Valérie remained standing quite still. Whatever was going on inside her – and Richard guessed it would be a cross between an earthquake, a tsunami and the Big Bang – she was determined to get it under control. This only made him worry more. He wasn't used to seeing Valérie trying to control her emotions; he didn't honestly think her capable of doing so, and he got the distinct impression that he was getting a front-row view of the working Valérie d'Orçay. The cool-eyed bounty hunter, the cold – alleged – assassin. It made him shiver. She suddenly seemed to notice him staring at her and her eyes blinked at a decision made, before her face broke out into the most beautiful, isn't life wonderful smile.

She put her arm through his and walked him towards René's bar. 'I am so sorry, Richard,' she oozed. 'To discover a body like that, it must have been quite a shock for you.'

He could have answered that it wasn't nearly as much of a shock as the look he had just seen in her eyes and he was aware also that she was piling on the sympathy, not a natural emotion for her. But he was also Richard, a middle-aged man separated from his wife, most of the world and quite often reality itself, so sympathy, false or otherwise, was always welcome.

'Oh well, you know…' he said, trying to brush it off airily.

She stopped walking suddenly then nudged him forcibly back towards his stall. 'We must take a look for ourselves while we have the chance,' she hissed, though loudly enough to wake the dead in Richard's view.

He thought about putting up a fight, dragging her away before they both got into trouble or, in his case, more trouble. But he also sensed an opportunity. That their relationship had been slightly distant since her supposedly dead husband had reappeared was, he was prepared to concede, only natural, but this was at least a chance to get the working side of things back on track. He nodded at her seriously, giving his approval, but she hadn't been paying attention.

'Oh come on, Richard!' she pleaded in that half-bored tone of hers, clearly expecting a reluctance on his part that he hadn't shown. 'You were just saying, not one hour ago, that we needed a case, an adventure...'

'I agree with you,' he interrupted.

'And now you stand there, so English. Something has landed in our laps and...'

'I rather landed in his lap,' he muttered.

'And yet you hesitate again...' She produced more forensic gloves from her bag, stock in trade presumably, and snapped them on.

'I am not hesitating!' he exploded, then, more slowly and with made-up sign language to underline the point that she hadn't bothered listening, 'I agree with you, let's take a look at the *buffet*.'

Valérie's face took on a look of extreme shock suggesting that it had been slapped with a wet halibut. 'You are not objecting?'

'No. I am not objecting.'

She paused and her forehead furrowed into a deep frown. 'Are you feeling well, Richard? Perhaps the shock.' She handed him a pair of gloves.

'I am perfectly fine, thank you. Now, we're wasting time.' He strode with determination back to the dresser, which was now under a hastily erected marquee with linen pegged on all four sides, two policemen standing at the front. Richard sneaked in at the back, followed by Valérie.

Slowly, he bent down at the door that had once housed the deceased Mayor Narcisse Planchet.

Valérie knelt down too and spoke without looking at him. 'Are you sure you are all right?'

'Absolutely certain,' he replied stiffly. 'You know you'd do well to update your files on me,' he said, flicking the latch and pulling the handle. 'I'm not as predictable as you seem to think I am.' As he finished his sentence with a flourish, Richard, for the second time that day fell backwards and emitted a high-pitched scream as the dead mayor once more half-tumbled out of the antique furniture.

'I mean really!' Valérie's dudgeon was high. 'I know it is a bank holiday, but you might have thought someone was available to remove the poor man.'

Richard, his composure partially recovered, sat up on his haunches once more. 'They probably have to wait for forensics to come down from Blois,' he said, simultaneously avoiding looking at the corpse while trying to make it look like he was peering hard at it. Planchet had always had a grey pallor to his skin, but he now looked almost transparent; all colour, and there hadn't been much to start with, had drained away like on shed snake skin. He also smelled badly, a mixture of perfume and death, and Richard pulled out a handkerchief to cover his mouth. 'What are we looking for?' he asked.

'Anything.' Valérie was concentrating hard while at the same time having a fairly rigorous rummage about. 'I wish Edmond were here,' she said, tactlessly ignoring the fact that Richard actually was.

'Yes, half a set more eyes would make a huge difference obviously,' he muffled tartly.

Valérie continued to frisk the dead man, whose expression in death continued to be the same as it had been in life, a mixture of disappointment and caginess, like an old deposed lion allowed to stay on with the pride. 'You don't like him very much, do you?' she said eventually.

Richard shrugged. 'I can't say I knew him all that well. Noel was the only one who saw him regularly.'

'I mean Edmond,' she snapped.

'Ah.'

Obviously he'd hoped for more, but he had no idea what to say. He had no claim on Valérie, so to all intents and purposes his toes hadn't been trodden on. He certainly would not admit to feeling jealous either; he even reluctantly liked the man, but there was something nagging him. He just didn't know what.

'*Martin Guerre*,' he said eventually.

She let out a deep breath. 'Who is Martin Guerre?' she asked, inspecting the underside of the dresser top with a gloved hand.

'It's a Gérard Depardieu film, a true story though!' he added quickly. 'A man returns years after leaving his wife and children. He claims to be the runaway husband. But there are, er, doubts.'

'Doubts?'

'Doubts.'

'What doubts?'

'Well. Someone claimed that Martin Guerre had lost a leg in the war with Italy.'

'And?'

'This Martin Guerre had two legs.'

She went back to her search. 'And what happened?'

Richard shrugged again, trying to exude an air of indifference. 'Well, to cut a long story short, he was found to be an imposter and had his head cut off.' She stayed silent. 'Where is he anyway?'

'I do not know, I am not his keeper, you know!'

Richard fought against the obvious sarcastic response of 'Clearly', and instead went with, 'He seemed to be enjoying the *brocante* anyway.'

She turned and narrowed her eyes at him in suspicion. 'Yes,' she said slowly. 'He collects ceramics; he tells me he still finds a bargain sometimes. I cannot find anything here!' She was flustered. 'I do not understand. Why kill Planchet? And then why stab him in the neck with a pen when he is so obviously dead?'

'And then why put him in a *buffet*?' Richard added.

She shook her head. 'OK, we had better go. Edmond will know what to do.' She stood up and patted the dust off her sleeves and capri pants. 'Put him back in, Richard, there is nothing here.'

'Oh great! Thanks.' As always, his caustic weariness was lost on her.

'I must find Edmond,' she repeated, not listening to him.

She sneaked out the way they had come in, leaving Richard to struggle with Mayor Planchet once more. For some reason, and Richard was never, ever in control of these things, his mind leapt to Louis Armstrong and the film *High Society*. Frank Sinatra is muscling in on soon to be remarried Grace Kelly; Bing Crosby is her lovelorn ex, while her fiancé, John Lund, rules the roost. Louis Armstrong is on Bing's side. 'There's a dark horse running in this here race,' Louis laments, 'and my boy's running a slow third.' Richard felt like Bing, he was running a slow third.

'I'm running a slow third,' he said out loud, which was swiftly followed by an 'ow' as he manoeuvred the dead man back into place. His hand had struck something hard and sharp. Reaching under the former mayor with his left hand he found the culprit.

It was a broken piece of terracotta ceramic. *Well now*, he thought, unable and reluctant to suppress a grin, *did you evah?*

Chapter Five

Richard hung back in the shadow of René's bar awning, hoping not to be seen. The view inside the bar wasn't very inviting and he was wondering if he was really needed at all. From his partially hidden viewpoint, the Commissaire looked like a lecturer at an adult education centre, standing in front of a dozen or so adults of varying backgrounds and abilities. Of course, Richard knew very well he had to go in and join the group. It was he after all who had found the body. Or, to be more precise, the body had found him. Either way he had been unknowingly guarding the deceased for most of the morning and at various points trying to sell the poor man off.

He took a deep breath, pulled open the glass door and was immediately hit with an icy blast. A blast that came not just from René's newly installed air conditioning unit, which sounded like a jumbo jet was landing nearby, but from all the faces that turned towards him. Richard rather got the feeling that he was being held responsible for this lecture from the Commissaire and that the least he could have done was to endure it as long as they had.

'Sorry,' he muttered in as English a way as was possible. That is, he didn't really know why he was saying it.

'Where have you been?' snapped Lapierre.

'Sorry,' he repeated. 'I think I'm in shock, I needed a walk by the river.'

The Commissaire raised his nose as though at a blind cheese-tasting event and turned back to the group. 'To answer your question about the deceased former mayor, Monsieur Mabit, the answer is just that, he remains deceased. Anything else will be revealed in the fullness of time.'

Noel Mabit, sitting at a table alone and slightly apart from the others, looked wounded, like a scolded child who didn't understand their crime. Richard felt for him and decided he would sit at his table in a gesture of support. Nobody else needed him as far as he could tell. The English *boules* team were at one table with Roddy, the aristocratic orangutan, translating for the other three. Three of the Avignon Arrivistes were at a neighbouring table, missing their ladies' world champion. Martin and Gennie were at the same table as Valérie and were holding each other the same way Valérie was holding Passepartout. Next to her sat Edmond, who had forsaken his sunglasses and reinstated his eyepatch. With his thick, wavy hair he looked like a pirate Sacha Distel.

'Rosé, please, René,' Richard said as he made his way to Noel's table, needlessly stooping as he did so like a theatre late-comer. He glanced up and caught Valérie's quizzical eye as he sat next to Noel, who also had a quizzical eye for Richard that was quickly followed by a brief nod of 'thank you'. It would be fair to say that Richard and Noel Mabit's relationship had hitherto been a testy one. Richard had always felt that Noel, pulling the bureaucratic strings, had tried to make life slightly harder for him. He had been fine initially, when Clare was still here, obsequiously fussing about her like a moth at a lamp. But when she left and Richard was alone, Noel seemed to regard him as something of a threat. To what, Richard had never actually worked out, finding the man's comic attempts to make him feel unwanted a mild irritation, even a game that he quite enjoyed. Only, Richard knew Noel better than the public servant realised. He knew what was said about Noel behind the man's back, what a figure of fun he had become. It wasn't Richard who was the outsider here anymore, it was Noel himself. Hence why the man was sitting alone.

'There are people here that I do not know.' The Commissaire still eyed Richard as he spoke, making sure that Richard knew he had tested his patience almost to the limit, especially when René cut across with a wine glass and a chilled *pichet* of rosé.

'Two glasses, please, René,' Richard whispered, though in the silence of the bar it sounded as though he had in fact hollered the request into a ravine.

The policeman theatrically wiggled his moustache, licked his pencil, still locking his eyes on Richard and repeated his statement. 'There are people here that I do not know. You, for instance.' He pointed his pencil at Roddy, who opened his large bug-eyes wide and smoothed the cravat that sat above a tweed waistcoat. 'Who are you?'

'Me?' the youngish man replied in a passable French accent. Richard guessed he was in his mid to late thirties, but it was always so difficult to tell with male aristocracy as they essentially wore the same outfit from late teens to late eighties. 'You mean, who am I?'

The Commissaire stood on his tip-toes briefly, a sure sign that he was beginning to lose his temper. 'That is precisely what I mean, monsieur.'

'Ah, right-o.' The man gulped visibly, his enormous Adam's apple bobbing up and down like a ball-cock in a toilet cistern. He also couldn't pronounce his 'Rs', which came out as 'Ws'. 'Er, well, I'm Rodney Darius Rougemare, fourteenth Duke of Anglethorp Spa, Marquess Shireholme, seventh Baron…' He tailed off, aware that the Commissaire had stopped writing and had simply raised an eyebrow. 'You can call me Roddy, everyone does.'

Richard hoped Lapierre wouldn't take him literally and call him 'Woddy'. 'So, monsieur, you are here with this *boules* team from England, is that right?'

'Well, yes, but we prefer the term *pétanque*, you see…'

'I agree with Woddy,' piped up the old lady from the Avignon Arrivistes. 'We're here to play *pétanque* not blasted *boules!*' She seemed to hold very strong views on the matter.

The Commissaire shrugged. 'Forgive me, madame.' He bowed in deference to her age. 'You are?'

'I am Agathe Deschanel and I am the President of the Féderation Internationale de Pétanque,' she said grandly. 'You'll no doubt notice the absence of the word *boules!*'

Richard was not alone in the room in realising that the nonagenarian Agathe Deschanel was not a woman to be trifled with.

'Are there not usually four in a *bou... pétanque* team? Where is your other member?'

'She wished to get changed.' A large, perspiring man on the end of the table, with a greasy and receding centre parting, wiped his brow with a paper napkin, revealing visible underarm sweat patches on his ancient-looking Johnny Hallyday tour T-shirt. 'She always wishes to get changed,' he added as though it was a personal inconvenience to him.

'And you are?' the Commissaire sighed.

'I am Philippe Gratin!' The way he said it put Richard in mind of Zorro; he wasn't just saying his name, he was announcing himself. 'I am ranked number three in France in *pétanque*!'

'*Men's* number three,' Valérie said loudly, putting a needle into the man's balloon of an ego.

'I say, we haven't been introduced yet, I'm Roddy.' Roddy stood up and leant over to shake Gratin's hand, but the Frenchman offered only his left hand, not his right.

'Excuse me,' he said, without any hint of apology. 'But my right hand is precious. It is insured for one hundred thousand euros!'

'Ah, right-o.' Roddy sat back down again.

There was a brief silence and the Commissaire saw an opportunity to continue his work. 'Your colleagues, Monsieur Woddy, they cannot speak?'

'Ah.' Roddy stood up again. 'They don't speak French, no, sorry.' He sat back down.

'I speak a little,' the elegant Jessica Fletcher look-a-like sitting next to him said. 'I am Angela Babcock. I am

41

secretary of the town-twinning committee of Anglethorp Spa. *Les villes jumelles*,' she added loudly and slowly.

The Commissaire frowned at her. 'You remind me of someone, madame. I do not yet remember who...'

'I told you, didn't I?' Gennie couldn't help herself. 'She was in that thing!'

'This is my niece.' If Angela had heard anything she rode right over it. 'Olivia Babcock. Say *bonjour*, Olivia.'

The pretty young woman looked terrified, but did as she was told, giggling nervously as she did so. Everyone returned the *bonjour*, even the Commissaire who admonished himself for doing so.

'On this team, that leaves you, monsieur.' Again, the policeman's pencil was directed like a sword, but the sullen man in the incongruous tam-o'-shanter stared back impassively.

'That's Derek,' Roddy offered; there was a slight hint of distaste. 'He doesn't speak any French.'

'He barely speaks any English!' Angela huffed.

'Derek?' In his French accent the Commissaire made it sound like Dalek and though Derek nodded, there was seemingly nothing else coming from the man. 'Last, but I hope not least, you, monsieur.'

'Alphonse Berlioz,' was the intense response, from a dapper man of middle age. 'I am Madame's secretary.' He nodded deferentially towards Agathe Deschanel.

'He's been a dear,' came a surprisingly soft response, 'while I have built *pétanque* into an international sport.'

Alphonse demurred and shrugged modestly, while at the same time managing to protrude his chin, which is Gallic body language for 'I agree entirely'.

'You know it really is too bad that we get an investigating officer who has no feel for our world,' Agathe concluded.

There was a slight pause while Lapierre digested this. 'Do you feel that your world, Madame Deschanel,' – his eyes narrowed – 'is somehow linked to the death of Mayor Planchet?'

The old woman responded immediately, snorting in derision. 'Of course not!'

'Pity,' the Commissaire replied morosely.

Richard was tired and running out of patience and the idea that *boules* – he was determined to stick to that name, no matter what – would be a cause for murder was beyond ridiculous.

'Why are you shaking your head, monsieur?' Lapierre pounced on him. 'Do you have something to add?'

Richard was suddenly aware that all eyes were on him in a way that a crowd feels relieved when the spotlight isn't on them; they had a victim. 'No, nothing,' he said.

'Please share it with the group.' In the absence of anything concrete to say, the Commissaire was being unnecessarily sardonic.

Richard caught Valérie's worried gaze and took a deep breath. 'It just strikes me as being highly improbable that Mayor Planchet was murdered because of bloody *boules*!' There, he'd said it and felt all the better for it.

There was a momentary silence in the room before it seemed like everyone responded at once with an outraged, '*PÉTANQUE!*'

Before Richard could reply, though he had no idea what with, the door to René's upstairs rooms opened and the tall, imposing figure of the missing Avignon Arriviste filled the doorway. She was quite the sight. Well over six feet tall, nearer seven if you added her amazing headwear, she strode into the centre of the group, a riot of colour in her flowing traditional Malian outfit, which was part dress, part enormous bow and with a corsage of yellow lily of the valley pinned to her breast. 'I am Fatouma Dembele,' she said confidently. 'I am so sorry that I am late.'

Again there was silence. Richard had seen some entrances in his time, but few to beat the impact of Fatouma's. The room was stunned. There was, however, a low rumble of noise coming from somewhere, perhaps suggesting that the air conditioning was breathing its last, though it was a throaty sort of humming, like a powerful engine wanting to rev harder. It was difficult to pinpoint the source until Gennie spoke up.

'Oh, Martin,' she said, rolling her eyes. 'Do stop that!'

Chapter Six

Fatouma first approached Agathe Deschanel and put a consoling hand on her shoulder, a gesture that the old woman reciprocated warmly by patting it gently. She then looked about for somewhere to sit and walked over to Noel and Richard's table.

'May I sit here, *messieurs?*' she asked, a relaxed smile breaking out while her warm, friendly eyes caught the sun through the window. Neither had the wherewithal for speech but managed to gesture their willing assent. With some practised style she managed to sit at the smallish alcove table without unravelling her costume and she reached over to pour some water from the *carafe d'eau*. It was clear to Richard that she knew all eyes were on her and that she was enjoying it too. 'May I offer my condolences for your loss, monsieur,' she said to Noel. 'Your welcome has been so generous and this is so tragic.'

For a moment Richard thought Noel might even cry; his face creased in a sort of emotional torture that Richard didn't know the man was capable of. The usual implacable façade soon returned though and he nodded his thanks vigorously rather than say anything. It then occurred to almost everyone else in the bar that no one had actually taken Noel Mabit's feelings into consideration at all. Mabit had been working closely with the deceased mayor for years, essentially fulfilling the role himself; one had to assume therefore that the relationship had been a close one and that Noel must be in terrible shock. Martin led the way with a 'yes, bad luck, old man', and soon the rest of the crowd followed suit. Noel continued to stare at the table until he gratefully accepted the glass of water that Fatouma pushed his way.

'Can we get on, please?' The Commissaire had tried to remain respectful as condolences were bandied about, but his face betrayed his continuing exasperation at the constant interruptions.

'What do you want from us, Henri?' Valérie asked, her frustration at what she no doubt saw as stifling inaction matching the policeman's own. 'You should be out hunting the murderer.'

'That is precisely what I am trying to do, Madame Masson!' he retaliated sternly, though he noticeably took a step backwards as he did so. If he was going to continue this tactic to keep Valérie at bay it was a dangerous one and Richard couldn't see it doing him any good at all in the long run. He was interested to see Edmond's reaction, however, and the man's one visible eyebrow had shot up into his pristine hairline in a cross between surprise and outright shock. This struck Richard as confirmation – he hoped anyway – that the couple had not actually settled back into traditional married life. For her part Valérie was once again trying her best to remain calm but the solid glass tumbler she was holding was in extreme danger of exploding under the pressure of her grip.

'Commissaire,' she said slowly, always a bad sign for the addressee. 'You have established who we all are; you have a rough time of death, the possible method of murder and the absurd theatrics of the pen in the neck. What do you possibly expect to learn from a mass questioning of two *boules* teams?'

'*Pétanque!*' The rotund figure of Philippe Gratin stood up surprisingly quickly in his anger. 'I repeat, *pétanque!*' he said, before wiping his face like an opera singer at the end of an aria and sitting back down again, slightly embarrassed.

Valérie threw her arms in the air. 'Pah! *Boules, pétanque!* Honestly, what is the difference?'

Richard had some sympathy with the question, but decided to join in with the majority in eye-rolling at her naivety.

'It's very simple, old girl,' Martin said. '*Boules* really is *pétanque*, you see...'

'It most certainly is not!' Agathe was having none of it.

'What is going on?' Angela, whose French had clearly been stretched to the limit, was feeling left out.

'There seems to be some kind of row going on.' Roddy seemed embarrassed on everyone's behalf.

'A row? What about? Is it to do with the murder of the mayor?' Richard noticed a glint of excitement in Angela's eye.

'No, 'fraid not,' Roddy explained. 'They're trying to establish the difference between *boules* and *pétanque*.'

'How extraordinary!' she replied, then she cleared her throat loudly, a sign that she was perhaps about to settle the argument. '*Boules*,' she began in faltering though pretty accurate French, silencing the room, 'is the collective name for a certain type of ball sports; *pétanque* is a specific ball-throwing sport.'

'Bravo, madame!' Philippe Gratin threw his considerable weight behind the definition.

'Yes,' Roddy added enthusiastically. 'Like *bocce*!'

'What is this *bocce*?' Valérie had had enough, but not obviously enough that her anger didn't strike the others as just natural curiosity.

The Commissaire turned in flouncing frustration towards the bar where a loitering René was waiting with a soothing whiskey.

'I've got this one,' Martin said, hoping to redeem himself. 'I know my ball games.' He sniggered at his own childish joke, unfortunately giving the opportunity for someone else to steal his thunder.

'*Pétanque* and *bocce* have the same scoring system.' It was the intense Alphonse Berlioz who took the opportunity.

'But different techniques...' Martin wasn't to be outdone.

Alphonse reacted sharply. 'In *pétanque* the ball is tossed,' he said quickly.

'Whereas in *bocce*...' Martin tried again.

'It is bowled!' Alphonse waited for the acknowledgement of his triumph.

'Though sometimes with a run-up.' Valérie said with the deflation of boredom and reading from her phone. 'How very silly!'

Valérie's dismissive attitude towards what was for many in the room their life and livelihood, brought a rather uncomfortable silence and the Commissaire saw his own opportunity. He didn't bother with a preamble.

'I am aware that ten of you had dinner together yesterday evening!' He went off at quite a pace. 'The two teams of *pétanque*, Monsieur Mabit and the dead mayor. I would like to know what was discussed, how the mayor was...' At last he had a chance to pause. 'I would like to know everything that went on, please.'

Valérie held up her hand. 'Henri, I understand why the players are here, why Noel is here. But why are the rest of us here?'

The Commissaire took a slow walk towards Valérie, acknowledging Richard as he did so. 'Because, Madame d'Orçay,' he conceded, 'the English team are staying with the Thompsons. And,' – he rode over an attempted interruption – 'I have decided to have you and Monsieur Ainsworth here because if you were not, you would no doubt try to sneak in anyway! Therefore it is easier this way.'

A sly smile emerged on Valérie's face. 'I do not believe a word of that. You have been ordered to have us here, haven't you, Henri?' This took Richard quite by surprise.

'Yes!' Lapierre replied emphatically and without taking his eyes off her. 'However, I did not invite this man!' He pointed at Edmond Masson.

'Oh, Richard and I can vouch for him.'

The Commissaire looked at Richard, who begrudgingly shrugged a sort of agreement.

The Commissaire went back to his position at the bar. 'Very well,' he said, regaining his composure. 'What occurred yesterday evening?'

There wasn't an overwhelming response until Roddy spoke up. 'I'm afraid I rather dominated proceedings,' he answered apologetically. 'You see, Angela speaks French pretty well if she has a run-up, as it were, like *bocce*, whereas Olivia, bless her, speaks rarely and Derek...' – he threw a hand in the direction of the impassive Derek – 'he doesn't have a lot to say. As a result I spent most of the time translating.'

Derek was vaguely aware that he was being talked about and raised a hand like a disinterested child hearing his name as the register is called.

'I can vouch for that.' It was Alphonse who confirmed. 'Without Monsieur Rougemare there would have been very little communication indeed.' It wasn't clear whether this was a compliment or complaint.

'Is Rougemare a French name, monsieur?' Lapierre asked.

'Oh rather, yes. It goes way back to when we probably owned most of this,' the Duke replied guilelessly. 'You know, the Plantagenets?'

'I see.' The Commissaire's coldness spoke volumes and also on behalf of most of the room. 'And so no one can report anything unusual about the evening, nothing at all?'

Again, a hush fell until eventually it was, to everyone's surprise, Noel Mabit, who spoke. 'There was something out of the ordinary,' he ventured nervously.

'Yes!' The Commissaire pounced.

'The mayor,' Noel said, almost in a whisper.

'Go on…' Lapierre sensed a breakthrough.

'Well, he turned up for a start.'

Ten minutes later, once most people had shuffled out and René had opened his door to the evening custom, Richard, Noel, Valérie and Edmond together with a morose Commissaire sat around the one table.

'I don't understand it.' The Commissaire spoke into his wine glass as much as to the table. 'Even I, and I think I know something of this town now, but even I, I am not sure that I would have known Mayor Planchet existed had he *not* been murdered! It is absurd!'

Valérie was running her finger around the top of her glass. 'Who ordered you to involve us, Henri?' she asked, her voice deadly serious.

The Commissaire snorted in reply. 'I do not know how high this goes,' – he shrugged – 'only that it is very high. For some reason the higher-ups want this kept as quiet as possible and resolved yesterday.'

'The mayor wasn't dead yesterday.' Richard would be the first to admit that his contributions were not always the most helpful.

'It is a diplomatic issue, I am told,' the policeman continued. 'We have here English aristocracy, a ladies' world champion player of *pétanque* from Mali, a dead public official and the President of the Féderation Internationale de Pétanque!' The way he listed these people made it sound to the rest of the group that Agathe Deschanel was definitely the most important diplomatically.

'That was quite some entrance that Fatouma made,' Valérie remarked, clearly impressed.

'It was the same last night,' a still sullen Noel said. 'She was a little later than the others and wearing a very flamboyant outfit. The mayor was quite taken with her.'

'Was it the same outfit?' Valérie asked.

'No, no, quite different.'

'Her luggage must be enormous,' Richard observed, also noticing a quick look of surprise from Edmond.

'It quite distracted the mayor,' Noel continued. He seemed mainly to be talking to himself. 'But then he hadn't been himself for a number of days.'

'How do you mean?' Lapierre asked, without much hope.

'Eh?' Noel looked up. 'Oh, well, I don't know, alert maybe? I don't want to insult the dead, you know?'

'You aren't, Noel, please tell us more.' Valérie laid a hand on the official's arm.

'More alert?' Lapierre prompted.

'Well...' Noel looked around the table. 'Sober,' he whispered. 'Like he was waiting for something. He was jumpy, he was sleeping less and less, during the day I mean. Drinking very little. It was most unusual.'

'It sounds to me,' Edmond said after a pause, 'that he was expecting something, or more likely someone.'

'From the past, you mean?' Richard tried to hide the acerbic edge to his question. 'You know, someone popping up after a long time to muddy the waters, so to speak?'

'Brilliant, Richard!' Valérie exclaimed innocently.

Chapter Seven

Richard sat in the cool shade of the hen coop back at his B&B, while Olivia de Havilland, Lana Turner and Joan Crawford pecked and fussed around him. He had been in there now for a good hour, not hiding as such, just making himself unavailable. Everyone knew where he was anyway, but also knew better than to disturb him when he was in conference with 'his ladies'.

It had been the first chance he'd had to properly examine his 'evidence' found under the dead mayor and the more he did so, the less evidential it became. A smallish triangle of reddish brown ceramic, it looked more like the fragment of a broken terracotta plant pot than a piece of a collectible. Of course, the question to be asked was: why was it in the dresser in the first place? But then the next question, and probably a more important one, was why the dead mayor was in the dresser in the first place. Eventually he hid the piece of terracotta in the bottom of the bag of hen feed and was, in theory, working out his next move. For that, he needed peace, quiet and the contented trilling of his Hollywood goddesses.

Usually if he had a piece of evidence, he would share it immediately with Valérie, but by her own words, this particular piece of evidence directly implicated her current former husband in a murder. He really wanted to lay aside his personal feelings and approach it in a cold-eyed investigative manner, but that simply wasn't possible. The arrival of Edmond Masson had massively disrupted his and Valérie's personal relationship – husbands do that – and even the vague suggestion that Edmond was guilty of killing the mayor would no doubt put something of a crimp on their professional standing too. Obviously he needed more evidence that Edmond was involved before he could confront them both; the last thing he wanted was to be accused of sour grapes and jealousy, even if that was the case.

'Are you ever coming out of there?' Through a gap in the wooden coop panelling, he could see his redoubtable housekeeper – prospective hospitality business partner, maybe even boss – Madame Tablier standing as ever with her hands on her hips in a double teapot stance, dusting cloth hanging from the front pocket of her floral house-coat, long grey hair pulled up into a hairnet.

'What do you know about terracotta pots, Madame Tablier?' he called from inside.

'I know they leave terrible scratches on wooden surfaces, that's what I know!'

'Good point,' he said, having nothing better to say.

'We need to talk!' she barked. 'I'm told you haven't cashed in that money yet?'

Madame Tablier had recently come into money. She was, not unnaturally for her, pretty uncomfortable with the idea and had therefore passed it on to Richard so he could settle his divorce with Clare and buy the *chambre d'hôte* outright. In doing so, the status quo would remain the same but with her becoming, for want of a better description, the silent partner in the B&B business. Clare though, having currently stalled the divorce proceedings, didn't need to be settled so Richard hadn't cashed Madame Tablier's banker's draft because it just didn't feel right to do so. He had opened a separate account so that it was safe, but he didn't want to tell her this because he didn't know how she'd react to the news of her, of her what? Demotion? It was all very complicated.

He sighed and stroked Lana Turner. It was just one more reason, in his opinion, to seek solace and comfort alone in a wooden box with distracting wildfowl.

'I'll be out soon.' He tried to sound bumptious and cheerful, but in reply he heard her tut loudly and then watched as she sloped off muttering to herself. She walked towards the sun terrace where, he now noticed, in the distance Valérie and Edmond sat opposite each other, sipping cocktails. He wouldn't be out soon, he decided, and settled in for the long haul.

He was awoken later by a loud squawk from Lana Turner, a sign that she had laid an egg. Richard, stiff after sitting in the same position for so long, stretched painfully and congratulated her. Outside there was a riotous sunset which he watched through the wooden slats, a glorious technicolour inferno of oranges and reds that filled the whole horizon. He liked to call these sunsets his 'Gone with the Wind' moments, reminiscent as they were of the scenes in the film when Atlanta was ablaze. Sometimes, as he looked, he could almost see Rhett Butler and Scarlett O'Hara – he preferred Clark Gable and Vivien Leigh – fleeing on their horse-drawn carriage. Daydreams, he smiled at the thought, just daydreams.

But this time there was something in the field, bobbing about in the vines and heading closer. It was the silhouette of a man, but with one very distinguishing feature, a tam-o'-shanter hat. Why on earth was Derek coming to his B&B and why not by way of the more traditional front door? Richard stayed rooted to the spot; hidden as he was in his coop, he knew he couldn't be seen and it was also obvious that Derek didn't want to be seen either, which made the wearing of a rather standout choice of headwear all the more remarkable. He watched as Derek, now at the fence and only a few yards away, looked about him for signs of life. Seeing none, he stealthily climbed the picket fence, briefly looked around as he sat on top and jumped down to the ground on Richard's property.

'Can I help you?' Richard asked, not unreasonably, but affecting a much deeper voice and staying hidden with his hens.

Derek, startled, ducked down, his eyes darting around in the fading fiery glow. Eventually his face turned towards the coop and Richard knew he would have to emerge. He grabbed a rather surprised Joan Crawford from her shelf nest and cradled her in the crook of her arm, stroking her as he did so. He had seen sinister cinema villains do it with cats and it spoke of calmness and power. Joan was having none of it, however, and flapped noisily out of his arms in a blaze of feathers and squawking as he pushed the door open with his foot.

'I said,' – Richard spat some feathers out of his mouth – 'can I help you?'

Derek stood up. He was slightly shorter than Richard but with wider shoulders. He didn't look at all fazed at being caught and looked inconvenienced rather than embarrassed. 'I am working in the course of my duties,' he said, his Scottish accent at least matching his headwear. 'I am on the trail of a criminal mastermind.' It wasn't just how he spoke that was sort of unpleasant, but the way he spoke, in a kind of mangled officialese English. His chin jutted out some considerable distance from his face like a snowplough and it was his bottom lip that did all the work, his top lip remaining static. It gave the overall impression of one of those old-fashioned ventriloquist's dummies.

'A criminal mastermind?' Richard couldn't help but sound somewhat sceptical. 'Here?'

'Yes, here!' It was clear Derek didn't go for Richard's tone.

'You don't think that, in reality, you're actually trespassing then?'

'The law knows no boundaries,' Derek replied pompously.

'That's not true though, is it?' Richard didn't take to the man at all. 'Law is very much all about boundaries, founded on them even. Now, why don't you go back the way you came, then go around to the front door and use the doorbell instead?'

Derek looked Richard up and down as though it were Richard who was the trespasser. 'What? And blow my cover?' he sneered, putting his chin even closer to Richard's chest.

'What cover? I've been watching your approach for the last five minutes. Did you think that a bobble-hatted tam-o'-shanter was going to blend in with the surroundings?'

Derek snatched immediately at his hat and dragged it down the side of his head, revealing the sort of wispy hair comb-over not much seen since the early nineteen eighties. 'Damn,' he said, this time a little less bullishly. 'I think I'm out of practice.' He then proceeded to draw a hip flask out of the pocket of his baggy grey trousers, and take a large nip. He fastened the top back on before remembering his manners and offering the flask to Richard who politely refused. In truth he'd have liked nothing more than the taste of strong liquor but he didn't trust the man at all.

'A criminal mastermind, you say?' Richard asked, returning the man's earlier sneer.

'Mind if I sit down?' Derek asked, and without waiting for an answer sat on the bench by the fence. 'I'm getting too old for this game,' he sighed.

'What game?' Richard thought the whole thing rather absurd.

Derek turned to look at Richard and seemed to be weighing him up. 'I am Detective Sergeant Derek Munro, retired.'

Richard paused before answering. 'And how's the retirement going? You seem rather busy to me.'

'I can't let it go, can I?' It sounded like a mission statement, but he didn't expand.

'Let what go?'

Derek took a big deep breath. 'I have been on the trail of a smuggling ring for years. I was seconded to the Customs and Excise unit a couple of years before retirement and they basically shoved me in a back office and asked me to do some filing. Desk stuff, whereas I am a man of action!' He took another draw on his flask. 'I began to get very interested in a file marked Wizard. Art smuggling to be precise. And the same name kept cropping up all over the place...'

'Edmond Masson?' Richard finished the sentence for him.

'How did you know that?' The man seemed positively insulted by the idea.

'A hunch,' Richard replied sadly.

'Well, it was a good hunch. I think you know more than you're letting on, my man!'

'And do you think he had something to do with the murder?'

Before Derek could answer the question, the pitter-patter of Passepartout's paws came trotting delicately around the corner.

'You must go!' Richard said quickly. 'Now!'

'Can't I just hide in the coop?'

'No! The hens will make a terrible racket. Back over the fence and we'll meet up tomorrow. Go!'

Derek put his flask back in his pocket and climbed over the fence, falling loudly on the other side. Richard picked up Passepartout and walked him back around the corner where he met an approaching Valérie.

'There you are, Passepartout!' she exclaimed, taking the small dog from Richard's grasp. 'I was beginning to get worried. Thank you, Richard, where did you find him?'

'He was sniffing about my hen coop,' he said, mustering some cheerfulness into his voice.

Valérie nodded slowly. 'And so disturbing your peace and quiet?'

'No, no not really. The hens seem to like the little scamp!' Even he could feel his false joviality fading.

'You have been hiding in there, Richard, I know it.'

'Well, er, sort of. I'm writing a book and er, just wanted some downtime. You know how it is?'

'Yes, Richard, I know how it is. And I know that you were hiding in there.'

'Yes. Yes, I was.'

'From whom?' she asked quietly.

'Erm, well everyone really.'

'Me?'

'You come under that bracket certainly, yes.'

'But why, Richard?'

His shoulders slumped as he felt a wave of honesty wash over him. 'I don't want to get in the way,' he said stoically. 'You two must have so much to talk about and I, well, I, you know, I just don't want to get in the way.'

She stayed silent for a moment. 'You do not like Edmond, do you?'

He gave out a brave, sarcastic chuckle. 'That's the problem, Valérie, I do like him.'

'But you think he's an imposter, that he isn't who he says he is. This Martin Guerre.' She wasn't angry, just establishing the facts.

'It's not just Martin Guerre,' Richard replied dolefully. 'There's Michael Redgrave as Captain Hašek in *The Captive Heart*. Richard Todd in *Chase a Crooked Shadow...*'

'Richard.'

'Right. Do you know how imposters are always unmasked in films, how they're always found out? Because they're much, much nicer than the people they're pretending to be, like in *The Scapegoat*.'

'Richard,' she repeated.

'I mean, was Edmond always as charming as he is now?'

She put a hand on his chest and to some observers it might have looked like a gesture of warmth. It wasn't. It was a gesture of stop, that's far enough.

'That is your films,' she said, sounding horribly like Clare with the use of 'your films'. She looked deep into his eyes. 'Do you really think I would not recognise my own husband?' She turned angrily and went inside leaving Richard once again alone, this time in the dark, the sun now having disappeared.

'There's nothing else for it,' he said quietly to himself. 'She's utterly blind to it. I'm going to have to protect her from this, from him.' He made a kind of vague promise to himself that that's exactly what he would do, protect her. It also occurred to him that to do so would mean outwitting her and that would not be easy, not very easy at all.

Chapter Eight

'What are your plans today, Richard?' Valérie asked distractedly, sipping delicately at her breakfast green tea. Passepartout dozed on the chair next to his mistress, occasionally whimpering or growling in his sleep as dogs do.

Richard was at the sink with his back to her. His English wine-tasting guests had already been picked up in their taxi and had ambitious plans to visit twelve vineyards that day to make up for the lack of wine-tasting options available the day before. He thought about her question before answering. What were *his* plans? Hitherto in their whirlwind partnership, it had always been 'our' plans, and she'd made them. When dead bodies had turned up previously, or people had disappeared, Valérie had been like a hunting dog, straining at the leash, goading Richard into joint action. Her question then was a signal to him that that was at an end. She certainly would not let the death of Mayor Planchet drift by without thorough investigation, but she would conduct that investigation with Edmond and not Richard.

'Well, I thought I would do some work on this new book I'm writing,' he answered eventually and as cheerfully as he could, giving the impression that there was really nothing else on his mind.

'A new book?' She sounded surprised, having assumed he'd made up the story of the book the night before.

'Yes, a new book.'

'What is it called, this new book?' She framed the question in a way that suggested she still didn't actually believe him. That she had good reason not to was neither here nor there for Richard. Damn it, he had his pride!

'It's called *Oh, To Be Ernest Thesiger!*' he replied grandly, though he had no idea from what cobwebbed recesses of his mind he had plucked that from.

'Oh. And what is it about?' She seemed slightly put out that he hadn't wilted under the initial question and admitted he was not writing a book at all.

He turned around to face her, leaning nonchalantly on the sink. If he had to fill time talking about film, he was in his element. *You want a book?* he thought. *I'll give you a book.*

'It's a quote from Sir Alec Guinness.' He paused. 'You've heard of him?' She shook her head and it wounded him more than he could say. 'Well, Sir Alec Guinness was one of the finest screen actors ever to grace the cinema. *Kind Hearts and Coronets? The Bridge on the River Kwai?*' Still nothing. He sighed in disappointment. 'Anyway, Sir Alec Guinness was also in *Star Wars.*' He avoided her eye in case the ignorance was continuing. 'He became a massive worldwide star because of it. He resented the attention though, the busier life. He wanted his quiet life back, the one he felt comfortable in.'

If she saw the analogy in what he was saying, she gave no indication. 'So who is this Ernest Thesiger, then?'

'He was a decent, unremarkable character actor. Never pestered by autograph hunters, rarely interviewed and therefore lived the life that Sir Alec Guinness yearned for.'

Madame Tablier bustled into the room, clanking bucket and mop as she did so.

'The quiet life?' Valérie asked over the din.

'Yes, exactly.'

'No excitement. The same thing day after day.'

'That's it.'

'And did he get his quiet life?'

Richard frowned. 'Well, he died.'

'You don't get much quieter than that!' Madame Tablier intervened. 'Now, we need more vinegar for the surfaces and I need a new head for my mop.'

'I'll also be doing some shopping,' Richard said without missing a beat, and turned back to the sink. 'Do you have any plans for today?' he asked airily.

Valérie put down her cup. 'I think the death of the mayor is quite important, do you not? But if you are too busy with your Guinnesses and your mop heads, Edmond and I will have to investigate without you.'

It was an indication of the state of Richard's mind that her anger was a source of comfort to him. He'd been wrong. She had obviously expected him to join them and was put out that he wasn't going to do so; he'd take that as a victory any day. Richard's priority, he had decided, though he clearly couldn't tell her this, was to locate Detective Sergeant Derek Munro and find out exactly what he knew about Edmond Masson and this art smuggling syndicate. If he was indeed to protect Valérie, and even the thought of that now sounded ridiculous, he had to know exactly what he was up against.

'Do let me know how you get on, won't you?' he said instead, and overdid his insouciance by whistling tunelessly. He plucked a large stainless steel ladle from the sink and in the reflection saw Valérie look first at a now awake Passepartout and then at Madame Tablier, who shrugged. As if he'd made up his mind about the whole thing, Passepartout began a low growl and bared his tiny teeth.

'Come in, Commissaire!' Richard called out, having cottoned on to the fact that Passepartout had a sixth sense regarding the law and became positively rabid whenever the policeman was in the vicinity.

A slightly bewildered Henri Lapierre opened the door and stepped through into the salon. His bafflement didn't leave him either as he looked around the room as though a trap had been set. He said nothing and instead made his way warily to the coffee machine and poured himself an espresso. 'How did you know I was here?' he asked, after a while.

'Never mind that, Henri.' Valérie didn't want to give the game away. 'Why are you here? Do you have news?'

The man shrugged annoyingly and took another sip. 'You were right, madame,' he said begrudgingly. 'Mayor Planchet died of *Convallaria majalis* poisoning, lily of the valley, specifically convallatoxin, which would lead to cardiac arrest. It was ingested orally.'

'So why the pen in the neck?' Richard asked.

'I will come to that, monsieur.'

'It is quite possible that Mayor Planchet drank the liquid voluntarily, of course…'

'Oh, Henri, that is nonsense!' Valérie threw her arms up in disgust.

'Bear with me, madame, please. As I say, it is quite possible that Mayor Planchet drank the liquid voluntarily. It is also quite possible that he then went to sleep in the *buffet* dresser. I have it on good authority from Monsieur Mabit that he did this often. He even kept a small pillow in the dresser and stretched out. He was a small man as you know.'

'I've heard of babies being kept in the top drawer if you don't have a cot, but a grown man taking naps in dining furniture!' Madame Tablier shook her head in disbelief. 'And to think I voted for him too.'

'What are you saying, Commissaire? That without the pen plunged into the mayor's neck this might not even be seen as murder?' Richard felt he was stating the obvious, but that it needed stating nonetheless.

'Precisely.' It was obvious Lapierre was angry.

'Death by misadventure or even suicide,' Valérie mused.

'We have a killer,' – Lapierre began to stride the room – 'and he is playing games with us!'

'More than that,' Richard concluded, 'he seems to want to be caught.'

Valérie took Richard's vague notion and ran with it. 'I see, Richard,' she said, no hint of a 'brilliant' this time. 'Why go back hours later and kill the man again?'

'Fury?' the Commissaire ventured. 'He kills the mayor and searches for something which he does not find. So he goes back to the body and angrily kills again.'

Richard shrugged. 'Well, it's a theory at least,' he said.

'And there were no fingerprints on the pen obviously?'

'None.' The Commissaire laid two photographs down on the table. One was a relatively recent photograph of the mayor wearing his sash of office and the other, a much older, faded picture, was also of the mayor taken some years ago, judging by the clothing. He looked exactly the same in both of them. Thin, wispy combed-back hair, small eyes and a nose so big that by rights it should have belonged to a much larger man.

'What do we really know of this mayor?' Valérie asked, looking at the pictures. 'If we get to know the victim better, it may reveal more about his killer I think.'

They all turned to look at Madame Tablier, who leant portentously on her mop as if about to regale the room with an epic odyssey. 'Lived here all his life,' she said. And that was that.

'Is that it, madame?' A suspicious tone in the Commissaire's voice suggested that Madame Tablier was holding something back.

'Ask around,' she huffed, 'there wasn't much more to know. I mean,' – she paused – 'he wasn't here *all* his life…'

'Ah!' An excitable Valérie sensed a breakthrough.

'No, he went off for three months.'

'When was this?' The Commissaire pounced.

'Oh, let me see…' It was clear to Richard that his old housekeeper was rather enjoying the attention. 'What are we now… so it would be, oh, about 1978.'

'Nineteen seventy-eight!' The three others all reacted at the same time prompting Madame Tablier to lift her mop in defence.

'Yes!' she cried, startled. 'For about three months.'

'Why?' Richard asked.

'Ah.' She put the mop back down. 'He got all fancy, didn't he? He won a scholarship to some art school up in that there Paris. There was quite the fanfare when he left.' She bent down to pick up a speck of dust from the floor.

'And?' Again it was left to Richard to do the prompting.

'Came home three months later, tail between his legs. Later on he stood for mayor and he's been drinking himself into furniture ever since!'

'But why did he come back?' Valérie asked, knowing there must be more to it.

'Tch.' Madame Tablier snorted in disgust, indicating that whatever the reason, she didn't approve. 'Love!' she said, as though it were some foul pestilence.

'Love,' the Commissaire repeated, an air of the romantic in his shrugging shoulders.

'Love.' Richard nodded, as if it were but a distant memory.

'Love?' questioned Valérie, sounding like a nutcracker successfully demolishing a Brazil nut. 'And do you know who he was in love with?'

'Oh, yes,' Madame Tablier confirmed and began mopping the floor.

'Madame, please.' The already tetchy Commissaire was losing his patience.

'Oh, right. Well, it was Monique Lafarge, wasn't it?' The other three looked at each other and shook their heads. 'Of course, you'd know her better as Madame Mabit.' The room fell into a stunned silence, the only noise being the mop swishing about in the bucket. 'He declared his undying love

68

for her on his return,' Madame Tablier started up again after her dramatic pause. 'Only she'd married Monsieur Mabit almost the day after old Planchet had left. You didn't hang around in those days around here. If you weren't married by the time you were twenty, you never would be.'

'Really, even in 1978?' Valérie was having trouble believing it.

'Yes,' the old woman snapped back. 'Monique and Monsieur Mabit were about the only two left in town of that age, apart from Madame Gondard, but she was a bit older and missed the boat too. Now she's his housekeeper, does a bit of shopping for him.'

Richard felt they were getting off the point. 'So Monsieur Mabit and Madame Lafarge married while Mayor Planchet was away?'

'They did!' She sounded almost proud for some odd reason. 'This isn't fancy pants Paris, you know? With your free love and God knows what else! Like I say… if you were twenty…' She became quite flustered. 'It's like shopping for food on Christmas Eve.' She left it at that.

'Sorry, what?' Richard wanted to know exactly what was like shopping for food on Christmas Eve.

'Marriage,' was the reply. 'It's like shopping for food on Christmas Eve; you take what you can get.'

There was a stunned silence until Valérie asked, 'And are there children?'

Madame Tablier looked offended at the suggestion. 'It wasn't that kind of marriage!' she said, and went back to mopping the floor.

Chapter Nine

'Are you OK?' Richard asked as Valérie tapped the brakes, changed down a gear and leant her soft-top sporty Renault Alpine carefully into a hairpin bend. If vexed and frustrated or even happy and relaxed she had a tendency in Richard's eyes to drive like a maniac. As a result, this careful, bordering on cautious driving had him at a loss he couldn't work her out at all. It wasn't that she needed time to think, surely; even thought to Valérie was done at breakneck speed. It occurred to Richard that perhaps she might be dragging her heels a little. They were on their way to Martin and Gennie's *chambre d'hôte* after all, she to pick up Edmond and he was joining her on the pretext of lending Martin a book, though he really wanted to follow up on Detective Sergeant Derek Munro's claims and he was staying there with the rest of the English team.

'Why would someone kill this Mayor Planchet?' Valérie asked eventually, as often answering his question with a question of her own, though it felt more like she was interviewing a witness rather than a discussion between investigative partners.

'And why twice?' Two could play at that game.

She sped into the next sharp bend and Richard was almost relieved to see something of the old Valérie returning.

'What do you know of him, Richard? This mayor.'

He gripped the door pull feeling as though the danger was just like old times. 'Not much,' he said through clenched teeth, as she put her foot down some more. 'He's been mayor for decades, though it's well known that Noel really runs things around here. Planchet got the title, Noel got the girl,' he concluded, giving it a romantic twist that he didn't really feel.

'I do not see any motive for murder in that.' She sounded flat, disappointed.

'I don't see Noel as a killer either,' he chuckled. 'Just think of the paperwork!'

'Paperwork?' she asked, taking her eyes off the road.

'I was joking,' he said with a grin. It really was like old times, his English humour flying straight over her head and into a roadside ditch. 'If their particular *ménage à trois* is behind this, I still don't see how Planchet fits in at all. It would be more likely that Madame Mabit would kill her husband. It's well known that she has little time for him.'

She pondered this a moment, waiting at a junction for a car to pass. 'We must speak to Noel Mabit ourselves I think.'

'We?' he asked. It was his turn to be cautious.

'I am glad we are in agreement, Richard!' She sped through the junction, misunderstanding his English 'we' for the French *oui* and therefore apparently pleased he was back on the team.

They drove in silence for a few minutes before Richard decided to address things head on. 'What are the facts?' he asked with determination. 'What do we know?' She started to reply, but he didn't give her chance. 'Mayor Narcisse Planchet, death by lily of the valley poisoning, possibly, *possibly*, self-inflicted. He is also stabbed in the neck, some hours after death. Time of death is late evening, early hours of the morning, after hosting, or at least attending, a civil dinner with Noel Mabit and the two visiting *pétanque* teams.'

'*Boules.*' Valérie's interruption felt almost involuntary, it was a natural reflex for her to be contradictory.

'I'm only trying to help!' Richard, it has to be said, was rather enjoying himself now. He had never previously had a devil-may-care attitude and he was finding it rather fun. 'The question for me is why? I mean, the man seemed to virtually not exist.'

'I think that's it, Richard! He was hiding!'

It was an interesting point of view and to Richard's mind neatly summed up the state of French bureaucracy. If you stood for public office almost anywhere other than in France, you would be front and centre, taking undeserved plaudits, kissing children and so on. In France, with bureaucracy a largely faceless monolith, a medieval fort built against openness and individual responsibility, there was nowhere better to hide than low-level small town officialdom.

'It's difficult to see what he was hiding from though; nobody seems to have really known him.'

'Maybe we should look at the time he spent in Paris. He may have made enemies.'

'That's not going to be easy,' he replied. 'It's over forty years ago and he was only gone for three months.'

She pursed her lips in thought. 'I agree. It is difficult to see what could be done, disappearing for just three months.'

Quite right, Richard thought, *you'd need to disappear for about twenty years to really create some mischief.*

Valérie stopped the car with a skid on Martin and Gennie's wide gravel driveway, throwing a few stones on to the adjacent *pétanque* pitch, much to the annoyance of Angela Babcock and her niece.

'Richard!' she cried, and for a horrible second he really was convinced that she had read his thoughts and was about to admonish him. 'Noel Mabit must be the only one who knew Mayor Planchet well,' Valérie said intensely.

'Well he would certainly have seen him more than anyone else. You know, it's very difficult to think of them as romantic rivals.' He spoke to her back, his seat belt still buckled, as she had already got out of the car leaving Richard and a still sleeping Passepartout behind.

'I must speak with Edmond.' He heard her say as she marched off, leaving him to his thoughts.

'You rather put my niece off her throw!' Angela Babcock was smarting about their gravel-throwing arrival, though the timid Olivia didn't seem at all bothered. 'I feel sure she would have won that end.'

Richard shrugged apologetically from the passenger seat, but in a way that made clear that it wasn't actually his fault. Angela turned back to the game in something of a flounce, the wide, flowing sleeves of her floral blouse billowing like a yacht at sea. In the meantime Martin had approached a still-sitting Richard, tip-toeing so as not to disturb the players.

'I thought I took the game seriously,' – he leant in close to Richard and spoke in a hushed voice – 'but these people… obsessives. Are you getting out, old man, only I'd like to have a word if I may?'

There was a nervousness about Martin that Richard wasn't used to seeing. You don't have the kind of brash personality of a Martin, nor get up to the kind of things he and Gennie got up to – and Richard really, really didn't want any details – by exhibiting any kind of nerves. 'Is everything OK, Martin?' He climbed out of the car.

'It's about Valérie,' he said, looking over Richard's shoulder to make sure Valérie was well out of earshot. 'You and Valérie to be exact. Well, you, Valérie and this Edmond fella to be absolutely pinpoint.'

A metallic thud sounded behind him and a 'Bravo!' as Angela congratulated a rather embarrassed-looking Olivia for scattering her *boules*.

Richard climbed awkwardly out of the car, a deep sense of dread enveloping him as he pondered what on earth was vexing Martin. For one awful moment he had the feeling that he was about to receive an invitation to one of Martin and Gennie's notorious 'singles' evenings and felt like jumping back in the car and driving away. 'What's up, Martin?' he asked eventually and with a deep sigh.

Martin sighed back in return and if Valérie had been present to witness this conversational prelude she'd have highlighted it as the most English thing that could possibly exist. Two middle-aged Englishmen avoiding a delicate subject and communicating solely through the use of mercurial exhalation.

'Well, thing is,' Martin started and then paused again. 'I mean really, it's none of our business, but... you see, well... where do we stand and all that?'

'Where do we stand on what?' Richard replied a tad haughtily and began walking towards the garden. If this was to be a personal question about the status of the Valérie-Edmond-Richard triumvirate, it was frankly (a), none of Martin's business and (b), not something Richard felt at all qualified to answer.

'Well, you see, it's just Gennie feels a bit sorry for old Edmond, stuck out here with us and these *pétanque* blighters, and she wondered if we might invite Val for dinner. You know, just the four of us?' Richard's heart first leapt at the thought of not being invited and then immediately sank at the realisation that he really hadn't been invited. Edmond and Val, as Martin called her, though not to her face, were the couple. Martin was just checking that was OK with the defeated beau. 'I hope you don't mind?' he asked. 'Gennie thought it best if I prepared the ground, so to speak. Man to man.'

'Just for dinner?' Richard couldn't help but ask the question.

'Oh, yes! No, absolutely. Dinner!' Martin seemed almost offended. 'Well...' he added wistfully. 'Yes, I'm sure just dinner.'

'Of course,' Richard replied quietly. 'They are married after all. I don't really know why they're not actually staying in the same place.'

'Yes,' Martin agreed. 'That had struck us too. Well, I'll go and give Gennie the good news.' He paused. 'I hope you don't mind, old man, had to ask you know?'

Richard gave as much of a smile as he could to Martin and shrugged off any potential issue there might be, and then watched as Martin strode purposefully towards the house and a presumably waiting Gennie. *What a very odd man*, he thought, not for the first time. *So correct and mannered in one way and yet so pervertedly uninhibited in others.*

'Richard, it is good to see you!' A smiling eyepatched Edmond was sitting at a large, wrought-iron garden table. Valérie sat impatiently at his side and directly opposite him was Roddy Rougemare, fourteenth Duke of Anglethorp Spa, Marquess Shireholme, seventh Baron of whatever, and looking every inch the aristocrat in a smoking jacket and paisley cravat. 'Roddy is teaching me the rules of bezique,' Edmond continued, holding up a hand of playing cards. 'And I am doing rather well!'

'Ha!' Roddy said. 'Beginner's luck I call it. Fortunately we're only playing for matchsticks or I'd have lost the estate and most of its contents by now. And there's really not much more to lose!'

Richard noticed Valérie roll her eyes and it was obvious that she wanted to speak to Edmond alone and not be involved in what she no doubt regarded as time-wasting frivolity.

'I thought you'd be practising with the others?' Richard asked the question as a light conversation piece, even managing a chuckle at the end of it.

'Well, ordinarily I would be,' Roddy said as he lifted a card from the two packs face down on the table, placing it carefully into his hand. 'But I'm waiting for our Derek to emerge. Peculiar chap, that one,' he added.

'He sleeps late, does he?' Richard tried not to sound too interested.

'Not usually, no. But I heard him up late last night in his room, rummaging around for something. Like I say...'

'Odd chap, yes.'

'A bit of a fantasist if you ask me.' Roddy watched Edmond intently as the older man rearranged his cards.

'Oh really?'

'Yes, kept saying this was more than a jolly. That there was more at stake than a silly *pétanque* tournament. I mean, I agree in a way, but he still took it all very seriously.'

'Interesting.' Richard tried to make it sound like anything but and studiously avoided what he knew was Valérie's own interested eye boring into him. 'Well, I'll leave you lot to it,' he added and moved off nonchalantly but in a definite direction. Having managed to avoid being seen by Angela and Olivia – the latter being given yet another lesson in wrist control – he sneaked in the backdoor of Martin and Gennie's separate bed and breakfast wing.

He tiptoed quietly up the stairs, memories flooding back to him of the time he and Valérie had searched the place while on the trail of the Mafiosi who had killed his beloved Ava Gardner. A sense of determination came over him as he remembered the assassination of his adored hen. He had no idea which room belonged to Derek and toyed with the idea of just calling out the man's name, but decided against it. Eventually he found the only bedroom door that wasn't locked and quietly opened it. The curtains were closed so he turned on the light, immediately regretting the decision to do so. Martin and Gennie might have tempered their behaviour while the *boules* team were staying, but there was always evidence of their peccadilloes. The curtains were a street scene, like an old fashioned movie backdrop before the invention of CGI. The street in question was a disturbingly accurate representation of Amsterdam night life, so realistic that Richard felt he'd been transported there. Taking a deep breath, he crept to the window and looked through the gap in the curtains. After the dark of the room, what first struck him was the sunlight as it hit him squarely in the eyes, temporarily blinding him. After a moment his eyes adjusted and through the window he saw that the garden card table was now empty. The next thing that struck him was the scene of devastation in the room. Every drawer was open, its contents strewn about. The mattress had been upended, suitcases left open. There had clearly been a frantic search, but had Derek lost something or was it altogether more sinister?

The third thing that struck him was something heavy on the back of his head and he fell to the floor.

Chapter Ten

Richard woke groggily and waited for his eyes to focus before checking his watch; he'd been out cold for about thirty minutes. He sat up warily in case his head fell off, but he had to admit he felt remarkably fine. It was just like he'd had one of those post-lunch wine-hazy power naps and, honestly, he actually felt oddly refreshed.

This of course was a bad sign, a very bad sign indeed.

Richard had been assaulted by a professional clearly, someone who knew exactly what they were doing when it came to disabling opponents. Of course, the place was absolutely crawling with professionals at the moment; besides Valérie and Edmond, there was the elusive Detective Sergeant Derek Munro, who presumably also had some sort of skill in that area. Now Richard began to feel sore. He felt wounded. Before Valérie had broken into his life he'd managed to sail through his fifty-odd years pretty much unscathed. There was the occasional visit to casualty as a child, a pot on the head, that kind of tradition. He'd had his appendix removed in his mid-twenties, but by and large he had bustled along injury free. Then a secret service trained bounty hunter and possible assassin darkens his door, and he'd been shot at, bombed, thrown down stairs at least twice, brained by various implements on half a dozen occasions and nearly lost what remained of his masculinity in a sword fight.

'Oh, to be Ernest Thesiger!' he said out loud, a new mantra bore repeating once more.

It was then Richard looked about him, closed his eyes tightly and re-opened them again. The untidiness that he'd encountered when he first came into the room was no longer there. Every drawer was neatly closed, clothes were folded, suitcases stacked, wardrobe doors unopened. Even the bed had been made. For a brief moment he wondered if he'd been dragged, unconscious, into a different room but no, the curtains were confirmation of that. He stood gingerly and peeked through them. The view was much the same as before only the card table was full again with Valérie, Edmond, Roddy and Martin; and two others were at the *boules* piste, Angela and Olivia.

He shook his head again, hoping it might rearrange his own brain furniture and help to make things clearer, but it didn't work. Either he'd had a dream, a hallucination and then passed out through lack of nutrition or some such or – and this was certainly the more likely explanation – he'd been attacked by a skilful professional who had then tidied up, a sort of ninja chambermaid. It was all too confusing and he decided to get out while he could and before he was put out of action again. Assuming he was still alone, but wary nonetheless, he approached the stairs with caution, stepping carefully on the thick carpet runner.

A shadow appeared behind the frosted glass door at the bottom of the stairs and he froze. He had only one choice in his mind and that was to, in the words of Michael Caine in *The Man Who Would Be King*, 'Brass it out!' He stood tall, took a deep breath and put a strong foot forward. His foot immediately hit an alien object that was not part of the sturdy safety of the carpet runner, and it shot forward unbalancing him and sending him sliding like an Olympic tobogganist towards the foot of the stairs, the carpet runner now acting like a sheet of ice, aiding his propulsion downwards. The door opened and a startled Gennie just had time to see Richard hurtling down towards her at some speed. She stepped nimbly to one side as Richard finally hit the ground floor, sliding just a little further forward so that his legs were outdoors and his torso on the indoor welcome mat. One hand above his head as though hailing a taxi and the other behind his back holding on tightly to the alien object that had literally caused his downfall.

He looked up into the face of a worried Gennie. It was fair to say that she had seen some sights in her time had Gennie Thompson, but a middle-aged man sledging down the stairs at her with some speed had flustered her somewhat. Richard decided to stay perfectly still, not admit to the absurdity of the situation and really attack the thing in what his nan would have called 'that keep calm and carry on nonsense'.

'Could you give me a lift back into town, Gennie, please?' he asked blithely and without bothering to stand up. 'I need to buy some bread for lunch.'

The start of the short car journey was admittedly somewhat awkward. Richard and Gennie, though very different people with certainly very different tastes and interests, were still both very English and both, for the first few minutes, chose to ignore what had just occurred.

It is what the English are so very good at and where their reputation for tact and diplomacy originates, a sort of conversational 'sweep it all under the carpet'. Eventually though, Gennie's more exotic side broke through and she appeared really quite upset.

'I don't like to ask,' she said, visibly gripping the steering wheel tighter. 'I'm very much a live and let live kind of person, but I don't like people snooping around and these *pétanque* players already have me on edge.'

'I'm sorry, Gennie,' he tried to sound soothing. 'Why do they have you on edge?'

'Ever since Valérie – and I like her very much, I really do – but ever since Valérie came into town things have changed.' *That was something of an understatement*, he thought. 'And now, what with this Edmond... and you all, all alone...' Her voice cracked.

'Honestly, Gennie, I'm fine, really.'

'Then why are you snooping about like that? Were you looking for Edmond's room? Were you going to plant something incriminating on him, get him out of the way?'

She really was in something of a state, but also very supportive too. 'No!' he said genuinely. 'I was looking for Derek actually. I don't suppose you've seen him today, have you?'

'No, thank you!' Her voice hardened. 'I don't like him. He's made some, erm, lewd suggestions.'

She didn't expand on that and Richard, not for the first time, was amazed by the contradictions in Gennie. She could be so demure, almost chaste at times, yet Richard had seen the other side, her and Martin's erotically equipped 'dungeon' for example. He liked her, for some reason felt sorry for her too, but there was no escaping the fact that she was part sexually-charged cabaret act and part rosary-clutching Mother Superior.

'I need to find Derek,' he said eventually, not really wanting to explore the upper limits of her lewd-tolerance.

'That shouldn't be too difficult, not with those silly hats he's always wearing. A different tartan for every day... really!'

'Indeed,' Richard replied dubiously and felt in his pocket for the object that had caused his stair fall, a tartan tam-o'-shanter.

Gennie dropped Richard off at the *boulangerie* and he was happy to be alone again. Nothing seemed to make any sense to him so to be back in the centre of town with its never changing French constants was a source of comfort. Old friends greeted each other warmly, commenting on the continued fine weather, then they would swap detailed accounts of their medical woes before the local gossip began. The queue for Jeanine's *boulangerie* went a good fifteen metres out of the door and was where all the news spread. Dominating the otherwise flawless skyline was the church, absurdly large for a town of Saint-Sauver's size, overwhelming, yet sturdy and on a scale even larger than the small chateau that was still being refurbished. The tables outside René's bar were once again full and he could see René himself gruffly taking orders. When you looked about like this, he told himself, you could feel that the world really was a wonderful place. Then he remembered that the mayor of this idyll had just been murdered and he himself had been clobbered by a highly trained professional. *Such a shame*, he thought.

Richard took a seat at an outside table at René's bar and distractedly ordered a pastis. An hour later and two more pastis into his thoughts, he was nowhere nearer working out what was going on and Derek, unfortunately, had not wandered by as he'd hoped. The crowds thinned out and René, with post lunchtime shift fatigue, came and sat opposite him.

'Are you all right, Richard?' René Dupont, a former 'strong-arm' in the Paris underworld, had a way of making even the most concerned questions sound like a threat.

'Me?' Richard replied, briefly taking his eyes off the door of the town hall, the *mairie*. 'Oh yes, fine. Absolutely fine.'

'Are you sure?' René leant in menacingly.

'Well, you know?' Richard tried to laugh it off. There was no point pretending that everything was hunky dory, because even when things were hunky dory, Richard rarely let it show. If he started bouncing about now like some Tiggerish optimist, people really would start to worry. 'Ups and downs,' he added.

René now leant in so close Richard could smell the stale cigarette smoke on his breath. 'I do know people, right?'

'Right.' Richard had no idea what the man, a good friend, was talking about.

'I can make him disappear again.' He winked, then leant back. 'Think about it.'

They were interrupted by a customer calling for the bill and a relieved Richard breathed out heavily as René barked the total at the now gibbering customer. The door to the town hall banged shut and caught Richard's attention. Monsieur and Madame Noel Mabit, rarely tolerating each other under normal circumstances emerged, arm in arm, from the *mairie*. They stopped as the sunlight hit them and Madame Mabit, Monique, put on some sunglasses while Noel took a smart beret from his jacket pocket and placed it on his head, adjusting it slightly to what could only be described as a rakish angle.

They walked, once again arm in arm, towards the bar, the very model of a respectable, loving couple. They both nodded a greeting to an open-mouthed Richard who couldn't hold back. 'I like your hat, Noel,' he said, trying not to sound sarcastic.

'Thank you, Monsieur Ainsworth.'

'I bought it for him on our honeymoon,' Madame Mabit cooed. 'It rather suits him, don't you think?'

They both giggled like nauseating newlyweds and went on their way.

'René!' Richard shouted. 'Just bring me the bottle!'

It arrived in what seemed like seconds. 'Thought about it, Richard?'

'What? Oh, still mulling it over. I'll let you know.'

He poured himself a large measure and added some water. *What else?* he thought. *What else could possibly turn this day upside down?*

There was a clatter as glasses clinked and a shadow fell across him. A fancy dog bed was placed on the table in front of him, a semi-naked miniature poodle in it, a look of displeasure and guilt on its face.

'Oh no,' he groaned.

'I've been looking for you,' Oriane Moulin said in a tone almost as menacing as René's. 'You owe me!'

Chapter Eleven

'So there we have it. We're up to date and you know as much as I do.' Richard looked intently into the keen faces of those watching who, it seemed, came to a conclusion as one and offered genuine, albeit low-level support. 'Thank you,' he said with heartfelt gratitude. 'That means a lot.'

It was Olivia de Havilland who went further and squawked loudly as if affronted on his behalf. Richard looked at her in agreement with the sentiment and then sat down in the corner. That his hens were a source of comfort was one thing, he realised, but to seek their counsel on highly personal and indeed homicidal matters was perhaps taking things a bit too far. Right now though, his options, he realised, were somewhat limited. The idea of confronting Valérie with the news that her nemesis Oriane Moulin was back in town, on top of suspecting her husband of murder, was too much to bear and would need some thought. Former colleagues in the French secret service they may have been, but there was no love lost between the two. He had thought about ringing Clare, but then told himself that it was time he stood on his own two feet. Once on his own two feet he had buckled and began to type the number of his daughter Alicia, before remembering that she was pregnant and could probably do without the hassle. Which brought him neatly back to the problem in hand and this audience with his poultry therapy team; 'emotional support animals' was the modern term he believed. He was intent on putting it all down to shock, left stunned as he was by the whirlwind conversational mugging from the infernal, troublemaking Oriane Moulin.

He didn't know her all that well but their brief acquaintance had borne bitter fruit. The folk-singing former model, ex-wife of a politician, had disappointed Valérie in not being guilty of a number of murders in their most recent investigation. She had seemingly dallied cruelly with the affections of Commissaire Henri Lapierre as well and, Valérie had told him, endangered the lives of comrades on a difficult covert mission in Libya leading to the loss, albeit temporarily, of her husband. Worse, in Richard's eyes, she had re-introduced the said husband, Edmond Masson, into Valérie's life equation, and left Richard himself bereft, angry and stuck in a classic film character rut of 'brave loser' that he was finding it difficult to get out of.

'You owe me!' Oriane Moulin had repeated angrily, before pulling a chair back and flouncing down on it like a sullen teenager.

His first thought had been, 'Great, that's all I need, another highly trained killer lunatic in my life.'

It transpired that she had just returned from the vet and that Zsa Zsa, her ludicrously sculpted miniature poodle, all cuffs and curls, was pregnant. The dog didn't look particularly repentant about this, even exuding a certain glow, but it was clear that Oriane felt violated on her behalf, and clear also where she lay the blame for this unblessed union: Valérie's Passepartout.

Richard's mood darkened again at the thought, his mind now back in the coop and, with classic horror film timing, he heard two crows fighting in the fields. *Yes*, he thought darkly, *even Passepartout was getting more action than he was.*

At first, and fortified with a decent quantity of lunchtime pastis, he had fought back. 'Firstly,' he'd said, slurring his words ever so slightly, 'Passepartout is not my dog. What the creature gets up to therefore is none of my business. And secondly, if you will name your dog after an actress who was married nine times, what do you expect?' He'd felt rather pleased with himself and, watching as the wind briefly left Oriane's sails, he'd taken a victory sip feeling that he'd earned the right. So far that morning he'd been first knocked unconscious and then knocked sideways as the Mabits engaged in what looked like a teenage romance; usually a heart-warming image, especially in a forty-year marriage, but which in this case felt oddly sinister. He had also singularly failed to locate Detective Sergeant Derek Munro, who was presumably conducting his enquiries elsewhere. And now, the scourge who had brought Edmond Masson into his orbit, crushing any chances he might have had with Valérie, was practically frothing at the mouth and blaming him for her ridiculous pooch being knocked up.

'There's only so much a man can take, you know?' he pleaded at his hens.

'Talking of multiple, multiple marriages,' Oriane had said slyly, her composure restored. 'Where is your partner? Your *business* partner, I mean.'

Oriane Moulin had smiled her way through the question so that if you weren't within earshot, you'd never know the undertone of malevolence attached. To the onlooker it looked like a polite question. And there were a lot of onlookers. Oriane was world-famous, or at least French famous, which to the French is the same thing. If Richard regarded Valérie as the epitome of French womanhood, as seen through the eyes of a boy who'd grown up in England in the 1970s, then Oriane was Bardot squared. He was aware that all eyes were on them both; she looked playful and happy and he had the look of a man who suspected there might be a gun under the table and it was pointed at his genitalia. Only metaphorically of course, but such was her outrage at Zsa Zsa's condition, he wouldn't have put it past her.

'I don't know where Valérie is,' he'd said eventually, trying to sound indifferent but knowing, after a few drinks, he just sounded hurt.

'Poor Richard,' she oozed through another glorious smile. 'No doubt they are getting reacquainted after all these years. Picnics on the river bank, walks in the woods…' She was gleefully twisting the knife while maintaining her beaming face and even, just for the crowd, sliding her foot up and down his shin.

'Maybe,' he said stiffly while sitting upright in his chair and moving his legs out of harm's way. 'I think they have more pressing issues actually, what with the murder of the mayor and all.'

It seemed highly unlikely to Richard that anyone within an internet's radius of Saint-Sauver would not have heard of the death of Mayor Narcisse Planchet, but Oriane looked shocked nonetheless. He rubbed the back of his head, just behind the ear, where the after-effects of his attack that morning were only now beginning to ache.

'Is something wrong with your head, Richard?' Her mood had changed, it was no longer aggressive, it was the opposite; it was warm and caring and therefore infinitely more alarming.

'I'm fine,' he replied coldly. 'Where were you this morning by the way?'

She leant across the table and held his hand. 'Why, did you need me?'

Whatever noise the Doomsday clock eventually has to make when it chimes, presumably a cross between air raid sirens, nuclear evacuation alarms and a thousand screaming souls in hell, that sound was now filling Richard's head. But he was also aware that one of the most desired women in France, her long auburn hair blowing gently in the breeze, was openly flirting with him and it was a salve to an ego recently more battered than a Friday night cod in Grimsby.

It all came pouring out. He told her about the mayor's death. He hadn't meant to, but he did. He told her about Valérie and Edmond, against his better judgement. He told her about the ceramic evidence, Detective Inspector Derek Munro and his suspicions of Edmond and seriously wondered if it was the right thing to do. But he did it anyway, albeit with some reluctance.

In the end, she had leant back and lit a cigarette with almost post-coital languor. 'I wonder…' she said eventually through a stream of smoke.

Richard had bitten. 'You wonder what?'

'I wonder if Edmond Masson is really who he says he is.'

She'd left the statement hanging in the air with the smoke which might have well swirled itself into a giant question mark.

'Don't you know?' he'd asked with a certain sense of exasperation. 'I mean, you worked with him.'

'That was twenty years ago. We have all changed and he has been through a lot in that time, wouldn't you say?'

Richard indeed would say. The story of Edmond Masson was now imprinted on his brain. The three of them, Valérie, Oriane and Edmond on a mission in Libya to rescue a French hostage. Unfortunately, however, and he realised belatedly that he only had Valérie's word for this, Oriane had gone gung-ho, the hostage was dead and Edmond taken prisoner.

'Surely you would recognise him?' he'd asked, looking for a sign of doubt.

She had shrugged. 'I remember a very dynamic man with a blond crewcut. This man has longer hair and an eyepatch.' Then she had paused. 'I *thought* that he was dead.'

'You don't think it's him? You think this man is an imposter?'

Again, the shrug. 'I do not know now.'

Richard had exploded. 'Well, thanks a bloody bunch! You might have made sure before you dropped him at my place looking for his ex-wife!'

'Wife,' she'd corrected him.

'Whatever.' His reply had been sulky.

Then she'd leant forward, stubbing her cigarette out slowly in the ashtray. 'Richard,' – she'd waited for him to look her in the eye – 'we must form an alliance, I think. Maybe this man is not who he says he is…'

'But…' he had tried to interrupt.

'Maybe Valérie is in danger.' Then she leant back and waited for his response.

Richard's shoulders had slumped, not so much in defeat but something close to it nonetheless. 'You know, I was really happy,' he'd began quietly. 'My wife had just left me, I'd bought a new cinema surround-sound system and some old cinema chairs; my only real friends were poultry. The world was finally how I wanted it. Then murders, secret service, free sex, violence, fraud, assassination… this isn't my world.'

'Free sex?'

'I added that bit for dramatic effect.'

'Oh.'

They had sat in silence for a minute or two. 'So what's the plan?' Richard asked her, hoping his last comment would be scratched from the records.

'Leave it with me,' was her determined response and with that she had stood, posed momentarily for the many phone cameras pointed in her direction, picked up Zsa Zsa and catwalked into the distance.

'And so,' – Richard turned back to his now sleepy hens, a pleading note in his voice as if asking forgiveness – 'I can't help feeling I've made a terrible mistake.' Lana Turner clucked disapprovingly. 'I know,' Richard replied immediately. 'And I'm glad you asked that question, but to be honest I don't know what the hell's going on either.

I do know one thing though,' he added, knowing that his next sentence would probably, and amongst pretty stiff competition, be the most English thing he'd ever uttered. 'I could do with a really good lie-in.'

'Richard!' It was Valérie just the other side of the thin coop walls and with a tone in her voice that suggested lie-ins would have to wait. 'Are you there?' He stayed silent, hoping she was either a figment of extreme tiredness or, if not, that she would just go away. 'We must go, Richard! The town hall, it has been burgled!'

Chapter Twelve

Neither Richard nor, he suspected, Valérie knew quite what to expect when they arrived at the *mairie* of Saint-Sauver, but some kind of official presence at the very least. Instead, apart from a dull light from an upstairs window, the place was shrouded in darkness. It was nearly two in the morning and Richard was wondering if Valérie had got all her facts quite straight.

'Are you sure he meant this town hall?' he whispered, as they walked towards the stone steps.

'Of course!' she hissed back.

'And you're sure it was the Commissaire?' he prodded, hoping to sound playful rather than irritable.

Valérie was about as playful as a rattlesnake with a hangover, however, and whirled on him, her torch, stronger than the illumination from a lighthouse, momentarily blinding him.

'I think I would recognise the voice of my ex-husband, Richard!'

In response, his eyebrow arched so high it almost certainly left the arc of Valérie's torch. Whatever she had planned to do next in her frustration they were both interrupted by the creak of the large wooden door and a shaft of light bathed the steps. Noel Mabit peered out and looked nervously about him, before silently beckoning them in.

'Are the police not here, Noel?' Richard asked reasonably as Noel closed the door behind them.

'What is going on?' Valérie demanded, her patience as usual somewhere near to breaking down.

'Monsieur Mabit is acting under my instructions.' The Commissaire emerged from the shadows rather like a pantomime villain. 'I do not want the whole town to know about this until I can establish some alibis.'

It seemed a reasonable thing to do under the circumstances but Valérie snorted derisively anyway.

'What *has* happened?' she asked again. 'You said there had been a break-in, Henri.'

'There has!' Inevitably the Commissaire's finger pointed in success.

Richard was a big fan of taking one's victories whenever and wherever they came, but it did rather seem that the Commissaire was feeling triumphant simply for having discovered evidence of a crime, and not the solving bit, which is surely closer to the point.

'And is anything missing?' Richard had spent a lot of time in the *mairie* – the sheer colossal weight of French bureaucratic paperwork demanded that he do so – but he couldn't think what might need to be stolen from the place apart from, of course, important documents.

The Commissaire didn't answer and instead nodded towards Noel, whose own small torch was now concentrated on a bare wall. It was clear though that the wall hadn't been bare for long. There was an outline of discolouration on the yellow wall showing that, until recently, a painting had hung there. Not a large painting, but a painting nonetheless. Richard tried to recall what the painting had been. All the time spent here and he hadn't noticed it at all.

Valérie walked slowly towards the wall, her worried look exaggerated in the torchlight. 'Turn the lights on, Henri, please. We must look around more carefully, not in the dark.'

It was Noel who moved off and within moments the shadowy darkness had been replaced by a slightly less shadowy darkness as the new eco-friendly LED lightbulbs seemed to resent being woken up at such an hour and took an age to actually illuminate anything.

'I can't remember what was hanging there, Noel? Remind me.' Richard took a step forward and ignored Noel's tutting at his lack of awareness.

'It was *Scène sur la Loire*,' Lapierre interrupted.

'By some Englishman,' Noel added peevishly.

'A Turner?' Richard was even more surprised that he couldn't remember it. 'A J.M.W. Turner? Here in Saint-Sauver? And you just let it hang on the wall in reception?'

'Was it an original, monsieur?' Valérie's eyes shone brightly with the excitement of it all.

'No,' Noel said simply and neither Valérie nor Richard could hide their immense disappointment.

'Tell them, monsieur.' The Commissaire was rocking gently on the balls of his feet, a sure sign that a major breakthrough was about to be revealed and he was in crowing mood.

'It was not an original Turner,' Noel began nervously, his brief attempt at bullishness having drained away with the darkness. 'It was an original Planchet.'

There was silence for a moment as Richard and Valérie took this in. 'So, he copied the Turner?' Richard asked. He was somewhat surprised. In his brief dealings with the late mayor he'd have struggled to imagine the man holding a brush still let alone forging one of the great watercolourists of the nineteenth century.

'Are you suggesting, monsieur, that the mayor was a professional forger?' Valérie didn't seem entirely convinced either.

Noel looked to the ground and shrugged like a naughty schoolboy.

'But why?' It was Richard who was prepared to ask the obvious question. 'Why steal a forgery?'

It was the cue the Commissaire had been waiting for. 'I think it is obvious that whoever stole this painting did not know it was a forgery!' He banged a clenched fist into the palm of the opposite hand.

'But why kill the mayor?' Richard had a feeling that the policeman was more interested in a swift result than actual facts.

'Ah!' It was clear that the Commissaire wasn't done yet.

'I think that Mayor Planchet was part of a wider network.' He began pacing the room. 'Someone in that network feels that they have been deceived...'

'You mean someone palmed them off with a forgery?' Richard asked, still unable to hide his scepticism.

The Commissaire ignored him. 'Someone in that network feels they have been conned. They didn't get the cut they feel they deserved, perhaps? Maybe there is an original somewhere and they want that back?' He was beginning to run out of steam. 'The mayor would not give this person their cut and so – pfft! – he is wiped out.'

'I don't know,' Richard mused. 'I didn't know Mayor Planchet very well but I do know he used a stamp instead of a signature on documents because of the DTs.'

'DTs?' the Commissaire asked.

'*Delerium tremens*,' Richard explained. 'The old man was a soak.'

While they pondered this seemingly unbridgeable gap between genius art copyist and gin-addled old lush, Valérie was at the door checking on the lock.

'This is obviously where they broke in,' she confirmed. The mess of splintered wood around the heavy Chubb lock was clear to see.

'Not very subtle, is it?' Richard said. 'Which at least rules some people out of the equation.'

He hadn't meant to sound quite so sure of himself, he was the kind of person who liked to leave room for doubt, but there was something nagging at him and while he couldn't say exactly what that something was, it was there. As a result he was merely thinking aloud, though at the same time allowing himself the illusion that he was Basil Rathbone's Sherlock Holmes explaining the elementary to those too blind to see it for themselves.

'What do you mean?' The Commissaire wasn't too keen on having his thunder stolen and eyed Richard with an air of mistrust. Valérie, on the other hand, was watching carefully, even encouragingly.

'Well, it's obvious, my dear Lestrade...'

'Lapierre.'

'My mistake. It's obvious. This break-in is crude. The door has been hacked at and from the front too. To my mind that's amateurish, so we rule out the five professionals.'

'And who are these *professionals*?' The Commissaire's eyes squinted in suspicion.

'Well, like I say, that's obvious. For one, Valérie couldn't have done it. Not subtle enough.'

This took the Commissaire by surprise, while Valérie's eyes narrowed in suspicion. 'I didn't suspect that she had,' Lapierre pounced. 'So why are you so keen to rule her out?'

This wasn't going quite how Richard had intended and it was clear Valérie expected a pretty good answer to the question as well. 'Then there's Edmond Masson,' he added quickly, ignoring the question, 'someone else with the skills to do a more subtle job.'

'You are ruling out this Edmond Masson?' The Commissaire looked surprised and a little disappointed in Richard. As was Richard, if he were honest. 'And where *is* your husband, madame?'

'How would I know?' Valérie scoffed. 'I am not his keeper!'

It was becoming quite clear why they'd lost contact for over twenty years, but Richard was keen to move on. 'Then,' he allowed a note of victory into his voice. 'We have Detective Sergeant Derek Munro of Scotland Yard!'

The three others looked at him in a mixture of awe and shock.

'But, Richard,' – it was Valérie who broke the silence – 'how do you know that this Derek is a policeman?'

'Well,' Richard stumbled. 'He told me. He's been on the trail of an art smuggling ring for years. He didn't say what exactly, but this certainly fits the bill.'

The Commissaire scratched his chin. 'I would like to speak to this Detective Inspector Derek Munro of Scotland Yard. He is operating on my territory!' Then he paused. 'So, that's three…'

'René,' Valérie said simply.

'Yes?' The timing was spot on. The minute Valérie confirmed René as one of the five professionals, the stocky, muscular figure of René Dupont filled the doorway. The former thumbscrew merchant for the Paris underworld always looked threatening anyway, but even more so with the moonlight behind him giving his silhouette a blue glow.

'Why are you here, monsieur?' the Commissaire asked sharply.

'I saw the light and wondered what was going on,' was René's equally sharp response. Officialdom didn't cow René Dupont.

'Yes, we did too.' Behind René was the entire Avignon Arrivistes *pétanque* team in various forms of pyjamas and nightwear. They had the look of a vigilante committee from some old horror film.

The Commissaire threw his head back in defeat and closed his eyes. 'We may as well have sold tickets,' he breathed out heavily.

'Something going on?' Martin Thompson appeared around the corner, still wearing his rather questionable baseball cap. He was also without Gennie, which surprised Richard, and was wearing a large lily of the valley flower tucked behind one ear.

'And why are *you* here?' The Commissaire was now sounding weary.

'I saw the light and wondered what was going on,' he replied unconvincingly.

The Commissaire buried his head in his hands. 'You saw the light from the village you live in?'

'Ah. Late-night stroll and all that, y'know?'

The Commissaire straightened up and took a deep breath. 'I must ask you all to go back to your beds, and in some cases, villages. There is nothing to see here…'

Richard left them to it and took another stroll around the town hall reception. He walked behind the counter and realised for the first that it had a raised floor. *These petty bureaucrats think of everything*, he thought. Then he trod on something that crunched loudly underfoot and he bent down to pick it up.

'Found something, Monsieur Ainsworth?' It was Noel hovering around his kingdom.

'What's this?' Richard asked.

'Isn't it obvious?' The officious little man replied, before pointing to a smashed display case in the corner. 'That was attacked too. We keep old earthenware pots that are dug up in the fields on display. Some are thousands of years old.' He puffed his chest out with pride.

Richard turned the piece over in his hand. It was almost exactly the same as the piece he'd found under the dead mayor in the dresser.

He put it in his pocket as he became aware that Valérie was approaching. 'That's four, Richard,' she said intensely. 'I do not understand. Who is our fifth professional?'

He could have broken the news more delicately certainly, but in his defence he was slightly distracted, still, 'Oh, didn't I tell you? Oriane Moulin's back in town,' was blunter than he would have liked even if the effect would have been much the same anyway.

Chapter Thirteen

Richard and Valérie had barely exchanged another word before frostily saying goodnight and things were still decidedly chilly at breakfast the next morning. Valérie was obviously brooding at the reappearance of her one-time colleague, now nemesis, Oriane, while Richard felt he hadn't received the glory he deserved for his professional/amateur thesis. Even less so when with the Commissaire's parting words were, 'It looks like this policeman of yours has absconded with a fake painting, monsieur!' Well played, he'd added sarcastically, '*bien joué!*'

Neither one of them felt they could talk, either. The wine-tasting Brits had rolled in noisily at about four in the morning and were therefore late for breakfast, meaning Richard and Valérie could be interrupted at any moment. Valérie though, inevitably, could hold it all in no longer.

'I do not like it,' she said, her tone suggesting the apocalypse was close at hand. 'What does she want now?'

In ripe mid-season form Richard might have ventured to lighten the mood with a breezy 'maybe she's dug up another husband for you?' but he strongly suspected this was neither the time nor the place, and wasn't sure even if the time or the place actually existed for such arch levity.

'I rather got the impression,' he said, trying to sound practical, 'that it wasn't really you she was looking for.' He placed a cup of coffee on the table in front of her. 'Was it old son?' he added, demanding the question of Passepartout. The small dog, sensing trouble, buried his head into his bed.

'What do you mean?' Valérie was immediately on the defensive, which meant that she was attacking.

'Well...' Richard wasn't now sure how to broach the subject, but knew it had to be in English, where he had a greater wealth of euphemism. 'It seems young fella-me-lad here has been getting his breakfast oats.' He nodded as if that were an end to the matter.

Valérie looked at him blankly. 'I do not understand. He's eaten something he shouldn't have?'

'Sort of. No, what I mean to say is, Passepartout's been shucking the oyster, as it were.'

'He *has* eaten something he shouldn't!' She grabbed the startled dog and hugged him to her chest.

'No, that's not what I'm saying, though in a way...'

'Oh, Richard! Just tell me what it is, I am now so worried!'

'Well, he's been having it away, hasn't he?'

'Having what away?'

'No. Look. Funny business. Hanky panky. Rolling in the hay. That sort of thing.'

'Are you OK, Richard?'

'He's knocked up Zsa Zsa,' he confessed eventually.

'Knocked up? Oh.' She paused, having finally penetrated his euphemism barrage. As the reality and no doubt the consequences dawned on her, her face changed. 'That hussy!' she cried. 'She must have attacked him!'

Steam was still metaphorically coming out of her ears as Richard's guests came noisily down the stairs their timing, to Richard's mind, perfect. Valérie snatched up Passepartout and took him outside. Richard felt a bit sorry for the little creature; he was presumably about to get a lecture on 'ladies of the night' and 'taking precautions', but it seemed a little harsh on the chap.

Madame Tablier came in through the door at the same time as Valérie left, and just in time to see the sight of the English guests who looked like their wine-tasting odyssey was taking its toll.

'Madame Tablier, could you take over, please? We have an emergency.'

She looked at the small, dishevelled group in front of her. 'Right,' she said, laying her broom to one side. 'Elbows off the table and sit up straight. If any of you have been sick in my bedrooms, you'll pay double. Coffee?'

Richard found Valérie sitting in her sports car, a contrite Passepartout, his head bowed in shame, on the backseat.

'Come on,' he said brightly, trying to shift her mood. 'We've got work to do.'

They decided that their first stop would be René's bar to check on the alibis of the Avignon Arrivistes. It was actually all Valérie's idea and she also seemed determined to break the land speed record in order to do it. When they arrived though, she sat rooted to her seat.

'Of course,' she said slyly, 'you may be wrong, Richard.'

He nodded vigorously, acknowledging from a lifetime's experience that the possibility was a strong one. 'It's been said often, but then, I'm not a vet, am I?'

'No. Not about that.' Her chin hardened. 'I mean about the locks on the door. Yes, it may be an amateur who broke in. But it might also be a professional trying to make it look like an amateur.' Richard sighed. He had a feeling he knew where this was going. 'Like Oriane Moulin, for instance.' She tossed the name into the air as if she'd just found it on the tip of her tongue and thought it might float nicely away in the breeze. Then she got out of the car taking Passepartout with her.

'Good point,' Richard muttered to himself. 'Or Edmond Masson, perhaps?' He got out of the car too and followed her. 'Or, maybe it's a professional, pretending to be an amateur double-bluffing as a professional?' he said, striding past her.

'Brilliant, Richard!' she exclaimed, standing still. 'You are right. Exactly the kind of thing Oriane Moulin would do, no?'

He couldn't help shaking his head, his mood obviously matching that of a morose René Dupont who was outside his bar smoking as they approached. 'They're out back,' he said, not happily. Valérie marched to the back garden and René turned to Richard when she was out of earshot. 'When do you think this will end?' he almost pleaded. 'They're driving away regular customers. Yesterday, they rearranged all my tables and started playing bloody *boules* indoors!'

'With the full metal *boules*?' Richard could only imagine the floor damage.

'No, those beach ones. But even so...' He shrugged as Richard began walking through to the rear patio area. 'These people are obsessed,' René added, making the same complaint Martin had made.

'I do not understand why you are asking these questions, madame.' Agathe Deschanel, perched on her walking frame which was presumably adapted to international *pétanque* standards, was in a petulant mood. 'I haven't had my usual twelve hours,' she moaned, 'and you come by asking the same questions as the Commissaire. Why?' She narrowed her eyes at Valérie in a way that suggested it was a power tactic she used often, but Valérie was not one to be brushed off.

'We want to make sure that everyone is safe, that is all. Monsieur Mabit has asked us to act on behalf of the council.' She looked to Richard for support.

'Yes, you know. What with the mayor being out of action, we're a kind of guest safety subcommittee.'

Philippe Gratin, wearing a different Johnny Hallyday tour T-shirt today, one that showed a silhouetted Johnny in crotch-breakingly tight denim, guitar slung over his shoulder walking into the sunset. Gratin crouched into a *boule* throwing position, not with any grace, his bulk wouldn't allow that. 'Are you the same safety committee that was looking after the dead mayor?' He let his *boule* fly through the air and it landed with a resounding crash, scattering his opponent's *boules*. He looked at Richard and Valérie and added a 'Hmmm?' to his question.

Richard couldn't help acknowledging that it was a pretty fair question.

'As we told the Commissaire,' – Alphonse Berlioz adopted the same throwing position as his teammate – 'we were all in bed from about ten thirty last night. We keep a very strict timetable. Then we heard this commotion.' He let go of his own *boule*, which landed right on top of the now vulnerable *cochonnet* and wiped a victory finger under his thin moustache.

'I wasn't in bed.' Fatouma Dembele had been standing apart from the rest of her team and quietly taking in all that was being said. She had an almost distracted look on her face, but a very playful twinkle in her eye. She was also almost a foot taller than everybody else and the only one to really give their matching tracksuits much sporting style.

'You were not?' Alphonse didn't look best pleased that a team curfew had been broken.

'No,' she replied at the same time as letting her *boule* go, dislodging Alphonse's leading ball. 'I went for a walk. I like the night.'

'Did you see anyone, madame?' Valérie asked.

'Oh yes, yes I did.' She bent down and threw her colleagues' *boules* back to them. It was a nicely timed dramatic pause and Richard felt, not for the first time, that Fatouma quite enjoyed the spotlight.

'Well, who?' Valérie asked impatiently.

It was Richard who answered. 'It wasn't Martin Thompson by any chance, was it?' he asked with a heavy sigh.

She nodded with a smile. 'It was, monsieur, and I must say...'

'Yes?' Valérie pounced on a potential snippet of information.

'He is a very peculiar individual.'

'That's one way of putting it,' Richard replied. He had a feeling that Martin's cat on heat night-time activities might get the man into trouble with this investigation. 'Dare I ask what you talked about?'

'I have nothing to hide. Mr Thompson had been watching a documentary about my country and wished to know more, that is all.'

Richard gave this some thought. On the face of it, it sounded perfectly reasonable; he knew very well that Martin was a bit of a history buff. On the other hand, meeting Martin late at night to discuss one of his 'documentaries' had entirely different connotations.

Agathe broke his chain of thought by wheeling her walking frame to the throwing circle. She was very thin, to the point of frailty, and didn't look like she could pick up a *boule*, let alone throw it. 'We had a team vote,' she said sternly, 'about whether to stay here or go home. It was unanimous.'

'When do you leave?' René asked hopefully from behind his outside bar.

'We are staying!' It was Philippe who replied. 'Whether the English will, I would not like to say.'

'And the vote was unanimous, you say?' Richard admired their spirit.

'Eventually.' Fatouma gave him a confident smile.

'In all honesty, I wanted to leave. I am worried about the stress to Madame Deschanel.' Alphonse threw the *cochonnet* about three-quarters down the piste.

'I wanted to go as well,' Philippe reluctantly admitted.

Agathe shrugged. 'It was Fatouma who changed our minds,' she said proudly. 'We represent our sport and nothing gets in the way of *pétanque*. That is why we have become such an international success in recent years, played all over the world.' She threw her *boule* which seemed to arc against the laws of physics before nestling next to its small wooden target.

If Richard had been concentrating he'd have concluded that the English team didn't stand a chance against these people. René was right, they were obsessives, but they were also highly skilled. He wasn't concentrating, however, as his mind was elsewhere. Fatouma had overturned a majority decision and it reminded him of *Twelve Angry Men*, a 1957 taut cinema classic about a jury being persuaded to change their own minds.

'*Twelve Angry Men*,' he said, as if in a dream.

Fatouma smashed Agathe's ball away with a perfect shot. 'Men are always angry,' she said, her smile dipping for a moment. 'The number is irrelevant.'

Chapter Fourteen

At Martin and Gennie's place, things didn't seem to have changed at all in the intervening twenty-four hours. Angela Babcock and her niece Olivia were still playing *boules*, Roddy and Edmond were at the garden table continuing their complicated card game and, more suspiciously, Derek had still not been seen.

'It really is most inconvenient,' Angela decried. 'One must build up a chemistry in a team. He really should be here.' She was sounding quite petulant about the whole thing rather than worried that anything sinister might be behind the man's disappearance.

'Do you really need chemistry?' Valérie asked slowly. Richard knew when she was in 'prodding the beehive with a stick' mode, which was at least ninety-nine per cent of the time.

'Of course you do!' Angela replied with such strength of emotion that Olivia even blushed. 'It's taken us six months to knock His Grace into shape...' She strained to control herself. 'Since his poor father passed away.'

Valérie didn't answer but turned and walked towards the card game. Richard heard her mutter into Passepartout's ear, 'Silly woman!'

'Has he disappeared like this before?' Richard asked.

Angela didn't immediately answer, but he saw her glance quickly at her niece out of the corner of her eye. She took a step back so that she was now behind Olivia and performed the classic 'he likes a drink' mime with a glass-empty hand to the mouth. Freeze-framed it might have looked like she was saying Olivia had a problem with alcohol, but he knew she was just trying to protect her. From what though? It was almost like the poor girl was being kept from anything interesting in the world at all. Olivia meanwhile arced a throw at a deliberately placed and fiendish *boule* set-up, smashing the ensemble to pieces and nestling her own ball by the *cochonnet*. Innocent she may be but she was also a demon player, for sure. Then it occurred to Richard what was going on; the poor girl wasn't being protected as such, she just wasn't to be distracted. She was being hothoused and kept focussed, like an Olympic gymnast from the old Soviet Union. Realising this, he felt sorry for her. She was about the same age as his daughter, Alicia, but she looked much, much younger.

He moved closer to Angela and out of earshot of Olivia. 'Did you know he's a policeman?' he asked quietly.

Angela looked at him seriously, but seriously as in, 'are you seriously asking me that?' And then out of nowhere came the most extraordinary laugh. It was a cross between the deep sigh of old plumbing and the sound two foxes make at night when they think they're alone. It was clear she didn't let herself go like this often and also clear to Richard that this was a genuine guffaw, because no one in their right mind would choose that outrageous brouhaha as a false laugh. She even slapped him playfully on the shoulder, but he remained unmoved. Suddenly she regained control of herself, cleared her throat and leant in. 'You must be joking?' she said, her face now stony and cold.

'He told me he was a detective sergeant for Scotland Yard and had worked in the Customs and Excise department tracking international art smuggling.'

She took a deep breath. 'Derek Munro has barely ever left Anglethorp Spa. He took over his father's rather dreary hardware shop at an early age and has fantasised about doing something different for the past thirty-odd years. And usually in the pub.' She sighed again; she really did have a touch of Jessica Fletcher about her. 'I'm afraid he's rather taken you in, Mr Ainsworth.' Abruptly she turned away. 'Six more ends before a break, Olivia, my dear. Then we'll massage those wrists.'

Richard still didn't want to believe that he had been hoodwinked quite so easily and while he ruminated he became aware of the presence of Martin at his shoulder. 'It's all in the wrist apparently,' Martin said a touch plaintively, and then reasserted himself. 'Listen, old man, I didn't want to say anything in front of Val, but we had that Moulin woman here this morning.'

Richard immediately snapped out of his Angela Lansbury reverie and back into a much more complicated real world. 'I appreciate the thought,' he said genuinely. 'I've told Valérie she's back in town though.'

'Really?' Martin was surprised. 'How did she take it? Balloons and lead involved, I shouldn't wonder.'

'Something like that. What did she want anyway? Oriane, I mean.'

'Well, most odd. Firstly she wanted to see if we were interested in having a puppy about the place; seems a bit impractical to me. You can imagine what a mess that would make of the *boules* piste.'

'Quite.'

'Then, the strangest thing. She sees Edmond walk into the garden and greets him like a long-lost friend and all that. They chat for about half an hour, she looked very touchy feely and all that, him less so. I didn't know they knew each other.' He paused. 'Small world, isn't it?'

'Very,' Richard replied tersely. 'Almost claustrophobic.' They stood watching Angela and Olivia continue their practice.

'Listen, about last night.' Martin's voice was now even lower. 'You know, me turning up at the *mairie* at all hours.'

Richard turned towards him. 'I was wondering about that,' he said.

'Well,' Martin looked nervously about him, 'strangest thing, old man. Fatouma asked me to meet her. She wanted to know more about the town.'

'Fatouma Dembele, world champion *pétanquiste* – if that's a word – wanted some tourist information at two in the morning?'

'Yes.' Martin blushed.

'From you?'

'Yes. I know how it looks. But we have quite a lot in common really.' Richard thought this very unlikely. 'We bonded the other day. I'd been watching this stuff on the History Channel about Timbuktu. Anyway, she was rather intrigued by my knowledge and erm, well, we kind of swapped notes.' Richard didn't believe a word of it. 'You see, thing is, you know the old woman and myself, we, er, dabble… with er…' Martin was being oddly coy.

Richard sighed. 'You're swingers, Martin. No details, please.'

'Oh no! No! I know the score.' He coughed nervously. 'Well, Gennie had gone to bed, migraine, she's very stressed at the moment, and I got this message on the, you know, the, er, well, we call it the Batphone.' Richard's spirit was sinking so low he was almost treading on it. 'So I went. But I hadn't got the old girl's permission and we're very strict about that. As Fatouma said, it's all very hush, hush.'

It was Richard's turn to sigh while he worked out how to word his next question. 'And?' was the best he could muster.

'So I did.'

'And?'

'We talked about the town. Tourism, as you say. And Timbuktu, did you know…'

Richard shook his head. 'No. You must have been very disappointed.' He tried to hide his distaste.

'No, not really,' Martin answered brightly. 'It was fascinating stuff, whole libraries hidden away. And anyway, I'd gone without permission, so nothing would have happened anyway. We have our standards, old man! Besides,' he added with a slight hint of regret, 'she really did want to talk tourism. It can't all be sex, sex, sex, you know!'

They walked across the lawn to the card table where Gennie had now joined Valérie, Edmond and the Duke. 'One more thing,' Richard asked quietly while watching

Edmond. 'Did you see anyone else skulking about while you were in town?'

'No,' Martin replied, 'only Noel Mabit. Said he was working late. Good for him, the world needs people like him.'

There appeared to be a tense atmosphere at the card table. Gennie looked bored, if not a little upset. Valérie looked frustrated at the inaction of it all while Edmond and Roddy, the fourteenth Duke of Anglethorp, were seemingly locked in card battle. Richard sympathised with Valérie's impatience and couldn't see how all this was getting them anywhere. He decided to do something out of character, go completely off-piste, and see if he couldn't stir the pot a little. He ran through a few things in his head first, and came up with a plan. Then he got cold feet and decided against it, before berating himself in a violent internal struggle and telling himself to just bloody well get on with it. He coughed, then opened his mouth to speak.

Before he could say anything Valérie's phone rang and she moved off quickly to a quieter corner of the garden where she wouldn't be overheard.

He coughed again.

This time Gennie and Martin, via some unsaid possibly telepathic communication both announced at the same time that they should 'think about getting lunch ready' and walked away arm in arm.

Whatever he was going to do, he'd better get on with it.

'So,' he said, slightly overdoing a touch of menace.

'Your Grace!' This time the interruption came from Angela. 'I say, Your Grace! It really is time you did some practising of your own, don't you think?'

Roddy looked at Edmond, who had his sunglasses on, presumably as much to help with his poker face as for protection for his one good eye, if indeed you need a poker face with *bezique*.

'Perhaps it is time we were more sociable?' Edmond said quietly, laying his cards face down.

'I agree,' Roddy replied, less jovially than usual and doing the same. Then, even further out of character, he used his phone to take a snapshot of the card table. 'Just in case the wind gets up!' Suddenly he was all smiles and dashed off to the demanding Angela.

For the first time that Richard could think of, he and Edmond were alone and he felt very uncomfortable. Whatever plans he had had to stir the pot were already somewhat compromised by the depletion in ingredients and co-chefs, but also he just didn't know what to say to the man. All that came into his head was some ridiculous notion to challenge him to an old-fashioned duel instead.

'I don't think our Duke trusts me,' Edmond said, while getting out of his chair with some difficulty.

'It looks like a very serious game.' Richard helped moved Edmond's chair out of the way.

'All games are,' he replied enigmatically.

'Still playing for matchsticks, though?'

'Oh yes!' Edmond laughed. 'It is absurd, no?'

Damn right, thought Richard. And then, quite unexpectedly something else emerged from his brain. 'You haven't thought of upping the stakes at all?'

'Money?' Edmond laughed again. 'I haven't any for one thing, and His Grace is a rich man. I may be a card addict, Richard, but I am no fool.'

They both laughed this time. Neither of them meant it.

'You could always work your way up to the high roller stakes,' Richard pressed, and then took an uncharacteristic leap. 'I don't know, start with matchsticks and move up to ceramics or something?'

Edmond stopped and turned to Richard; his glasses, doubling up on the eyepatch, were still masking his eyes but his thin, tight lips gave away something of what he thought and he didn't look happy.

'Mr Ainsworth!' The badgering Angela Babcock was a master of the mistimed interruption. 'Mr Ainsworth! Could we borrow you?'

'I think you should go, Richard.' Edmond's voice was low and just erred slightly on the side of menace, a feeling underlined when he placed his gloved hand on Richard's shoulder. 'And please, my friend, be very careful.' He turned away leaving Richard like he'd just received the kind of icy blast you got from René's glacial air conditioning.

Inevitably he found it very hard to concentrate on a game of *boules* after getting what he regarded as a physical threat. Not least because he seriously doubted whether the hens, in their end-of-day debrief, could take the sudden ramping-up of tension. He played anyway and did his best to be sociable; he even won a couple of ends, which only deepened his shock.

However, it was not a comfortable ride back home with Valérie.

Chapter Fifteen

'So,' she began after a few kilometres of silence. 'Your Derek apparently is not a policeman. The Commissaire spoke to Scotland Yard and they have never heard of him.' There was no triumph or gloating in her voice but the way she said 'your' Derek was again the way Clare used to say 'your' when distancing herself from what she considered his mundanity or pig-headedness. It was a signal of complete disassociation; don't contaminate me with 'your' stuff, it said. With that in mind, once again, Richard felt very much alone. Even more so after Edmond's threat as he didn't feel able to tell Valérie about it. Whatever he felt about Edmond Masson – and he was willing to concede that jealousy might just be playing a part somewhere – he hadn't expected a warning with menaces. This wasn't a film, this was a very real threat and from a trained agent of the French secret service too. OK, so the man had one hand, one eye and a pronounced limp, though Richard still couldn't decide which leg was actually damaged. It all added up to potential weak spots in terms of a battle, but he wasn't fooled. Richard remembered a one-armed Spencer Tracy beating up a very two-armed Ernest Borgnine in *Bad Day at Black Rock*, so he wasn't willing to risk anything remotely physical, even if that were his style. Even the self-defence techniques that Valérie had once taught him from the Krav Maga discipline wouldn't be enough he suspected.

He was beginning to regret not taking up some form of martial art when he was younger, just as his over-protective mother had urged him to do. He sat up straight. *What am I thinking?* he thought. *Am I really going to take this lying down?*

He slumped down again. The short answer to that question was very much in the affirmative. He tried to think of a film quote, one that, far from lending him some bravado, would just cheer him up instead and his mind settled on Bob Hope. Asked if he was a dirty coward, Hope had replied, 'No. A clean one!' Richard chuckled to himself and tried to think what film it was but, unusually, the title didn't immediately spring to mind. *It's the stress*, he thought, *I'm losing my grip*, just at exactly the same time as Valérie's vintage sports car did the same and a loud bang saw them career off the road and into a ditch.

'He's shooting at us!' Richard cried. 'Duck!' And he grabbed Valérie and pulled her down below dashboard level.

They stayed in that position for a few minutes, waiting for any further shots, Richard breathing heavily, trying to control his heart rate and blood pressure. Valérie cooed through the front seats to Passepartout in the back, asking him to be quiet and keep his head down. For himself, Passepartout being the old pro that he was stayed fast asleep.

Eventually, with apparently no more attacks forthcoming, Valérie asked the obvious question.

'Who is shooting at us?' Her voice was calm and the enquiry framed in the same tone one might ask, 'Anyone for tennis?' There was a lightness in her voice, a touch of 'I know what you're going to say, I just want to hear you say it.' It was therefore infinitely more worrying to a near-hyperventilating Richard than if she had been hysterical or angry, which for any sane person would have been the natural reaction to being shot off the road.

Should he tell her now about Edmond's warning? There would be no coming back from it if he did. You don't go around telling wives that their husbands are murderers and expect it just to be shrugged off. He needed to think this through; there were going to be consequences.

'Edmond bloody Masson, that's who!' he babbled. 'And he obviously doesn't care if you're collateral damage!'

'I see.' Valérie slid smoothly out of the car, keeping her head down as she did so. 'Stay there,' she hissed at him.

He could hear her move to the back of the car and stop. 'Can you see him?' he whispered.

She ignored his question. 'You can come out, Edmond,' she said coldly. 'He knows it is you. I have him covered.'

Richard thought that his heart had stopped working. All his suspicions about Edmond Masson, the sudden appearance, the death of the mayor, the disappearance of Derek, the ceramics... he had convinced himself that somehow he needed to protect Valérie from him. It had never for one moment occurred to him that they were in it together.

His heart pounded like a steam drill. His brain flooded as though a dam of injustice had burst. He was frightened of course, terrified even. But most of all he felt really bloody annoyed. He'd been used; he didn't know for how long, but he'd definitely been used. Dragged along in a whirl of mendacity and falsehood, laughed at, eaten up and spat out. And what irritated him even more than that, he'd enjoyed it too. Suddenly it was all too much for him.

'Well, that's just bloody typical, isn't it?' he bawled, struggling on to his knees on the passenger seat, his hands already in the air. 'I should have known,' he added with a sneer, purely for theatricality.

Valérie remained standing still, though adrenalin was causing her to tap her foot and, through the smoke from what looked like a burst engine, he saw a look on her face strongly suggesting that a quick bullet from a sniper in the woods might be infinitely more preferable to what was about to unleash itself in his direction.

'Has he gone?' He smiled weakly trying to pretend it had all been a joke. Valérie didn't take her eyes off him and reached into her bag. 'Don't shoot!' he cried.

Valérie retrieved her phone and pressed at the screen. 'Monsieur Foulon? It's Valérie d'Orçay.' She was horribly, terrifyingly calm. 'Yes, 1979 Renault Alpine V6 that's right. It looks like the big end has blown.' She listened to the mechanic on the other end, while Richard wished Martin had been present for the 'big end' part, so that he and Valérie could join forces against a common enemy, just like old times. 'No, I don't know where I am exactly. Wait a second. Richard!' she barked.

'Yes,' he replied, narrowly avoiding adding 'Sir'.

'Where are we?'

Richard briefly thought about adding levity to the situation and treating the 'Where are we?' question as an existential query into the nature of their relationship, the case and, dammit, even the world itself but instead he wisely restricted himself to, 'On the D956, about two kilometres south of the bridge over the Follet.'

Valérie repeated Richard's words, still without taking her eyes off him, not in a threatening way, which he reckoned he could just about have coped with, but like a parent unsure of the punishment for a very, very disappointing child. 'That is very kind of you,' she said to the mechanic. 'Also, could you bring a hire car with you? I need transport urgently this evening. *Merci*. I will see you in thirty minutes then.' She put her phone back in her bag. 'Put your silly hands down, Richard!' she snapped.

He did as he was told and clambered awkwardly out of the car, stretching his legs after the uncomfortable position.

'You had me going there!' he laughed. The laugh was hollower than a flute.

'Why,' – her voice was low and menacing – 'why, would you think that Edmond Masson would be shooting at us?'

'I was joking!' Again he laughed.

'You were not joking!'

He stayed silent, looking at the floor.

'Richard! Were you joking?'

'No.'

'Well? We have thirty minutes to wait and I want an answer.' She was tapping her foot again.

'I don't trust him!' Richard said eventually, though this time with defiance.

'So he must be *shooting* at us, then!' In Richard's opinion, and it was something for which he took full credit, she had become exceptionally good at sarcasm. It had been a foreign land to her when they had first met, now she wielded it like a pro.

'I think he's dangerous!' he pleaded.

'So do I!' she shouted back.

'Ha! You see!' His hands went back up, this time in triumph.

'So do I. We both do.'

'Ah. Good point.'

'Why on earth, Richard, do you think he would try to kill you, or me? Why?' It wasn't a plea as such, but he did see some emotion to her question. Maybe she wasn't sure about Edmond either, and she needed Richard's suspicions to confirm her own.

He took a big, deep breath. The kind you take when you plan to spend a long time underwater. 'Why would he try to kill me? Because he told me he would, that's why.'

'That he would what?' She looked confused.

'Kill me.'

'He said he would kill you?'

'Yes?'

'And me?'

Richard didn't like the way this was panning out. She was supposed to be on his side by now.

'Well, you didn't actually crop up in the conversation to be honest.'

'I see.' Her eyebrow was now so arched it looked like it might actually fall off her face. 'And when did this threat happen?'

He put his hands in his pockets and kicked at the ground. 'Earlier on, at Martin and Gennie's. And yesterday someone knocked me out while I was searching Derek's room,' he added, as if that were damning evidence.

'Someone knocked you out?' The way she asked the question frankly hurt. Pupil had turned master in the acerbic mockery stakes and it was clear that she didn't believe him. 'Why didn't you tell me?'

It was a fair question. 'Well...' he began.

'It's because you do not trust me anymore, am I right?'

'Well, I wouldn't go...'

'But you trust Oriane Moulin...'

'I...'

'And her degenerate poodle?'

'If you trust Edmond so much, why aren't you living with him then, eh? Answer me that.' It was premature to add a note of victory, but that's how he felt and physically she relaxed a little and was less aggressive. She raised her chin, however, in a curiously very English show of stoicism. He must have taught her that too.

'That, Richard, is none of your business.'

He nodded but said nothing. She was right, it wasn't. She had never pried or asked about him and Clare, she had drawn a line at that and the reason was now obvious. Richard and Valérie had very different opinions about the other and Richard felt like a fool.

He smiled as warmly as he could, nodded and said quietly, 'You're right, Madame d'Orçay, it *is* none of my business.' He turned slowly and began walking; he didn't want to wait for the mechanic and then be driven home. He needed to be alone and to think, and maybe reassess everything he now was, where he was, figuratively and literally. He left Valérie standing there and, though it was a struggle, he didn't look back.

Chapter Sixteen

It actually felt good to walk away and for once he wasn't just thinking about film endings or screen heroes. He had been deluding himself about their, for want of a better word, relationship, so to have the strength just to turn on his heels and walk into the sunset to begin afresh was actually rather appealing. At least it was for a while. Then the weather turned.

The storm came from nowhere and with it the change in mood. It was a perfect meteorological representation, as Richard saw it, of his state of mind and the state of his life. While ordinary, weaker men might have buckled under such heavy imagery, Richard, however, briefly felt grateful for it; not much, but a little. Now it really was pure cinema, pure cliché perhaps, but cinema nonetheless and whatever his mood that would always cheer him a little.

Some thirty minutes later, however, he'd had enough of cinematic allegory, was soaked to the bone and sorely regretting his John Wayne walk into the distance hissy fit. On the one hand it was perfectly natural after being threatened – and he was convinced that was exactly what Edmond had done – that you should feel under fire. The man had been in the secret service for heaven's sake; it was perfectly within his capabilities to search out a convenient grassy knoll and take a potshot. Maybe not at Valérie as well, but there was no telling the man's state of mind. Of course she was bound to defend him, that was only natural, but it meant that she wasn't seeing straight either. He thought back to the last image of her and concluded that if indeed she was a woman in emotional turmoil, she was doing a damned fine job of hiding it. Frankly, the look on her face suggested that if turmoil came knocking then he'd get pretty short shrift.

The rain became heavier and his jacket, now pulled over his head, was blocking his vision as the fierce rain, mixed with hail, bounced off the tarmac. For the last ten minutes, in what he knew was a futile gesture, he had held his thumb out, hoping to hitch a ride but no car had even passed him, let alone stopped. Then a sleek and silent black vehicle took him by surprise, but drove past him anyway, not stopping. Richard swore at the driver who at the same time braked some fifty metres down the road and Richard looked briefly to the dark skies to thank the patron saint of unheard expletives.

He ran to the passenger door and opened it, climbing in quickly.

'Thanks for stopping,' he said gratefully, removing his jacket from his head. 'I'm sorry, I'm… Oh. It's you.'

Valérie was sitting, dry as old paper, in her plush beige leather driving seat, the lights from the dashboard illuminating her perfectly but with a state of panic on her typically beautiful face. 'Richard,' she begged urgently, 'I need your help!' Her voice was earnest and pleading, almost breaking with emotion. So, he thought, his initial conclusions had been right all along. The car might have indeed blown its big end, but there was something else too. Valérie must have taken the time waiting for this replacement to examine what he'd said and come to the same conclusion as he had: that Edmond was indeed a wrong 'un.

'What? What is it?' He'd never seen her this desperate.

'This silly car! It will not do as it is told!'

They drove in silence for a few minutes. The only noise being the insistent and incessant electronic chirping from the ultra-modern driver assistance system, a series of hectoring warning beeps. In the centre of the dashboard was a screen showing their position and a whole host of graphs indicating performance and handling, percentages of this, that and the other. The screen was so big Richard half-expected a middle-aged musician to rise from the gearbox and play some cinema entrance music on a Wurlitzer organ. Only there was no gearbox either.

'It's called a driver assistance system.' He tried to sound knowledgeable but got a fruity beep from somewhere within the on-board computer.

'I don't like it.' She was definitely rattled, but not unfortunately in the way he had imagined.

'Let's hope it doesn't have an ejector seat, anyway!' He knew she wouldn't get it, but it cheered him up.

'What is the silly thing saying now?' she remonstrated.

It was true, the thing had seemingly got itself into something of a tizzy and was making a series of howls and whoops that reminded Richard strongly of Cheeta the chimpanzee in the Johnny Weissmuller *Tarzan* films.

'I think it's warning you that you're in the middle of the road,' he replied, trying to be helpful.

'But it is a one-track road!' she shouted, vexed to the limit.

She moved over slightly anyway, placating the onboard computer in the process, which quietened it down, but only briefly. It then said something in a low voice in French.

'Now what?'

'Would you prefer if I drive?' Richard asked genuinely.

'What is the silly thing talking about?'

The computer, now sounding like HAL from *2001: A Space Odyssey*, was making monotone warnings about water on the road.

'It says that there's water on the road.'

Valérie screamed in frustration. 'Men!' she shouted. 'I know there is water on the road! It is raining, of course there is water on the road. What a stupid thing to say. Men build cars after their own image and so they mansplain everything.'

'I think he's only trying to be helpful, just looking out for you.'

Valérie didn't answer straight away, thinking over what Richard had said. 'Maybe you can tell the computer that I have been doing this a long time. If I am in danger, I will let him know.'

'I don't think that will stop him,' Richard replied carefully. 'He feels it's his job and in a funny way cares for you.'

Out of the corner of his eye, he saw a smile flicker on Valérie's face. 'I suppose I should appreciate that at least.'

The storm had stopped by the time they reached home and steam was rising pleasingly from the roads, almost as it was from Valérie's frazzled mind. The storm had cleared the air, so it was fresh as they got out of the car and their brief coded conversation had done much the same to them. They were still being awkward with each other, however, unsure of where they stood as a team or even as friends.

'I suppose you will feed your hens now.' She wasn't mocking, and it wasn't even a question.

'Better had,' Richard replied. 'They'll be hungry,' he added unnecessarily. There was silence but neither turned away. 'You never know,' Richard half-chuckled, 'Detective Sergeant, or whatever he is, Derek Munro might even turn up in the coop again.'

'He was here?' This was news to her obviously.

'Yes, didn't I tell you? I saw him approaching from the fields at the back. You could see his hat a mile off!'

'From that field?' She pointed.

'Yes, just where those crows are shooing off that buzzard. They're probably fighting over a carcass or something.'

She looked at him and he looked back at her before his shoulders slumped and his head flopped forward into his chest.

Moments later they had climbed over the fence behind the chicken coop and were cautiously making their way to where the crows were looping in the air, now fighting amongst themselves.

'I don't like this,' Richard said quietly. 'It doesn't look good.'

'Why don't you wait at the coop?' Valérie replied innocently.

'I don't mean this this,' he tried to explain. 'I can do this this. I mean that this.' He pointed at the birds.

'Ah, I see. No, I don't like the look of it either. If it is what we think it is, it doesn't seem to make sense at all.'

Richard had other ideas though. Derek Munro had been throwing around some pretty weighty accusations the night before and it looked like someone hadn't taken very kindly to it. Richard knew who that someone was, but he wasn't going to bring that up again now.

It didn't take them long to find the body. Poor Derek Munro hadn't gone very far after his conversation with Richard, and he certainly wasn't going to go any further now. He lay face down in the soil, the young vines standing like a guard of honour around his body. Richard shook his head unhappily as Valérie nudged the bloodied tam-o'-shanter with her foot.

'Do you have your phone, Richard?' Her voice was respectfully quiet.

'Yes,' he replied, taking the phone out of his back pocket. He was about to dial the Commissaire when he handed the phone to Valérie instead.

'Look,' he mumbled. 'Can you tell the Commissaire this time? He already thinks I'm a jinx on humanity.'

She took the phone from him and dialled the number while Richard shooed the scavengers away.

Chapter Seventeen

The next morning, Commissaire Henri Lapierre was making quite a show of his frustration. He was also, Richard couldn't help but notice, making his show of frustration with Richard's coffee, baguettes and leftover breakfast croissants. All of which, the whole world couldn't fail to notice, were re-forming themselves on the man's shirtfront.

'So, excuse me,' he muffled, releasing another avalanche of pastry like a digger releasing dirt, 'but I need to get my facts in order. After twenty-four hours of apparently looking for the missing Derek Munro, you *remember* a clandestine meeting with him at your house and – pfft! as if by magic – his body turns up, and near to your house also.'

Richard wasn't altogether keen on the man's tone.

'Are you sure that it is him, Henri?' Valérie asked, offering Richard a little respite from what was turning into an uncomfortable interrogation. 'We didn't turn over the body obviously.'

The Commissaire brushed some crumbs off his tie. 'I have his ID, madame.' He solemnly produced a small leather wallet and unclipped the fastener. 'Munro, Derek. Detective Sergeant, CID.'

'Ah!' Richard brightened up at this potential vindication. Then Lapierre showed him the clearly homemade ID card. 'Do you think he coloured that in himself, monsieur?' he asked disappointedly.

The Commissaire continued. 'Munro, Derek,' he intoned, 'air traffic controller.' He gave Richard a disappointed look. 'Munro, Derek. Archaeologist. Munro, Derek. Archbishop.'

'But, Henri...' Valérie tried to interrupt.

'Please, madame, I am still on the As.'

'Well, he was undercover.' Richard was feeling somewhat morose.

Lapierre shook his head. 'You ask if I am sure that the body is him, but I don't think he even knew who was him.' He looked rather pleased with himself for that witticism.

'Roddy did say he was a fantasist,' Richard said bleakly, walking to the window.

'Roddy?' The Commissaire looked confused.

'The Duke. He said he thought Derek was a bit of a fantasist.'

'Oh, this Woddy. Yes. Well, no doubt when I get to the Fs, there will be a childish little business card for fantasist too!' He gave an unpleasant little chuckle.

'There is no need for that, Henri.' Valérie was behaving with more solemnity than the policeman, whose attitude verged on the disrespectful in Richard's eyes.

'No.' The Commissaire sighed. 'I apologise. I have been up all night and it was not a pleasant sight, this murder. He was hit on the head. It seems he was attacked from behind,

133

from the, er...' – he looked at Richard – 'the garden side of the field.'

'And do you know what with?' Valérie was ignoring, for now at least, the policeman's obvious insinuations about the garden side.

'Oh yes.' From his leather holdall he produced a large colour photograph. It was obviously the murder weapon, covered in dried blood and matted hair. 'A *pétanque!*' he said in triumph.

'A *boule*, Henri. *Pétanque* is the game, the *boule* is the...'

'Yes, yes, yes,' he said irritably, annoyed that he had ruined his own big reveal.

Richard took a closer look at the evidence bag, which he regretted as it made him feel nauseous. 'Do you have any idea whose it is?' he asked quietly.

'No, monsieur. I was going to ask you that question.' Again, it was a heavy-handed insinuation but Richard was too numb to react defensively to it.

'Well, it's not mine. I don't think I even own a set of *boules*.'

'Think? You do not *think* that you own a set of *boules*?' The Commissaire pounced on the ambiguity, but Richard could only shrug in response. Firstly, he and Clare had taken on the house partly furnished and secondly, this was France; the chances were that at least ninety per cent of rural houses would have an old and rusty set of *boules* hidden in an outhouse somewhere, sitting in a warped wooden box and covered in cobwebs.

'You're more than welcome to have a look, Commissaire.' Richard stiffened slightly, now realising that, at least for form's sake, he should be taking some level of umbrage at the official's suggestions. 'I have nothing to hide,' he added giving it the required touch of melodrama.

The policeman took a long sip of coffee. 'Tell me again, monsieur, why did this Munro, this Derek come to see you?'

'Oh, Henri!' Valérie interrupted. 'What difference does that make? The poor man was obviously deluded, so for whatever reason that he came here, it would be irrelevant.'

The Commissaire was having none of it. 'That is perhaps true, madame, and no doubt your partner here appreciates your defence, but fantasist or no, delusional or no, the man was brutally murdered just metres from where I stand and after a clandestine meeting with the monsieur here.' He looked at Richard. 'Oh yes, you made a big show of looking for this man yesterday, but I put it to you that you may have known that he was, in fact, already dead!'

'You don't believe that really, Henri?' Valérie wasn't her usual confident self. 'Do you?'

'Pah!' The Commissaire exploded in frustration. 'No! Unfortunately I do not, but this man is a menace!' He now pointed at Richard, who looked a little hurt. 'He may not actually be a killer himself, but everywhere he goes, everything he touches, ends in someone being murdered. Please, monsieur, I beg you, go home. Go back to England. I hear they always complain about over-population there, you could be of some use, perhaps.'

The sarcasm was overblown, but Richard also couldn't help thinking the man had a point. The Follet Valley, rural France, was supposed to be his quiet retreat into dotage and even greater insignificance. He had even planned a nondescript headstone for his grave. 'Here lies Richard Ainsworth, doing what he tried to do in life, rest in peace.' But the fact of the matter was very different. Lapierre was right, he was bad luck. He was a one-man massacre machine and if he didn't leave the area pretty sharpish there might be very few people left in it, and he really didn't want that on his conscience.

'I told you,' he said quietly. 'He told me he was a policeman with customs and excise and on the trail of what he called a criminal mastermind, some art smuggling ring.' He paused. 'He was very believable and I fell for it. I'm sorry.'

'And he gave no hint as to who this criminal mastermind might be?' the Commissaire scoffed.

Richard said nothing. The truth was that although he had repeated this half a dozen times already, he had so far managed to leave out the identity of Munro's suspected criminal mastermind.

'Richard,' Valérie prodded, 'you must tell us. At the moment it is you who is suspected.'

Richard took a deep breath. 'He said that the same name cropped up in all the files…'

'The files that do not exist?' Lapierre was sneering again.

'Yes. So there you go, what difference does it make?'

'Monsieur,' he said gravely, tapping his nose as he did so, knocking some crumbs from his moustache. 'This nose tells me one thing. Oh yes. This nose tells me that you are hiding something, someone. That you are protecting someone. I demand to know who that someone is!'

Richard sat down and made sure he didn't catch Valérie's eye. 'Edmond Masson,' he said quietly. 'He told me that the name that turned up in all the files was Edmond Masson.'

The tension in the room was suddenly unbearable; far from just being able to cut it with a knife you could walk into it, a swirling fog of resentment, hurt, incredulity and betrayal. Nobody knew quite what to say next until Richard decided to try and redeem himself.

'Like you say, the files don't exist and Munro wasn't a policeman, so any accusations he made are absurd.'

'And yet he is dead.'

Both men were waiting for Valérie to say something. 'Richard.' Her tone was cold and businesslike and Richard didn't like it one bit. 'You say that Derek Munro was very believable, how so?' The smile she managed to add to the question was probably the most worrying of all. This was 'work' Valérie, the highly paid bounty hunter/assassin. She might look like she'd just stepped right out of a subtitled and elegant French film from a classier decade, but her eyes were as glassy as a shark's, the smile about as friendly as the Spanish Inquisition and, Richard knew, as did Henri, that just below the surface, hellfire was waiting to be unleashed.

'Well,' he began. 'Er. The thing is...' He didn't want to betray her in front of the Commissaire, but the truth was he'd been attacked, probably by Edmond, warned off, definitely by Edmond and had evidence, hidden in the chicken coop, that Edmond was probably at least present at the death of Mayor Planchet. Apart from the threat though, it now all seemed pretty thin.

She walked silently towards him. 'I suspect, Richard,' – her voice was low and quiet – 'that you wanted to believe him, isn't that so?'

In truth, he would have preferred hellfire to this. This was immense dismay on a scale even Richard hadn't previously attained; she suspected him of a stab in the back, a friendship-destroying act of treachery and mistrust that he couldn't actually, if really pushed, argue against. His mind was swimming. Had the Walter Mitty-ish Derek Munro said the name Edmond Masson first, or had Richard prompted him to do so, willingly filling in the gaps in his detective fantasy? He couldn't remember. But she was right, he had certainly wanted to believe it.

'What was the time of death, Henri?' She asked the question but didn't take her eyes off Richard.

Lapierre needlessly opened his notebook, secretly pleased that he was only a witness in this particular byplay. 'According to the pathologist's notes, the early hours of Friday morning,' he read, 'around two am.'

'I was with my husband.' Valérie's voice verged on the robotic.

Richard didn't feel like openly questioning her at this point, but he was fairly sure that Valérie and Passepartout had remained at his B&B, while Edmond was staying a few miles away at Martin and Gennie's place. *Was she really inventing an alibi for him?* he asked himself. Then in the next thought he decided that she was and that she was in some considerable danger if that's how deeply she felt.

'And you, monsieur? Where were you at that time?' It was clear that the Commissaire had moved on from feeling awkward and slightly embarrassed to enjoying himself immensely at Richard's expense.

Richard decided to stare down Valérie. He had to let her know that he was strong, that he would see this through.

'Answer the Commissaire, Richard.' He barely recognised her voice.

'I was with Rita Hayworth,' he said, ingesting it with just the right amount of salaciousness as to hint that it was a night of carefree wild abandon, and not a DVD of the film *Gilda*.

'Another one!' The Commissaire shook his head. 'And this Madame Hayworth, she can confirm your story, yes?'

Richard nearly buckled at this. The questioning of the Commissaire combined with the Medusa-like stare of an angrily defiant Valérie was already too much, but the fact that neither of them had heard of the cinema goddess Rita Hayworth nearly dragged him under.

'I'll ask her,' he said eventually, just about remaining upright.

'And you, madame? You have witnesses that you were with your husband?'

Finally Valérie took her eyes off Richard, releasing the grip she had on him. 'Don't be disgusting, Henri!' She seemed genuinely offended.

'Madame d'Orçay,' he said slyly. 'I have met Monsieur and Madame Thompson, I know of them. I think it a reasonable question for me to ask.'

Richard sat down, relieved to be relegated to the sidelines for a moment. He then watched the promised and unbridled hellfire unleash itself on the recently supercilious official. She needed to let it out, he realised, and thanked his lucky stars that it wasn't directed at him, at least for now. He sneaked out halfway through her storm to check on the chicken-protected evidence. Lifting Lana Turner gently, he dug down into her hay bed.

The terracotta piece was no longer there.

Chapter Eighteen

It was an ashen-faced and suitably contrite Commissaire Lapierre who drove himself and an equally ashen-faced and suitably contrite Richard back to Martin and Gennie's house to interview Edmond Masson. Valérie was in the car in front, driving erratically as she no doubt wrestled with her violent emotions and also an insubordinate driver assistance system. In the end, Richard hadn't been spared her paroxysm and after the furious dressing-down of Lapierre, revealing some fairly personal inadequacies on his part, it had been Richard's turn. Still in shock from his missing evidence, he was too stunned to fight back. It had started with a fair bit of hen-baiting and insults based on his national traits, sedentary nature, the way he combed his hair, his alcohol consumption and his fondness for a really poor omelette. She had then, to his horror, officially disbanded their detective agency partnership, picked up Passepartout and told both men that she would meet them at Martin and Gennie's and that if they tried to get in the car with her, they would end their days needing to have all meals served as soup.

It had been quite the performance.

'Has she always been like this?' Richard asked eventually, as Valérie nearly drove into an oncoming group of Lycra-clad Sunday cyclists.

Lapierre turned towards him, a surprised look on his face that suggested he'd completely forgotten he was even carrying a passenger. He pursed his lips in rumination.

'No,' he said definitely. 'I think that perhaps she has mellowed.'

'Blimey!'

'It was never easy, monsieur,' the policeman said morosely. 'But it was always exhilarating.'

The way he uttered the word 'exhilarating' made it sound like the Commissaire was most certainly not a fan, in any way shape or form, of exhilaration. It was something he and Richard had in common. The two of them lapsed back into silence watching the active volcano that is Valérie d'Orçay swerve her hire car around corners as if the corners themselves were being impertinent.

There were a couple of uniformed police officers to meet them when they arrived some five minutes after Valérie, who was already in conference with Edmond. He had a rather amused look his face which Richard couldn't understand. If pushed he would admit to not understanding very much about Edmond Masson anyway. He seemed to take diffidence to almost Olympic levels and constantly wore a half-smile that, were Richard that way inclined, was immensely slappable. If he had come back looking to pick up where their marriage had left off, why was he staying at Martin and Gennie's place and not with Valérie at his B&B? Surely it couldn't be discretion? The man was French after all. And though he doubted Madame Tablier, in her role as prospective part-owner, would have allowed such a thing anyway, he had tried to question Valérie on that specific point. She had talked awkwardly about 'taking things slowly' but had entirely missed Richard's point when he'd suggested another thirty years would be about right in his book.

'Ah, Richard!' It was Angela Babcock who for once had eschewed formality and was using his first name instead. She was the kind of domineering, no-nonsense serial organiser that meant the sudden dropping of protocol always set alarm bells ringing. 'We're still a player short, I'm afraid. Would you mind filling in again?'

'They've been told about Derek, haven't they?' Richard whispered to the Commissaire.

'Yes, naturally.' Lapierre was as taken aback by her blithe attitude as he was.

'If you'll partner Olivia, and I will play with His Grace?'

Richard wandered over, but made a point as he did so of saying loudly that he had no *boules* of his own. Lapierre just shrugged and went with his officers to continue their examination of Derek's room.

'It looks like you'll have to join the team properly,' Roddy said, at least having the tact to look a little sad. 'Poor Derek,' he added.

'Yes, poor Derek,' Olivia agreed, while vigorously polishing her *boules*.

Angela, however, couldn't have sounded more cheerful. 'I was going to ask you about that. Will you join our team for the tournament? Now that Derek is no longer here.'

She made it sound like Derek Munro had just hopped on a plane home, rather than had his head stoved in with heavy-duty sporting equipment.

Richard didn't fancy it one bit, especially after what had happened to the last incumbent of the role, but he knew Angela was not going to take either no or prevarication as an answer. He tried anyway, 'Well I...'

'I mean, when all is said and done, it really is your patriotic duty, I feel. You are English, are you not?'

Roddy and Olivia were also giving him 'King and Country' type looks leaving him with very little choice.

'I have an Irish passport too,' he said weakly. Along with a few hundred thousand others he had in recent years searched his ancestry for anyone more European.

'I'm relatively new to it myself.' The Duke slapped him on the shoulder. 'We can be novices together.'

'You don't really play *boules* either?' Richard asked.

'*Pétanque!*' Surprisingly, it was Olivia with the admonishment.

'*Pétanque*, sorry.'

'Lord no! I'm absolutely hopeless at this sort of thing,' Roddy laughed. 'The old man was a bit of a whizz at it by all accounts, but not me. Not a lot of call for *pétanque* on oil rigs!'

Olivia handed Richard a gleaming set of *boules* that looked like they hadn't seen much action.

'You worked on an oil rig?' he asked, taken aback. He had always assumed, in a kind of benign, ill-informed way, that the landed gentry tended not to go in for work at all, let alone the harsh, lonely world of an oil rig.

'That was the last job I had. Father and I fell out after I left Eton, so I went on a gap year. Well, eighteen gap years to be precise because I never went back!' He snorted at his own joke. 'Then Angela caught up with me once the old man copped it, and here I am. Certainly beats being a pump hand somewhere off the coast of Aberdeen!' He threw the *cochonnet* down the other end of the piste and invited Olivia to play first.

Her ball landed right in front of the target, obscuring it from Angela's view, who threw next. From what Richard understood of the game, hers was also a good throw, the *boule* nestling into the shingle–clay mix some thirty centimetres beyond the jack, waiting, should the jack be dislodged. She threw again, with the same result. As they were still furthest away it was her partner's turn to throw next. Roddy's first throw went embarrassingly beyond the end of the piste, but his second lay in between the target and Angela's *boules*. Richard's first shot managed somehow to dislodge Olivia's ball, sending the jack rolling towards the opponents, his second was only marginally more successful in that it didn't do any further damage, but they were three down with one ball to go. Olivia stepped forward, a look of intense concentration on her face. She took a deep breath and sent down an Exocet that scattered Angela and Roddy to the four corners of the piste, while at the same time somehow managing to leave Richard's second ball as the closest to the *cochonnet*.

'That's what I call teamwork!' Roddy cheered. 'Obviously tough on old Derek, but you two have what it takes, I'd say, wouldn't you, Angela?'

'Indeed I would, Your Grace.' Angela looked very pleased with herself.

'Oh, please!' Roddy rolled his eyes and frowned with exasperation. 'I keep telling you, none of that "Your Grace" stuff here.' He turned to Richard and winked. 'Honestly, the woman was wiping my backside as a baby; you'd think that would put an end to formality!'

It was an arresting image. 'She was your nanny, then?' Again, Richard had always kind of thought that nannies were a fictional creation and with either the bright demeanour of a Julie Andrews or a demonic Bette Davis. He wasn't sure he'd actually met a real-life nanny before, nor one of their wards.

'Oh, yes,' Roddy beamed. 'First face I remember seeing as a lad. Every boy should have a nanny,' he added seriously as though issuing a decree.

Richard couldn't disagree. His life right now felt like a tsunami of misfortune, a meeting of numerous violent currents, dragging him under and then tossing him about. A nanny would be a most helpful source of solidity and comfort. With his current form though, he'd get a vengeful Bette Davis, not a Mary Poppins.

A solemn-looking Commissaire reappeared and strode straight past the *boules* players towards Valérie and Edmond, who were still in serious conference. Richard watched as the three of them entered into an animated discussion that was made worse by each one occasionally glancing in Richard's direction. Their glances were not filled with warmth and bonhomie.

'It's your turn, Mr Ainsworth.' Olivia really didn't need anyone else's help; she was quite clearly a skilled player, but she was following the form and an uneasy Richard, aware that the French contingent of secret service, bounty hunter and top-level policeman were making their way solemnly towards him, took his spot. He gulped and threw a *boule* so badly that Angela Babcock only narrowly avoided being struck by it.

'Yes, if you can avoid killing another member of the team, Mr Ainsworth, that would be useful I think.'

Under the circumstances, it was an unfortunate thing to say.

'Monsieur Ainsworth?' The Commissaire had a look of the hanging judge about him.

'What's going on?' It was Martin approaching with Gennie and a mistimed tray of tea and local *patisserie*.

'Monsieur Ainsworth,' Lapierre started again. 'I am arresting you for the murder of Derek Munro. You have the right to remain silent, etc., etc.' Really, the man's heart didn't seem in it at all.

Richard blinked in confusion. He looked from the Commissaire to Valérie, who at least had the decency to look embarrassed, and then to Edmond, who may as well have been wearing two eyepatches such was his emotionless demeanour.

'It's my throw,' he said weakly, before turning stiffly and lobbing his *boule* aggressively and almost baseball-like at the other *boules* gathered in a cluster and strewing them to all four corners.

'Bravo!' cheered Angela, clapping; it seemed she simply could not be distracted from the game.

It was by far the greatest *boule* throw of Richard's life and offered him a brief injection of confidence. 'May

I ask what evidence you have?' he demanded haughtily of the Commissaire, suddenly adopting a ramrod-straight posture and lifting his chin in the air as if he too had grown up with the poise and aplomb that only Eton and a nanny could give.

The Commissaire sighed. 'We have searched the late Monsieur Munro's room,' he began wearily. 'There is nothing out of the ordinary, the same set of fingerprints are on everything. They are his fingerprints, we have confirmed that already.'

'And so?' Richard was already finding the aristocratic pose quite tiring and his back was beginning to hurt.

'There was one other fingerprint, monsieur. On the door handle and on the light switch.' The Commissaire didn't look happy about the breakthrough. 'Your finger-print, monsieur, which, as you know, we have on file.'

'Oh, yes, I remember. That would be from the last time you had me wrongly arrested!'

The Commissaire nodded sadly also remembering the time when the two had first met and Richard had been suspected of murder after vegan cheese was slipped into a *Michelin*-starred dessert.

'Richard.' Valérie spoke quietly. 'Perhaps it would be best to go with the Commissaire for now.' She moved forward to stand at Edmond's shoulder. 'We will find the real murderer for you, won't we, Edmond?'

Edmond nodded slightly though not in an overly encouraging way.

'Well, you won't have to look too far!' Richard suddenly erupted in pure exasperation. 'You're standing next to him!

Yes, I went to Derek's room. I opened the door and turned on the light. The place was a mess, someone had got there before me. Then bam! I was hit on the head and knocked out. Look.' He pointed to a lump behind his ear. 'Proof. Somebody hit me! Somebody who knows where to hit.' He looked squarely into Edmond's one good eye. 'When I came to, the room had been tidied up.'

'You have any proof, monsieur?' the Commissaire asked.

'Well—' Richard looked around. 'Gennie! You were there!'

'Yes!' Gennie was enthusiastically helping out. 'You fell down the stairs!' She beamed. 'That's where I found you!'

'At the bottom of the stairs?' Edmond's voice was classic villain cold. 'You fell, you were not hit then?'

'No! I fell *after* I was hit. When I woke up. Don't trust this man,' Richard barked. 'He threatened me, told me to stay out of things.' Everyone turned to look at Edmond whose own posture seemed to have withered slightly, exaggerating his injuries and incapacities. He was also, and Richard didn't know how he'd done it, wearing a set of impressive medals on his jacket. 'Where did you get those?' Richard cried. 'Did you buy them at a *brocante* or nick them from the town hall? I mean, have *none* of you seen *The Prisoner of Zenda*?' He paused and looked at each face in turn. 'I'm talking about the Ronald Colman 1937 version obviously. Stewart Granger in 1958 was cold and the Peter Sellers 1979 effort was woeful.'

It was fair to say he was losing his grip and the support of the crowd.

'Richard…' Valérie stepped forward, her hand outstretched. 'It is for the best, I think.'

'Don't come near me!' he warned, while backing away, 'I've seen your work before and I always end up on my back.'

Martin coughed and got an admonishing look from Gennie.

A stand-off seemed to be reached with nobody quite sure what to do next until Angela Babcock stepped forward.

'Inspector?' she asked.

'Commissaire, madame.'

'Commissaire, that's right, I do believe that after the unfortunate death of your mayor, our respective governments were in contact with one another, am I correct?'

'Yes, madame, but this is…'

'And that for the duration of the *pétanque* tournament the English team are to have diplomatic immunity, am I still right in thinking that?'

Richard, while his head was still swimming, had to admit that Angela was channelling pure Lansbury, with a bit of Joyce Grenfell thrown in. The Commissaire said nothing.

'Mr Ainsworth,' she continued, 'is a member of our team, Commissaire, and is therefore subject to that very diplomatic immunity.'

'Since when was he a member of your team?' It was Valérie who demanded to know.

'Since about five minutes ago, madame.'

'But this is a murder investigation!' The Commissaire was matching Richard in levels of vexation but Angela stared him down.

'You see?' Roddy whispered in Richard's ear. 'Every boy needs a nanny.'

The Commissaire turned to Valérie and Edmond. 'I did what I could.' He shrugged. 'The evidence was always insufficient anyway.' He walked towards his car.

'You wanted me put away?' Richard sounded hurt at the dawning realisation that Valérie and Edmond were behind the attempted arrest. 'You two wanted me out of the way!' he cried, and then at Valérie, 'This partnership is definitely over!'

Chapter Nineteen

In the end, it had been a rather straightforward decision. Once home, thanks to a smarting and silent Commissaire, he had literally barricaded himself in his cinema room. He had shoved a chair under the door handle and chosen a film that suited his mood. Initially he had thought Hitchcock, *The Wrong Man*. A musician falsely accused of murder is left powerless as his life spirals out of control. But the spiralling was too slow, brilliantly done of course, but it had nothing on the sheer bungee-jump, one-hundred-mile-an-hour elasticity of his own situation as it currently stood. The choice then, among thousands of DVDs, hard drives, dusty VHS tapes and even a laser disc became, very quickly, blindingly clear.

Arsenic and Old Lace.

Until it had morphed into his everyday existence, Richard hadn't been a huge fan of farce, French or otherwise. It all seemed a bit frenetic and contrived. But the idea that a perpetually suave Cary Grant – in this instance an author of books on the futility of marriage – should consistently and maniacally lose his wits when he discovers his favourite aunts are serial killers and that his psychotic long-lost brother has returned *after years away*, just to make things even more complicated, resonated somewhat. It was him, Richard, on the screen and out of all control whatsoever, pushed and pulled in various directions by several psychopathic lunatics. All it lacked was an amorous chihuahua and a poodle up the duff, but even Hollywood couldn't provide that.

He'd settled in with a box of wine, not prepared to risk running out of alcohol and having to leave his safe room, and relaxed into the film, feeling for Cary every step of the way. Then it finished, so he pressed play again and went for a refresher at his wine box.

There was a knock at the door. Not a quiet, nervous, sorry to disturb you knock, but a confident, I know you're in there and I don't have time for this knock.

'What do you want, Madame d'Orçay?' he barked, affecting an air of irritation, which served to hide his actual nerves.

'Can I come in?' she asked, her tone not in any way encouraging him to open the door.

'You can't, sorry!' he replied. 'And don't try and force the door either, I've jammed a chair under the handle.' He took a victory sip of wine, just as the door smashed wide open, the chair legs snapping under the force.

Momentarily stunned, he quickly regained enough composure to stand and adopt a position of high dudgeon. 'Right,' he said, 'well that's going on your bill!' He had meant it to sound at least a little sarcastic but then he saw, through the doorway behind her, that she had indeed packed her bags. Valérie d'Orçay, a look of dudgeon on her own face even higher than his and matched by that of Passepartout, was actually moving out.

'What are you doing, Richard?' she asked, unreasonably in his opinion as she was the one who'd barged in.

'*No, I'm not drunk, madam, but you've given me an idea!*' It was Cary Grant on the big screen and filling in perfectly for him.

'What he said,' Richard added.

'So, you are dreaming again, is that it?'

'No!' He reacted with a hint of anger, not having Cary Grant's lightness of comedic touch. 'No. Once again you misread the room, I'm not dreaming, madame, I'm hiding.' He was very pleased with that. It was exactly the kind of thing that would be a killer line in a classic screwball comedy and therefore, proud as he was, he also knew it would have no effect on Valérie.

'It is the very same thing!' she retorted, not without vindication. 'Turn that silly man off.'

He muted the film. 'Are you leaving?' he asked tetchily, determined not to let his mood drop.

She paused before answering. 'Yes,' was her equally defiant reply and she turned to go.

'Well, take care, then!' His raised voice matched the screen persona he'd adopted. 'I think you're making a mistake though.' She half-turned back. 'He's not who he says he is, Valérie. He's not your husband and he is dangerous.' His eyes dropped to the floor under her withering gaze and his body bowed slightly. 'I don't want to see you hurt.'

She put her hand on his arm, a brief gesture of warmth amid the warring. 'I know what I am doing, Richard,' she said quietly, though not softly. 'You must trust me. It is you who needs to be careful.'

Now he looked at her, in some confusion and not a little hurt. 'Is that a threat, Valérie?'

'No, no. A warning, Richard. Neither of us really knows what we are dealing with.'

'It sounded like a threat!'

'Oh, Richard, if that means that you take me seriously then, yes, it is a threat!'

She turned around and bumped directly into Madame Tablier, who unusually was loitering in Richard's house and not in the B&B.

'You off, then?' The old woman was trying to hide her delight but not doing it at all well. 'I saw the bags. I've already cleaned your room out.'

Richard closed the door and placed a new unbroken chair under the handle. He had no desire at all to get involved in whatever occurred on the other side, but he had a feeling it wouldn't be pretty and that he'd get the blame anyway.

Ten minutes later and he was still in shock. Not so much in shock that he hadn't unmuted the film and refilled his glass, but a sort of numb bewilderment nonetheless. Cary was still up there, coping farcically with his own stressful situation, surrounded by innocent-looking murderers, imposters, spurned wives, incompetent police and an irate taxi driver. He was doing it perfectly and brilliantly, a masterclass of comic performance and timing as he descended into lunatic bafflement and maniacal helplessness. Richard wished he had that performative aplomb. Instead, as the images reflected on his glasses that he usually forgot to put on, every few minutes or so he just kind of whimpered, like a puppy with separation issues. He had absolutely no idea what was going on at all and though this was not an infrequent feeling by any means, it was rarely at this depth of cluelessness.

The actors broke out into a loud fight on the screen, guns were pulled, furniture and glass were smashed, cries of 'Look out!' punctuated with the dull thud of punches hitting their mark. Suddenly his own door smashed open again and Richard cried out as the shock had him falling off his chair.

'Richard! Richard! Are you all right?'

The fighting on the film came to an end and it was only then that Oriane Moulin realised what was going on. Nothing was going on. Richard looked at her like he had been expecting her all along, his reactions by now bordering on catatonic. To him it was just one more unexpected turn of events and therefore, in a sense, highly predictable.

'Do you people have no respect for privacy at all?' he asked, his apparently unflustered demeanour making Oriane worry all the more.

'I heard fighting and thought you were in trouble.'

On the face of it, it wasn't an unreasonable thing to assume but she missed Richard's deeper concern.

'Yes, well obviously, but why were you in the vicinity in the first place? That's what I'd like to know.' She started to reply, but he wasn't in a mood for listening. 'I mean, obviously, if you were standing on the opposite side of that door there and you heard the sound effects of the film, naturally you might conclude that there was indeed some kind of fracas, a rumpus, a ballyhoo...'

'Richard, are you unwell?'

'But the nub of the question, the crux, if you will, is this.' He took a deep breath. 'WHY WERE YOU ON THE OTHER SIDE OF THE BLOODY DOOR IN THE FIRST PLACE?'

It was obvious from her reaction that Oriane was happier with Richard effectively losing control of himself. She smiled at him as if him sitting on the floor surrounded by the wreckage of chair and door, his glasses askew but wine glass in hand was the norm, and that everything was indeed OK.

'You want to know why I'm here?' she asked calmly, as Zsa Zsa, with her absurdly trimmed moonboot-shaped paws, tiptoed around the detritus and took a long disapproving look at Richard.

He returned the dog's haughty expression and turned back to Oriane. 'Yes, if you wouldn't mind?'

She stood up and helped him to his feet. On screen the bit part actor playing the irate taxi driver exclaimed, *'I knew this would end up in a nuthouse!'* and Richard nodded in agreement.

'Can we turn that off for the moment, please?' Oriane asked with exactly the same look of disdain that Valérie had shown not long before.

Richard paused the film again wondering just what it was that highly trained French secret service operatives had against Cary Grant films. It reflected badly on the nation as a whole was his conclusion. He slumped back into his chair, while Oriane slid in elegantly at his side and Zsa Zsa jumped on to the seat to his left.

'Should she be doing that in her condition?'

Oriane ignored the question. 'Richard,' she hissed, as if they were being overheard, her voice suddenly very urgent. 'I think you are in danger!'

If he was meant to feel alarmed by this, it didn't show. He'd had his brief flirtation with shouting and expressive emotion and was now, on the face of it at least, back to the Blitz spirit of his English roots, upper lip stiff as a statue's.

'In danger, eh?' He weighed up the possibility. 'From former French secret service agents with a penchant for smashing furniture, or did you have someone else in mind?'

'I thought you were in trouble!' She looked hurt by his lack of gratitude.

'Which brings us back to my original question.' He sounded like a bored interrogator with an unrelenting witness. 'Why are you here?'

'Because I think you are in danger!' she repeated, unable to fathom his apparent fortitude.

'From whom?' he asked slowly.

'From the killer of the mayor and of this Derek Munro obviously.'

'Oh, you know about all that, do you? Hard to keep something like that quiet, I guess.' He toyed with the remote control for the film. 'Who specifically is the killer then, any idea? Because I appear to be top of the list of suspects, you know?'

'I heard about that too.'

'Yes, of course you did. I'm only a free man because of my standing as an international *pétanque* player, diplomatic immunity, don't you know?'

She shook her head. '*Are* you unwell, Richard? Have you had a blow to the head or something?'

'Several, if you must know, so maybe there's a cumulative effect taking place on my sanity.'

'We must be very careful, Richard, very careful indeed I think.'

It wasn't the portentous warning that had Richard worrying, it was the 'we'. 'We?' he asked nervously. 'As in, "we"?'

'Yes.' Her voice was immediately hard-edged, another trait she had in common with Valérie and it signalled that a decision had been made, without any consultation naturally, and that action would be taken. 'Do you have a spare room?' she asked, in a manner suggesting that if he'd said no, she'd have built one on the spot.

'Well...' He didn't know how to finish the sentence. 'Sort of, you see... Valérie has moved out.'

She didn't look surprised. 'To be with her *husband*?' The way she stressed the word husband showed that she definitely shared the same doubts about Edmond Masson as Richard. He nodded, trying to give nothing away. 'Then I will move in,' she stated, and stood up. Richard followed her to the door wondering how to put it delicately and politely that he'd really rather her not move in at all and that he would prefer to try and hover, at least temporarily, between frying pan and fire. It was then that he noticed her enormous suitcase just the other side of the door. And behind it was a disbelieving and clearly very disapproving Madame Tablier.

'You don't waste much time, do you? It's not a bloody harem you know?' the old woman growled.

'There is no need to help me, madame.' Oriane ignored her and strode past, dog under arm and reading Madame Tablier's moods as badly as Valérie. Yet another thing they had in common. He pressed play on the film and decided to hide for a bit longer. He wasn't so numb as before though and he winced internally at a sudden realisation. He wasn't jumping out of the frying pan into the fire at all; the fire was jumping into the frying pan with him.

Chapter Twenty

It was a relief to get back to the mundanity of breakfast. Richard's routine was a well-practised one: the alarm would go off at about six; he would shower, dress and make his way over to the *chambre d'hôte* for about seven fifteen. He would lay the tables, put out fresh juice, yoghurts and large glass jars containing cereals. He would then fire up the coffee, jump in his car and go to the *boulangerie* for fresh baguettes, croissants and *pains au chocolat*. Guests would descend, drawn by the traditional and magnetic continental morning aroma at about eight fifteen. He couldn't claim it was an exciting life, he couldn't even say it was his ideal existence either, but in the current climate it offered a solidity and regularity that he very much needed.

That's the thing, he told himself as he opened the door to the breakfast salon, *exotic, highly dangerous French women were all well and good, but you knew where you stood with a coffee and a pastry.*

There was a strange smell in the salon as he opened the door. Well, not a strange smell as such, it was just coffee, but the fact that the place was already filled with the smell of coffee was what was strange. Also, there were baguettes and other assorted *patisserie* laid out on the counter. One of the croissants was half-eaten. Had Madame Tablier arrived early? She sometimes did, but she had never prepared coffee before. In itself, it wasn't troubling, but Richard had geared himself up for a new start. If his partnership with Valérie had been dissolved, so be it, he would therefore take a step back from the world of murder and assorted intrigue and let others dwell upon the deaths of Mayor Planchet and Derek Munro. If indeed there was something going on with the *boules* teams – he was petty enough to no longer use the word *pétanque* – it was their problem. He would throw his *boules* as part of the tournament, but that was his limit. Yes, he was grateful to have diplomatic immunity and therefore not currently languishing in a prison cell charged with murder, but enough was enough.

His habitual breakfast routine was meant to herald a break from all that excitement, but someone had already scuppered his plans for a return to the unremarkable.

He went about the rest of the drill, a frown perma-nently in place. He doubted Oriane would have gone out for breakfast stuffs, the English wine guests even less so. Valérie, maybe? In some kind of very Valérie-type unspo-ken apology? That didn't seem likely either. Contrition was not the word that sprang to mind after their last exchange.

He looked at the finished preparations and shook his head. This was not the clean break from thrills and danger he'd been looking for. He decided to spend a few minutes with the hens instead, that usually did the trick.

'Hello, ladies!' he hailed as he approached the coop. 'You're up early!' Lana Turner, Joan Crawford and Olivia de Havilland were all outside, scratching at the ground, and all three greeted Richard's arrival with an avalanche of clucking and flapping. They looked like hotel guests who'd been waiting for the duty manager to arrive before embarking on a litany of complaints. *This happens*, Richard told himself, *occasionally a larger bird would land and try to steal their feed, or they could sense a fox in the field.* He calmed them down, refilled their water and went into the coop.

'What the...?' Richard didn't have a temper as such, but this was an invasion bordering on the personal.

'Ah, monsieur, I thought that you might be up earlier than this.' If Commissaire Lapierre felt any sort of embarrassment at being found in another man's hen coop, he was doing a damn good job of hiding it. Just for added effect he removed a half-eaten croissant from his jacket pocket and took a bite, glaring at Richard as he did so. It might even have been quite a threatening expression if it weren't for the fact that, as usual, flakes of pastry were stuck in his moustache and there were feathers on his head.

Richard tried not to look upset. 'I'm not sure of the terms of diplomatic immunity,' he began slowly and through gritted teeth, 'but tampering with a fella's hens seems pretty high up on the intrusion stakes, if you ask me!'

Lapierre didn't even blink. 'You have something to hide, monsieur?'

Confidently, having remembered that his one piece of solid-ish evidence implicating Edmond Masson in the murder of Mayor Planchet had been stolen, Richard replied with a haughty, 'Absolutely not.'

The smile that spread slowly across the pastried face of the policeman was not a good sign. It appeared in slow motion, almost like a leak. 'So this is what, then?' He held up the piece of terracotta that Richard had recovered from under the mayor's corpse. 'Are you teaching your chickens pottery?'

'Where did you find that?' Richard asked, surprised. 'I thought someone had stolen it.'

'It was hidden in the hen food, monsieur.' This simple statement was accompanied by a look of smug triumph.

'Of course! God, I'm an idiot! The feed!'

This wasn't the broken-down, tearful supplicatory confession the Commissaire had been expecting.

'You don't deny you have it?'

'No. I was going to show it to you before, but I forgot I put it in the feed. I thought I'd hidden it under Lana Turner.'

'Lana Turner?'

'One of the hens.' Richard frowned again. 'You've never heard of Lana Turner, have you?' The Commissaire shook his head. 'Honestly, you people! Have you been living under a rock?'

Finally the stress of the morning, the total up-turning of his plans, the coffee, the hen intrusion, it was all too much for Richard. Added to that, what finally broke him was the fact that one of the great luminaries of the Hollywood era, albeit dead some thirty years, was now virtually unheard of, albeit in rural France.

'Out!' he cried. 'Get out of my hen coop!'

'Monsieur, I must...'

'Do you have a warrant?' Richard was now totally exasperated, and on the verge of losing control. 'Well, do you? Sneaking around making coffee, delivering bread and tampering with a fella's hens! I shall make an official complaint.'

'I did not tamper with your hens!'

'I'll know if you did!' Richard had no idea what he meant by that.

The Commissaire took a deep breath. 'I shall wait for you outside. I suggest you calm down, monsieur.'

He exited the coop causing a commotion with and getting a mouthful from Richard's ladies as he did so.

Five minutes later Richard found the policeman sitting at the outdoor table, toying with the shard of terracotta. In front of him were two cups of coffee and a neat plate of breakfast pastries. It was a strangely genteel set-up and made Richard feel slightly guilty about his very un-Richard-like outburst. He sat opposite Lapierre.

'I did not know if you take sugar or milk, so I brought them out,' he said, not lifting his eyes from Richard's evidence.

'Thank you,' Richard mumbled.

'Where did you find this, monsieur? I am no expert, but it looks to me the same as was found broken at the town hall after the break-in. Did you remove evidence from the scene of a crime?' He didn't ask it in a threatening way, quite the opposite, he was being remarkably friendly.

Richard told him where he'd found it, under the body of the unfortunate and dead, Mayor Planchet.

'I see,' the Commissaire ruminated. 'But why did you take it? At that point, why did you think that it was of significance? Why hide it with your Lana Turners?'

He was a shrewd man, no doubt. Commissaire Henri Lapierre was down at heel, covered in pastry flakes and wore suits that looked like they'd been designed with creases and stains already built-in, but he was no fool.

Richard sighed. 'Valérie told me that Edmond Masson is a collector of ceramics, I don't know, terracotta stuff. So, when I found this...' His voice trailed off, expecting another admonishment from Lapierre.

'And you did not tell me about it.' It wasn't a question. 'I know why. Valérie d'Orçay is a very persuasive woman. Even if she has not asked you to do something, you do it. I know.' He sighed. 'What is going on, Monsieur Ainsworth. May I call you Richard?'

Richard nodded in surprise. 'Honestly, I don't know. And, yes.'

'You and Valérie are playing games?'

'No! It's certainly not that. I mean she tried to have me arrested yesterday for the death of Derek Munro.'

'They, Richard, *they* tried to have you arrested.'

'They,' Richard repeated morosely. The two men sat in silence for a moment. 'Why kill Derek, anyway?' Richard asked eventually. 'He seemed harmless to me. Yes, a fantasist, a daydreamer, but so am I.'

'Maybe he told a fantasy to the wrong person?' The Commissaire looked Richard in the eye.

'You mean, he let slip the undercover smuggling case and someone believed him, then got him out of the way?'

'It seems plausible, no?'

'Poor Derek.'

Again silence. 'I too am a *rêveur*, a daydreamer.' He sat back. 'I have told you before. I thought a posting to the Follet Valley would be ideal for me. A quiet backwater, where nothing ever happens. A few years of fishing with the occasional parking violation or hunting accident, then retirement.' He snorted unhappily. 'I should have checked to see if Valérie d'Orçay was living here beforehand. If I had known, I would have transferred to the most violent neighbourhood in Paris just for the peace and quiet!'

The policeman smiled and Richard joined him. 'How long were you married?' he asked.

'Oh, not long. Two years. We loved each other, it was genuine. But Valérie, she cannot be harnessed. All of her husbands, this Masson aside it seems, have to let her go at some point. You cannot keep an exotic bird in a small cage.'

'I guess not.' Richard found it a rather depressing thought.

'Men like us, we are attracted to women like that, like moths to a flame. And we get burnt. Like this Oriane Moulin, you remember her?' Richard didn't like to say that she was currently sleeping about ten metres from where they sat. 'A dangerous woman. I would be very wary of anyone who falls under her spell.'

Richard thought it best to move the conversation on. 'What about Masson, then? Do you think he is involved?'

The Commissaire smiled. 'You would like him to be, I think. Then he would be out of the way?'

'Nothing like that, no,' Richard lied.

'He certainly wants you out of the way. That is my impression. Why else would he try to have you arrested?'

'And Valérie too.'

'Maybe. I think she was trying to protect you perhaps. I do not know for sure. It was Masson who did most of the talking.' He finished his coffee. 'It is very difficult, Richard. He is a decorated war hero, an invalid, injured for the cause of France. Accusations against him will be defended by people who do not even know him. That is France.' He stood up. 'I will have this terracotta examined; if it is antique it is perhaps evidence of Masson's involvement.'

'Is there any coffee left?' Oriane Moulin stood at the salon door, shielding her eyes from the morning sun. Her long auburn hair was in a loose ponytail and she wore only a grey T-shirt that just about reached the top of her thighs. Zsa Zsa sniffed about at her bare ankles.

The Commissaire's demeanour changed immediately. His face became stoney, his eyes cold and Richard remembered what he'd just said about people associated with the dangerous Oriane Moulin.

'What is going on here, monsieur?' he asked quietly, stressing the word monsieur. 'Perhaps you are attempting to make a fool of me?'

Richard tried to laugh it off. 'No, not at all. And really, Henri, it's not what it looks like!'

'Commissaire, if you please.' And with that he strode off, his heavy tread crunching on the driveway gravel.

'Hello!' This time the interruption came from one of the English guests, smartly dressed in shorts and a polo top. 'I'm afraid we're a man down today, Mr Ainsworth. You don't mind if Steve stays here in bed, do you? Bloody lightweight.'

Richard tried to sound concerned. 'No, of course not,' he replied, unable to take his eyes off Oriane.

'Shame though,' the guest wittered on. 'Steve's the only one of us who speaks a bit of the local lingo. We're short a translator now.'

A gleam came into Richard's eyes and with it the thought of temporary escape.

Chapter Twenty-One

Richard lay still, trying not to further aggravate the angry swarm of hornets currently conducting some kind of heavy-metal karaoke concert inside his head. Just when he thought he'd reached a position where the clamour was just about tolerable, the hornets would move up a gear or the noise would change altogether. Briefly it had been the same noise his bicycle used to make when he pegged an ice lolly stick to the wheel spokes, a memory-inducing tumult that would normally give him a warm nostalgic feeling. This morning, however, it made him feel sick. And he clung on to the bed as it span violently like a fairground attraction. More childhood memories. 'The louder you scream, the faster we go!' repeated a hollow DJ voice above the disco beat of the music. The teenage flashback was accompanied by the smell of candy floss and toffee apples which he felt sure would tip him and his stomach right over the edge.

There was though a silver lining to this darkest of clouds. Yes, it hurt. Yes, he might never be quite the same after it. And yes, he would never touch a drop of alcohol again for the rest of his life, the current projection of longevity being roughly twenty-five minutes. But, like Edith Piaf herself, he had absolutely no regrets. He realised of course that getting inebriated to forget his current travails was neither big nor clever. It was, in fact, childish, irresponsible and bordering on cowardice.

It had worked though.

Rough as he felt, yesterday's antics had provided a welcome, all too brief, hiatus from what he saw as his now quite insurmountable problems. None of which, he convinced himself, were of his own making. He was being used like a traditional maypole had been his conclusion. He just stood there, still and strong, while various other parties danced around him and tied him up in knots. Yesterday he had, for a short while at least, thrown off those shackles and he would repeat the adventure in an instant. Well, maybe not this instant but an instant some time in the future when his head didn't feel like it was being grated for a side-salad.

The thing is, though it had been a temporary respite and though it had served its purpose, it was time now to tackle things head on. Get back in the game. He had come to some pretty big decisions the night before, none of which he could now remember, but as soon as he did so the world had better look out. Richard Ainsworth wasn't going to take this lying down anymore. Though he thought it best to wait until he could stand at least.

He opened one eye. Then closed it immediately, not having liked what he saw. It was entirely possible that he was still a little on the wrong side of completely sober and, therefore, what he saw was some sort of wine-fuelled mirage. He took a deep breath, opened both eyes and closed them again. It was not a mirage. It was definitely a haughty though attentive-looking poodle showing early signs of pregnancy and it was sitting on the pillow next to him.

'Why, Zsa Zsa, why?' he groaned. 'What fresh hell is this now?' The dog, crueller than the twin dogs of Hades, yapped right into his ear. Richard briefly had dark thoughts in response to this and wondered if any court would convict him if he carried them out. He decided that they would and that he probably didn't have the strength anyway. 'What do you want?' he whined, opening his eyes urgently and in anger and, as a result, noticing that Zsa Zsa had a note attached to her collar. Unravelling the piece of paper, he was just about able, through still blurred eyes, to read the pencil scrawl. 'Log in to the Saint-Sauver Facebook group,' it said. It was signed, 'O.M.'

Zsa Zsa then ate the note. Richard couldn't work out if this was the result of some form of secrecy training or that she had already developed peculiar pregnancy cravings. Whichever it was, she jumped gingerly off the bed and made her way out of his room. Richard grabbed his laptop from his bedside table and opened up Facebook. The Saint-Sauver group had been set up in a flurry of excitement by Jeanine, the *boulangère*, a couple of years earlier and had attracted a couple of hundred locals initially all with the same intention in mind, to promote each other's businesses and bounce around tourism ideas. That it had swiftly descended into petty little complaints and point-scoring, the sort of 'would number 42 rue du Lac remember that bushes must be trimmed TWICE a year...' variety was the reason it had lain virtually dormant for over twelve months. Most of the posts were now written in capitals from angry people with nothing better to do than look for things to moan about. The fact that Oriane Moulin then had not only known about the group but also the Facebook Live event now happening on it, once again set alarm bells ringing for Richard. The bells didn't help his thumping headache one bit; neither did the jittery camera work that was showing the inside of the *mairie* as people began arriving for what looked like an emergency town meeting.

One day! Richard admonished himself. *I take off one bloody day and things move on without me!* His head was still too foggy to contemplate that there might be a connection between the two and he concentrated on what was happening on the screen instead.

It was clear to Richard that it was Madame Mabit holding the camera phone for the Facebook Live event and she was doing a good job of making sure that everyone who attended had their moment in the sun upon entry. However, she was either unaware that she was making incessant barbed comments that were being broadcast to the world, or she didn't care. It was entertaining though. Richard didn't know everyone who was there, but he now knew that the retired vet, a Monsieur Lonsdale, must have done some unspeakable things to some of his patients if Madame Mabit's comments were to be believed. Also that Madame Gondard, who according to Madame Mabit was a premature and unwitting spinster, was thoroughly deserving of her current nervous condition on account of the amount of homes she'd wrecked in the eighties, presumably out of revenge, and also that she liked a drink and was the worst *femme de ménage* in town. René was there, as was Jeanine, who was quietly accused of cutting the quality of flour in her baguettes, a heinous crime, and of dishing out foreign coins in her change. The English and French *boules* team were in attendance as well, suggesting that whatever this meeting was about, it was probably to do with them. Fatouma looked as flamboyant as ever in vibrant colours and wearing a multitude of beaded necklaces for good measure. Philippe Gratin was inevitably wearing a Johnny Hallyday tour T-shirt; Agathe sat on her walker, while Alphonse fussed about her. Angela and Olivia sat at the front, which Richard thought odd, while the Duke, Roddy, nibbled at a croissant and chatted with a tired-looking Valérie. It didn't look like Edmond Masson was there.

There was a banging sound off screen, before Madame Mabit adjusted her position to take in the table at the front of the room. Her husband Noel was banging his gavel to bring order and attention, and Madame Mabit herself was clearly impressed with his efforts. 'Finally, the man I married,' she oozed. Next to Noel sat a clearly unhappy Commissaire Lapierre; whether he was unhappy at being there at all or because of the unsatisfactory nature of the Facebook Live event it was difficult to tell, but he shifted uncomfortably on his seat.

Noel's efforts with the gavel were going largely ignored, much to the chagrin of his wife, who took it personally and increased her invective as a result. In fact, it seemed that only Richard himself was paying attention and he sat up, his pains momentarily forgotten. He would no doubt have gone to the meeting if he'd been aware of it, but he also realised he had the best seat in the house where he was and decided to dress, make a coffee and just enjoy the remoteness of the experience. Even some five minutes later as the coffee aroma filled his salon, Noel was still struggling to get the crowd silenced. Richard knew why. It was nothing to do with Noel's abilities and everything to do with the gathering being mainly French. Some of these people wouldn't have seen each other for a few days and the gaps had to be filled in before official business could even be contemplated.

Eventually it was the Commissaire who lost his patience, grabbing the gavel from Noel and beating it with such force on to the table that it sounded like a gunshot. It worked and a hush descended finally.

'*Mesdames, messieurs*,' the Commissaire drawled. 'Er… Monsieur Mabit.'

'The mayor presumptive, Monsieur Mabit,' Madame Mabit added tellingly.

Noel Mabit stood up, a solemn look on his face. '*Mesdames et messieurs*,' he repeated. 'I have called this extraordinary meeting here today, which is being broadcast live to the rest of Saint-Sauver and, thanks to a spark of inspiration from Madame d'Orçay, to our newly built EHPAD down by the river.'

Richard didn't like the sound of that at all. He had no idea why he didn't like it, but he didn't. Firstly, it sounded like this whole Facebook thing had been Valérie's idea.

Why? What was her interest in it? And secondly, why did she want it broadcast to the EHPAD, the old people's home?

'What are you up to?' he asked aloud as he poured his coffee. 'What's your game?'

The doors opened and an apologetic Martin and Gennie entered. They wore matching T-shirts with the Saint-Sauver *boules* logo emblazoned on them. They didn't look happy though. Madame Mabit greeted them and there was some even shakier camera work as they all greeted each other with a kiss.

'Sorry we're late,' Martin grumbled, off camera.

'Is everything quite all right?' Madame Mabit whispered, thrusting the phone in a visibly upset Gennie's face.

'Someone keeps smashing up my auricula theatre!' she sounded exasperated. 'All of my pots and my violas.'

'And her lobelia's dried out.' Martin just couldn't help himself.

'Not now, Martin,' Richard and Gennie said simultaneously, though three kilometres apart.

'At first we thought it was that Derek chap, but obviously not. Poor Martin's been very jittery as it is since the team arrived; they stay up until all hours!'

Noel banged his gavel again, asking for silence and the camera turned back on him. 'At the request of Commissaire Lapierre, who I'm sure you all know, we are continuing with our town celebrations!' His note of triumph seemed a little extreme, given there had been two murders, Richard mused. 'As a committee we have decided that this coming Thursday, May the eighth, Victory in Europe Day and a national holiday, we will hold another *brocante* and move our *boules* tournament to this day also.'

'*Pétanque!*' someone shouted in exasperation.

'*Pétanque*, yes of course.' A grim, official look came across Noel's face. 'We have not taken this decision lightly, but after due deliberations the committee decided that this is precisely what the late, much loved Mayor Planchet and er, the late, er...' He looked at his notes. 'Derek Munro, would have wanted. Commissaire?'

Noel sat down and the Commissaire rose wearily. 'I have instructions for the *brocante*,' he began without preamble. 'Everyone who had a stall last Thursday must have the same stall in the same place this coming Thursday.'

'Will the match of *pétanque* be played at the same time?' A worried-looking Philippe Gratin asked. 'I didn't get to see all the stalls...'

'Can't you think about anything other than Johnny Hallyday recordings?' Agathe asked ferociously.

'Even the murderer, Henri, will he be required to attend?'

Though off screen and nowhere near a microphone, Richard recognised Valérie's heavy-handed sarcasm and this was confirmed as Madame Mabit turned the camera in Valérie's direction. Edmond Masson was now standing next to her, his eyepatch in place and even more medals on his chest than Richard remembered seeing before. He also wore a beret with a parachute regiment insignia on the front. *He's really hyping up the war hero chic!* Richard thought, and was pleased to see Passepartout, lying uncomfortably in Edmond's arms, mirroring Richard's own expression of guilty suspicion. Also, as the camera panned around the room, Richard noticed that Fatouma was no longer sitting down with her team. She was moving along the panelled walls and Richard could see exactly what she was seeing. The pictures, as with the Turner that used to hang in the *mairie* reception, had obviously been recently changed, the dark patches of larger frames visible on the wall. Then he thought he saw something else: was there a quick glance to someone in the crowd? He was certain there was, but frustratingly he couldn't see who it was to.

Then the camera re-focussed on the Commissaire who decided wisely to ignore Valérie's question and carry on. 'Everything,' he said with dour seriousness, 'will be as it was on May the first. Is that clear? We want to get a better picture of movements on the day. Everything must be the same.'

This struck Richard as a bit far-fetched and judging by the hubbub coming from his laptop, so did everyone else. It seemed very unlikely that the murderer of Mayor Planchet and Derek Munro, if they were the same person, would stumble forward or even attend. *Unless*, Richard banged his coffee cup on the breakfast bar, *this orders the murderer to attend and if they don't, their presence would be greatly missed!* He raised his arms in triumph. The Commissaire had taken on board everything that Richard had told him, the ceramic piece itself must have proved damning. He was setting a trap for Edmond Masson. *Clever!* he thought, allowing himself a victory sip. *Very clever.*

The hubbub from the *mairie* grew from general chat to disquiet, then it ramped up further to a brouhaha and a shouting match. The Commissaire gavelled them into silence again. 'What is going on?' he asked.

Madame Mabit scanned the crowd with her phone and Richard saw immediately where the source of the trouble was. Oriane Moulin, who he had quite forgotten about, was now standing next to Edmond Masson and appeared to be giving Passepartout something of a lecture on decency and ungentlemanly behaviour. Richard just caught the end of her outburst in which she said something like 'keep it in your trousers', totally flummoxing the diffident chihuahua.

Valérie, unsurprisingly, was somewhat miffed at this and responded with some smart comments of her own about 'street dogs' and 'poodle floozies'. Edmond looked stoic, though embarrassed. The Commissaire smashed the gavel again, demanding silence. Noel spoke up too. 'This is neither the time nor the place,' he pleaded. 'We must show respect for Mayor Planchet and for er...' he looked at his notes again, 'er, Derek Munro.'

'This is very much the time and the place!' An angry Oriane Moulin shouted back. 'You think that you will see this man again after today?' She pointed at Edmond Masson, who looked surprised by the accusation. 'You have given him warning to escape and not face justice for what he has done! Two murders!'

Even Richard was taken aback by this turn-up. It had certainly escalated quickly from dog shenanigans to accusations of double murder. Valérie was silenced too.

'These are very serious accusations, madame. Do you have evidence for this?' the Commissaire shouted over the din.

'My business partner has!' Oriane shouted back, while not removing her glare from the still non-fussed Passepartout.

'And who is your business partner?' This time it was Valérie who sneered.

'Monsieur Richard Ainsworth!'

A silence fell on the room. A silence that Richard knew would be banging around the Facebook audience and certainly the old people's home. He, Richard Ainsworth, a sort of pillar in this rural French community, generally liked and popular in a benign way, was publicly accusing, albeit in absentia, a decorated French war hero – who, on screen, seemed to be clutching at his heart – of double murder. It was not a good look. In fact, it was a very bad look indeed and Richard whimpered in front of his laptop as his jaw hit the breakfast bar.

However, he wasn't the only one aghast at what he'd seen.

Elsewhere, and across the channel, a former member of the Saint-Sauver Facebook group snapped shut her own laptop. Clare Ainsworth still had a business in Saint-Sauver, to whit a high-end *chambre d'hôte*, and she was going to defend that investment and defend it strongly, even if that also meant defending her man.

Chapter Twenty-Two

Valérie had once explained to Richard that Oriane Moulin was a loose cannon. That she was a talented operative in the service wasn't in doubt, but she lacked judgement, dangerously so and especially for her colleagues. Her role in what was seen, at least by Valérie, as an operational fiasco was proof of that. And now even Richard, a man preternaturally given to offer almost everyone the benefit of the doubt, was in agreement. So much so, that his carefully crafted reputation for curmudgeonly sometimes slightly sozzled insouciance was hanging by a thread. The woman was a human cluster bomb. There was now a debate going on in town about Oriane's very public accusations of a favoured son of the republic and Richard's standing, at the very least, hung in the balance. Not that far beneath the surface he hoped that the town of Saint-Sauver would weigh up the evidence in front of them and give Richard himself that much vaunted benefit of the doubt. After all, it wasn't him personally that had accused an invalided war hero of murder, not publicly anyway. It had been Oriane Moulin, who seemed anyway to regard such acts as some way down the list of atrocities from canine romance.

Richard's hopes on the fairness of the debate were immediately squashed as some people, admittedly only acquaintances, crossed the street to avoid him. Nobody had done that, even in COVID times. For most people it was clear that Richard was very firmly on the wrong side of the argument. He was the traitor, it seemed, and not Edmond. The first signs of a backlash appeared at the *boulangerie*, where the locals were not hiding their feelings on the subject. He'd decided to start there because he knew that Jeanine had a soft spot for him and that he would therefore be on fairly friendly territory. It had not gone to plan. What Richard had failed to take into account was that just because he had shut his own laptop and closed the scene playing out in front of him, that hadn't been the end of things in the *mairie* nor on Facebook. Specifically, his new 'business' partner was currently cooling her heels at the *gendarmerie* in one of their cells. Apparently the charges against Passepartout had become more vociferous, to the extent that Valérie's dog had been accused of quite despicable, ungentlemanly behaviour matched only in heinous criminality by Edmond Masson's treason and murder. Then things had turned physical when a uniformed officer had asked her to control herself.

Richard stood stoically in line, greeting everyone with his usual enthusiastic '*Bonjour!*' only to be met with either stony silence or some colourful under-the-breath mutterings. One such muttering he caught was 'not fit to eat a brioche'; on the face of it a fairly low-level insult, but in rural France the kind of thing that carried weight. He tried to take solace in the fact that, in some ways, he could be seen as a unifying figure. He noticed members of the Lafarge and the Vernon families even speak to each other, thus, at least temporarily, ending a long-term feud. The two families hadn't spoken for generations, some said since before the Second World War, yet Richard and their joint enmity towards him had broken that silence.

He was feeling very self-conscious and was almost relieved when he saw that the Mabits, still arm in arm and quite lovey-dovey, didn't cross the road to avoid him. They didn't greet him nor show him any warmth either and, if truth be told, it was a calculated flypast designed to make Richard feel that he no longer existed. 'When things quieten down, darling,' Madame Mabit began, her nose in the air, 'and you are officially mayor, we need to crack down on vicious gossip.'

Well, that's a bit rich, Richard thought, *coming from someone who's just done a David Dimbleby-style royal commentary in the guise of Joan Rivers.*

'I'm surprised you can show your face!' Madame Gondard was the first person that morning to speak to him directly and he was almost relieved by the break in tension. He wanted to reply along similar tart lines and, after what he had heard Madame Mabit say about the woman, that in the eighties she'd had more flings than the Highland Games, he had the ammunition to do so. It wouldn't be right though. He looked at her, forty years on from her dallying prime and he simply couldn't reconcile the two. Instead, he lifted his chin and went with a tried-and-tested Bogart quote.

'I have a lot of character in my face,' he spoke calmly, resisting the temptation to add the Bogart lisp. 'And it's taken an awful lot of late nights and drinking to put it there.'

To Richard it was the perfect repost. Noble, witty and honest. To the rest of the bread-waiting queue, however, it was confirmation that Richard was not only a slack-mouthed slanderous interloper, he was an absolute soak and the more dangerous for it.

'Perfidious Albion,' he heard someone mutter, before Madame Gondard turned her ire elsewhere, specifically Jeanine.

'You've given me a foreign coin again!' she blasted, handing it back to a red-faced, apologetic Jeanine who changed the coinage.

Then things turned nasty. Madame Filbert, who had once run the *presse*, paid for her baguette and began brandishing the thing at Richard like she was a strike breaker with a baseball bat. She was also shouting loudly at him, dislodging some ancient dentures in the process. The effect was that Richard received just a lot of spray rather than vitriol; it was like standing on a pier while a storm brewed up. Jeanine calmed her down with some *petits fours* 'on the house', but it was a tense moment nonetheless and had left Richard not only shaken but in no doubt as to where he currently stood and that Bogart quotes were perhaps not the way forward. The way forward, he knew, was to find the killer, be it Edmond Masson or whoever, or get out of town. Maybe even both.

When things had quietened down, Jeanine had asked two very simple questions of him. 'Are you sure this Moulin woman is right for you, Richard?' and 'Do you think that that so charming Edmond Masson is really a murderer?'

In response he would have liked to explain that it really hadn't been his decision on the Moulin front and that while he did harbour strong doubts as to Edmond Masson's character, he was also some way off the evidence presentation stage. He would have liked to have said all of that, but a still angry Madame Filbert returned mob-handed and Jeanine bundled a shaken Richard out of the bakery back door for his own safety.

He badly needed an ally and he walked more in hope than expectation towards the Café des Tasses Cassées. It was busy with a lunchtime crowd when he got there and he was grateful that a small table was free in the shade. René greeted him with a warm smile, which was unusual and had Richard's brittle confidence immediately fraying at the edges. He regarded René as a friend, for sure, but warmth wasn't his strong point.

'This way, Richard,' he said, more loudly than he needed to.

Richard looked up confused. 'I'm quite happy here in the shade. I just want to keep my head down.'

René leant in and whispered. 'I know you do, mate. Follow me.'

René Dupont wasn't the sort of person you argue with even if he declared that day was night, so Richard followed him, studiously avoiding any glances from the tables, which all went silent as he passed.

René led Richard to a discreet corner table for one at the back of the room. 'I can't really have you outside, can I? People see you and they'll take their business elsewhere.'

So that was it. 'There's nowhere else to go!' Richard replied, starting to feel exasperated at the situation.

'Even worse then, they'll go hungry and blame you for that, too!'

Richard took his seat at the table. 'No, not there mate. Can you sit this side so no one can see your face?'

Richard once again began to sit down; like a naughty schoolboy, he was facing the corner. 'No!' he cried, standing up straight and turning on René, something he would never have done without severe stress. 'I won't have it!'

An enormous ugly grin spread across the face of René Dupont, so wide that Richard noticed for the first time in their friendship that the man had two gold teeth. It was the kind of fearless taut grimace that would have left Parisian bad debtors of old with a laundry problem, but fortunately for Richard it was the only grin René had.

'I was just joking, Richard! What a load of old nonsense, eh?' The man gave him a terrifying hug. 'Come and sit at the bar, let's have a chat.'

A grateful Richard sat wearily on a bar stool and ordered a Perrier.

'Things are that bad, are they?' René asked sympathetically. 'Oh, that bloody team are out the back by the way, if you want to have a game.'

Richard shook his head definitely. He could do without anything *boules* related for one day. 'I've never been an outcast before,' he mused. 'I mean, I've been cast out, but not outcast. I feel like Randolph Scott in *Ride Lonesome*.'

René dried a wine glass on his red-chequered tea towel and looked carefully for any smears. Without looking at Richard, he said, 'Well, mate, that's your own fault, isn't it?' Richard didn't understand and shrugged in response. 'I offered you a way out, didn't I? And you didn't take it.'

For want of anything meaningful or even tactful to say, Richard raised a glass in René's direction instead. What a peculiar little town this is, he thought. Currently a vast majority of its population wanted to string him up from a lamppost while someone else was offering to kill for him. Oddly, it gave him a warm glow inside while also asking the question he'd had before and very recently. Maybe it really was time to move on and find the quiet life again? This was all getting far too exciting.

René hadn't finished though. 'Instead we have to go through this malarkey again, the *boules*, the *brocante*... all exactly the same!' He chuntered something under his breath, which sounded threatening. 'I suppose I'll have to give this back, too.' His voice was morose as he produced a small wooden box from the side of his till. 'Shame.'

'What is that?' Richard asked, trying not to be distracted by the cheering coming from the outdoor *boules* piste.

The box was quite ornate with inlaid marquetry and contrasting woods, and René opened it gently. 'I bought it from Noel the other day, on that stall you had. It brings back memories, I can tell you.'

Inside the box and neatly laid out were sets of antique pen nibs, palette knives and small jar-like receptacles.

'It looks expensive,' Richard said, not really knowing what it was.

'Fifteen euros, mate. Bargain!'

'What is it? It looks like a calligraphy set.' Richard was having trouble reconciling the delicate art of decorative handwriting with the enormous and scarred ham-like fists of the former underworld enforcer in front of him. Or, that something so refined and needing of a steady hand had belonged to the late mayor.

'Sort of calligraphy, I suppose, yeah.' He leant in conspiratorially. 'I knew a guy once in Paris, forged money the old way, by hand, initially anyway. He had a set like this.' He stood up again. 'Maybe I'm getting sentimental in my old age.'

Richard smiled at him. 'Still, fifteen euros is a bargain.'

'Ha! Damn right it is! Noel Mabit wanted fifty! I said, mate, this is a *brocante* not the Chambord Antiques Fair!'

Richard looked dolefully at the box of tools. It was a pretty thing for sure and probably not used for years as the dead Mayor Planchet's shaky hand couldn't have coped with calligraphy; but then, hadn't he forged some paintings in the past? At least one of which was now missing?

'Can I have a closer look?'

René pushed the box across the bar and Richard picked it up carefully. The velvet cushion that housed the tools was slightly faded but still a regal red and made the gold of the tools stand out even more. Richard closed the box and held it up, looking at it carefully, though he had no idea what for. He opened the lid again and began to take the tools out one by one. The velvet shelf was definitely higher than the base of the box, possibly hiding something underneath. He felt around for a button, or something that would release the shelf, before René intervened and pushed two sections of marquetry on the side at the same time.

The shelf flipped up.

Inside there was a piece of paper, quite brittle to the touch, suggesting its age. Richard carefully picked it out and read it aloud.

My dear Narcisse,

I write this with a heavy heart. It was never my intention to come between you and Monique, and I know now that our marriage was a mistake. A mistake for both of us and one made in haste. Monique has married the wrong man, and I hope you may find it in your heart to forgive us.

Your loyal friend, Noel

René whistled and shook his head.

'Do you hear that sound, René?' Richard asked without looking up. 'That's the sound of cats among pigeons.'

Chapter Twenty-Three

The discovery of the letter meant that Richard, now in a fog of concentration and deep thought, was able to ignore the cold-shoulders that came his way as he walked back to his car. He'd replaced the letter and asked René to hide the box until he knew what to do with it. If anything.

What did it mean, though? On the one hand it was a personal issue and quite possibly nothing to do with the two murders that had occurred. On the other hand, the letter was possibly in a forger's calligraphy set, and Richard was certain that forgeries of some sort were behind whatever was going on. The disappearing pictures from the *mairie* suggested as much; Planchet's background as an artist, his ownership of the calligraphy set and specifically the letter threw up a number of questions.

Was it genuine for a start? Was it really from Noel Mabit to Mayor Planchet? If not, that would suggest that Planchet had written the letter to himself. Why? Because the note contained everything that he wanted to hear; or maybe he produced it to, as Richard had said, put the cat among the pigeons?

He wished he had Valérie to bounce these thoughts and questions off. She didn't always make sense, but in these situations where it is often said that two heads are better than one, her experience and knowledge really meant she had one and a half heads to Richard's half. He tried looking at it from her point of view. On the one hand he could see her shrug it off as a very French *ménage à trois*, and therefore conclude that most of the world were at it. On the other hand, she would also realise that there was very little else to go on and something must be done. That something, he knew, would be to break into the town hall as somebody else had already, and have a right good look around.

Should he ring her? He doubted that she'd be very receptive after the public, practically worldwide accusations he had, albeit by proxy, levelled at her husband, but he could try...

His own phone beeped instead and it was an incoming text. 'Meet me at the tinned goods aisle at the supermarket. Valérie.'

It was something that he had always feared about Valérie, that she lived permanently in his head. Now though, he couldn't be more delighted, even if the follow-up text read, 'Wear a disguise. I don't really want to be seen with you.'

Some time later and it was clear that his rather thin disguise – a pair of sunglasses and a battered old Panama hat – were insufficient cover as people were talking about him and pointing at him as he entered the supermarket. He didn't care. There was very little he could do about it and he even barked impatiently at one couple, saying petulantly, 'What do you want? Even pariahs have to eat, dammit!'

He tried to skulk his way through to the tinned goods aisle, making sure he didn't make eye contact with anyone, trying to work out what was going on and wondering just how good a disguise Valérie had chosen. Previously, he had always thought that Valérie herself had been gung-ho and reckless, but it was now abundantly clear that next to her former colleague she was a model of restraint and probity. He was excited to see her, nervous too, he realised, and wondered again if his suspicions about Edmond weren't solely the result of jealousy, or whether there was even any truth to them at all.

'Richard?' The very recognisable hiss came from around the corner. 'Richard!' Valérie repeated.

He approached the end of the aisle in as nonchalant a way as possible and found Valérie pretending to peruse some two for one offers on tinned sweetcorn. She was in her usual disguise, which everyone knew. A headscarf tied under the chin and sunglasses so big she looked like an Elton John tribute act.

'If you're stocking up on tins, you must be going into hiding for a while,' he joked weakly.

She turned away but as she did so, she whispered, 'Please do not make it obvious you are talking to me! You are not very popular, you know?'

'I know!' he cried, then lowered his voice. 'I bloody know! And exactly whose fault is that?'

'Well, it certainly is not mine!' she reacted, angrily throwing some tins into her basket as she did so.

'Yes, it is!' Richard would be the first to admit that the stress of the situation was getting to him.

'How is it my fault?' she argued, half-turning. 'You accuse my husband of double murder and no sooner am I out of your house, you move Oriane Moulin in!'

'I did not move Oriane Moulin in!'

'She invited herself, I suppose?'

He took a deep breath. 'Yes, she rather did actually.'

'Oh, Richard.' Valérie shook her head. 'You really must start to stand up for yourself, I think.'

'I really don't…'

'You are too easily led, Richard.'

'Yes, but…'

'And that is why you are now in this situation.'

'I know, but…'

'If you ask me…'

'Will you be quiet!' he shouted.

'Well, really!'

He couldn't remember if he had ever raised his voice to Valérie d'Orçay before and it felt like an awkward thing to have done.

'Now, please listen,' he said more calmly. 'I'm well aware that Oriane Moulin is using me to get at you or, more specifically, at Passepartout. But I am also convinced that Edmond is involved in the murders somehow and I do think it's related to art, or at least forgeries.' He paused, waiting for her interruption, which never came so he went on. 'Something is going on here and I think your husband knows more than he's telling.' He paused again. 'You're making me nervous, why are you not arguing with me?'

She lowered her glasses a little so that he could see her dark eyes. They looked worried in a way he had never seen before. 'I think you are right, Richard.' Her voice sounded as though it were about to break.

'Oh. Really? I wasn't actually expecting you to say that.'

She put her glasses back in place and once again pretended to look at products on the shelf.

'I found him this morning. He was smashing pots on Gennie's auricula theatre.'

'Right,' Richard replied. 'What *is* an auricula theatre anyway?'

She looked at him again over her glasses. 'I had to ask that too. It's like a bookshelf for plants.'

'I see. When you told me he was interested in ceramics, I thought you meant antique ceramics. Why does he smash terracotta pots?'

'I do not know,' she said quietly, putting a hand to her forehead.

Richard thought about this for a moment. 'Let's assume that he is your long-lost husband.' He took a step back when Valérie plucked a can of *salsifis* from the shelf. Richard had seen her work before and knew just how devastating she could be with a weapon in her hand.

'Go on,' she said, not looking at him.

Richard pretended to read the label on a can of reduced salt kidney beans and continued. 'Well, my question is where has he been? Why is here now? He might be smashing pots because, because he's not well.'

Valérie replaced the sweetcorn and went for a large jar of peas and carrots instead. 'Not well,' she repeated, though not as a question.

'Yes, you know. No fault of his own and all that but a bit like Dana Andrews in *The Best Years of Our Lives...*' Now she turned towards him in frustration. 'I know, you've never heard of it,' he said defensively. 'Only at the time the highest grossing film since *Gone with the Wind*, but it's passed you by...'

'Richard!'

'Right. What I'm saying is PTSD. You know, post-traumatic stress disorder. It affects people in different ways. I had an uncle who was in the Falklands. He went to the bar to get my nan a port and lemon, and disappeared out of the toilet window. We never saw him again. What I'm saying is, Edmond might not be responsible for his actions.'

'Are you finally admitting that he might be my husband, then?'

Richard took a deep breath. 'Where has he been, has he told you?' He asked the question as delicately as he could.

She took her time in replying and Richard let her do so. In fact she took so long, he wondered if he'd overdone the delicacy and she hadn't actually heard the question.

Eventually, and after tutting at the price of a jarred *confit du canard*, which she nevertheless placed in her basket, she answered him. 'He has been the whole time in Mali, a prisoner, a hostage for most of it, taken there by his Libyan captors. Yes, he will have the PTSD, that would be natural, no?'

Richard nodded in agreement mixed with defeat. The simple truth was this: if Valérie was convinced that Edmond Masson was who he claimed to be, then for obvious reasons he had to accept the same. It didn't mean that the man wasn't a danger though.

He became aware of a smaller figure standing at his side and immediately recognised his nemesis Madame Gondard from the *boulangerie*.

'Kidney beans, is it?' she spat. 'You shouldn't be eating pulses, you should be eating your words! Is he bothering you, madame?'

Valérie shook her head. If she found the situation amusing, there was no sign of it and she moved off further down the aisle.

A few minutes later, Richard caught up with her in Kitchen Towel and Tissues.

She shook her head again, this time visibly upset. 'Richard,' she urged, 'we must not be seen with each other, but I am worried.'

Richard wanted to tell her about the calligraphy set, the letter, the paintings and the terracotta under the mayor's dead body, but when he noticed Madame Filbert gathering up a posse in Pet Food and Cat Litter, he realised there just wasn't the time. 'Leave it with me,' he said, though he had no idea what that meant.

'Do you have a plan?' she asked.

'Oh yes,' he lied.

'Richard, be careful, please.'

He shrugged with apparent sangfroid, while at the same time wishing people would stop asking him to be careful.

'Of course.' She turned to go, before turning back quickly. 'Yes?' he asked, taken by surprise.

'Richard.' She hesitated. 'Richard, can I use your car, please?'

His shoulders dropped at the mundanity of the question. Something romantic would have happened in a film. 'Why?' he asked. 'You hate my car.'

'Yes, but I need a car that does not answer me back!'

He held out his key and in response Valérie gave him a small, flat plastic object wrapped in white tape. It looked like a large vitamin pill.

'Is that it?' he asked, disbelief in his voice. 'Am I supposed to take it with meals?'

'It is not all of the key.' She shrugged, but with a touch of defiance in the gesture. 'I tried to destroy it.'

'But it still works?' Richard wasn't surprised.

'Of course. Everything you need is there.'

He raised his eyebrows. 'You two must have a smashing time at home!' he joked. She didn't laugh but downed her basket and walked away. Richard looked at the tiny key-disc she'd left him with, and made a mental note not to swallow it with his blood pressure tablets the next morning.

His phone beeped again and he hurried to see the message, hoping it was a parting *adieu* from Valérie. It wasn't, it was from Angela Babcock. 'Practice four pm. Down by the riverbank. If you wish to keep your diplomatic immunity I suggest you be there.'

He didn't reply. Richard Ainsworth was getting very bored with being pushed around, but he felt even more strongly now that Valérie needed his help. In a way she had rescued Richard, from what exactly he wasn't the one to say, but he was going to do the same for her. At the very least he would try and he was determined not to let her down. Well, not on purpose anyway.

Chapter Twenty-Four

Maybe it was precisely because Richard was used to being bullied and badgered almost interminably that the constant, chivvying noises coming from various parts of Valérie's car's dashboard simply washed over him. His own car, his beloved vintage 2CV, constantly fought back with mechanically truculent gear changes and almost toddler-like poor handling. It also leaked. Valérie's replacement vehicle on the other hand just made demanding noises that he was able to ignore while thinking of something else entirely. Both cars in a way reminded him of his marriage, something he was aware didn't necessarily reflect him in a good light. Either way, he enjoyed the short drive to *boules* practice and had to admit, somewhat guiltily, as he thought of his dear old Citroën, that the drive was smooth and easy, comfortable and relaxing in a way that the battered 2CV was not. Noises could be ignored, something he'd always found quite easy.

It was only when the car started growling at him that he suspected something might actually be amiss. He scanned the dashboard, which was just a series of illuminated dials, eco figures, temperatures and averages, none of which meant anything to him and none of which screamed a warning. That's when he began to miss the simplicity of his own car. These modern machines were all very well, but he was just dawdling his way to a *boules* practice session, not trying to land *Apollo 14*. He slowed down, sped up, even did an emergency stop, but the low rumbling continued. Then the thing seemed to bark at him and he felt a presence at his shoulder: Passepartout. This was worse, this was even more unnerving. It was one thing to be worried about Valérie, though deep down he knew she could take care of herself, but if, in her anxiety, she had 'mislaid' Passepartout, then things were very serious indeed. He parked at the riverside car park, noticing the rest of the team marking out a piste on the Saint-Sauver river's 'beach', and texted Valérie.

'Is everything OK?' he wrote, not wanting to alarm her.

The response was immediate. 'Of course. Please look after Passepartout. I know he will be safe with you.'

'Why on earth would he not be safe with you?' He fired back and waited a full five minutes before giving up on a reply.

She knows she's in danger, that's why! was his reasoning. He sighed and looked Passepartout square in the eye. 'Just you and me, kid,' he said to the dog, who cocked his head in answer. 'No pressure.'

Richard placed Passepartout on the table between him and Roddy, Duke of Anglethorp, and sat down heavily on the wooden bench. 'Sorry I'm late,' he said, unable to hide the reluctance he was feeling at being there at all.

'Oh, don't worry about that!' the terminally cheerful aristocrat replied. 'What a gorgeous spot this is though, isn't it?'

From where they sat on one of the municipal picnic tables they had the shimmering River Follet in front of them, its flat sandy beach a hot spot for locals in high summer. To their left was the old stone aqueduct bridge that led into town and on the opposite bank, set back and behind a high wall, was the small chateau, which was currently being restored.

'Yes, it is,' Richard replied, almost as if noticing it for the first time in years.

'I mean to say,' Roddy continued, 'you can see why a chap like Turner would spend so much time here.'

The reference knocked Richard out of his reverie. 'Turner?'

It was the Duke's turn to be surprised. 'Yes, Turner. Surely you've heard of him? Joseph Mallord William Turner, English watercolourist, landscapes mainly.'

'Yes, of course,' Richard replied cautiously. 'You can't move for Turners around here. I didn't know you were into art, Your Grace.'

'Oh, please, none of that stuff. I was going to study art history at Cambridge, that's why me and the old man fell out. I love Turner. It's the brushstrokes, the light. The old man used to have quite a few of them, bloody beautiful they were too, but he gave them to the Tate.'

Richard thought back to the missing Turner copy at the *mairie* and the pictures that were also missing in the town hall meeting room. *Were they all Turner copies too?* he asked himself.

'Was your late father a collector, then?' he prodded, more to buy himself some thinking time as much as anything.

'Not so much of the Turner variety, no. Though he did leave Angela a couple of pretty good copies. He inherited a lot of the classics obviously. His own area was Islamic art and culture, the ancient stuff. He was an expert in all that, called all over the world for it.' He stood up and stretched his legs, taking in the view. 'You know, just between you and I, Richard, it seems a damn shame to spoil such a lovely spot with more of this damn *boules* stuff.'

Richard couldn't have agreed more. 'I know what you mean,' he concurred. 'I wouldn't like to cross Angela, though!'

'Ha! No, quite. A formidable old girl. That's why the old man kept her on long after there was no need for a nanny. She became a kind of secretary, companion almost.'

'And you've done the same?' Richard was thinking aloud.

'God, yes! I wouldn't be able to run things without her. She organises everything, you know? It was her and Dad who first set up the town-twinning thing with that Planchet fella. He loved it here by all accounts.'

'Mayor Planchet? Yes, well he was born here.'

'No, I meant the old man. He tried a bit of painting here himself, back in the day. By all accounts he was pretty rotten. I often think that's why he got rid of my Turners; they sort of mocked his lack of talent.' He looked wistfully at the scene in front of him again. 'Some people feel the need to try and create beauty rather than just appreciate it for what it is, I suppose.'

'I hadn't considered it that way,' Richard answered thoughtfully.

'I like you, Richard.' The Duke beamed a grin at him. 'I think we're alike. We're watchers, not doers.'

'Your Grace! I think we're ready now.'

The Duke rolled his eyes. 'I don't *constantly* need to be reminded. Coming, Angela!'

Richard picked up Passepartout and they all walked down to the ad hoc *boules* piste on the beach. Olivia was drawing a circle at one end with a stick, while Angela was opening the cases containing the *boules* themselves.

'Ah, Mr Ainsworth, so glad you could make it. Now, I've set aside this set for you. I want you to take them home with you, practise, get a good feel of their weight.'

'Right-o,' he said, feigning enthusiasm.

'I often think, Mr Ainsworth,' – this time Olivia joined in – 'that all *boules* have individual characteristics, they're all different.'

'Really? If you say so. I'll do my best,' he replied doubtfully.

'I'm sure you'll be just fine.' Olivia said this with no real hint of encouragement in her voice. To Richard she really was the most intense person. He'd met intense people before obviously, Valérie for starters, but there was joy in Valérie, her intensity lit up her eyes. Olivia was cold; *boules* seemed to be the only type of conversation she could muster. 'You be pointer,' she added. 'I'll be shooter.'

'Whatever you think works,' he answered, not having a clue what she was talking about. He tried to catch Passepartout's eye as he did so, looking for some kind of support. What he saw instead was a very alert chihuahua, excitedly wagging its tail. For a moment Richard wondered if Valérie had changed her mind about leaving her beloved pooch behind with him and had come to redeem the dog instead before any harm could come to him.

It was not Valérie he saw though. On the opposite bank, some thirty metres away across the river, and clearly not keen on Passepartout's suddenly yapping attentions, was Oriane. At her feet was Zsa Zsa, who was clearly as excited as Passepartout at the prospect of a reunion.

Oriane shouted something across the river. It didn't look particularly polite to Richard, but whatever it was somehow became lost among the excited pooch noises and the river wind. Presumably someone downriver would shortly be on the receiving end of a salty earful.

'I say,' Roddy said, shielding his eyes to get a better look. 'It's that dreadful woman again. She's like a bad penny, that one.' He turned apologetically to Richard. 'Sorry, old chap, isn't she some sort of partner of yours?'

'Kind of.' Richard's shoulders slumped. 'She probably wants to arrange a DNA test.'

The blood drained out of the Duke's face. 'Whatever for?' he asked.

'I hope she isn't going to disturb us, Mr Ainsworth,' Angela interrupted and her tone suggested it wouldn't be a good thing for Richard if she did.

Richard slowly put his *boules* down at his feet and picked up Passepartout. 'I'd better go and see what she wants,' he said, rolling his eyes, suggesting his own annoyance at the interruption. 'Tch! Just as we were getting started,' he added dramatically. He then turned to walk off, before walking back and handing Passepartout to a startled and distinctly unimpressed Angela Babcock. 'Better leave him here,' he said by way of explanation, 'just to be on the safe side.'

He cantered off to the bridge where he met an irate Oriane, who was intent on getting to Passepartout instead and not at her erstwhile business partner. 'I want to talk to that dog!' she screamed, her eyes wide in anger.

'I don't think that's wise!' Richard retaliated, blocking her path. He was determined not to let her pass. It was pressure enough looking after Passepartout on Valérie's behalf, but he knew damn well his life wouldn't be worth living if he let Oriane Moulin get hold of the creature. He tried a distraction technique. 'So, erm, when did you get out? Nice weather for it.'

She stopped and looked him directly in the eye, squinting as she did so. 'What?' she asked, her question suggesting there might be something wrong with him.

'Like I say, nice weather for a... you know, er... jailbreak. Release! Sorry, I meant release! You have been released I take it?'

'What?' she spat again, then relented a little. 'Sort of, yes.' She took a deep breath. 'I want to speak to that dog! Look!' She pointed at Zsa Zsa, who was straining at her jewelled leash, no doubt eager to see her beau.

'I think she looks well on it,' Richard babbled.

'Well on what?' was the feisty reply.

'Erm, you know. She's blooming, definitely suits her.'

Oriane lifted her chin very slowly and took a menacing step closer to Richard. 'Are you mocking me, Richard?' she hissed.

'Oh no! No, no, no, no, no! No.' He tried to laugh, but just sort of gurgled instead.

'Then let me pass.' Oriane's voice was disturbingly calm. 'I don't want to hurt you, Richard.'

'Ah, right, you see, I'm not sure it's a good idea. Getting past me I mean, or hurting me really, to be honest.'

'Angela's asking how long you will be, old man.' Roddy had put on his poshest voice for the occasion and something in his tone stopped Oriane, who blinked and slowly moved her head to look at him. Her movements seemed oddly unnatural like the model Tyrannosaurus rex in the 1933 *King Kong* film or Ray Harryhausen's cyclops in *The 7th Voyage of Sinbad*.

Jesus! Concentrate, man! Richard admonished himself.

'I believe you two have met,' he said quickly. 'But proper introductions are always good, I think. Oriane Moulin, this is Rodney Darius Rougemare, fourteenth Duke of Anglethorp Spa, Marquess Shireholme, seventh Baron of, er, somewhere.'

This had the effect of stopping Oriane completely in her tracks, which Richard was grateful for. Before a total calming-down could happen, however, sirens suddenly wailed as a police car came speeding on to the bridge. A uniformed officer jumped out and Oriane turned to run, but ran straight into Roddy, who was just in the wrong place at the wrong time. A few seconds later, he was still in the wrong place at the wrong time as Oriane, thinking the poor man was deliberately blocking her way, threw a knee up into an aristocratic groin.

It took two officers to bundle her into the car and they sped off without another word. Richard looked down at Zsa Zsa who returned an innocent look before pelting off, lead in her wake, towards an excited Passepartout. Richard sighed, and then realised he should probably aid the prostrate Duke.

'Are you OK, sir?' he asked, awkwardly.

Roddy had an enormous, wide-eyed grin on his face. 'I say!' The grin got wider. 'I say, what a gal!'

Richard sighed again and helped the still grinning Duke to his feet.

Chapter Twenty-Five

Richard wagged his finger and stamped his foot. He'd never been very good at laying down the law. Clare had been the disciplinarian in the relationship, the parental bad cop to Richard's good one. It came more naturally to her, Richard generally running shy of that sort of confrontation. Needs must however and he repeated his point.

'I get it,' he said sternly, 'the damage has been done. But I want no hanky panky, understood?'

Passepartout and Zsa Zsa cocked their heads in unison like a synchronised swimming partnership. Then Passepartout wagged his tail, something Richard rarely saw him do and which suggested mischief, the exact opposite of the theme of his lecture.

'Look, I have to go out,' he remonstrated, 'so just behave yourselves, OK? Please.' There was more cocking of the heads and this time both wagged their tail. 'Hopeless,' Richard concluded, 'bloody hopeless.'

The dogs' confusion may have had something to do with Richard's attire. Passepartout had seen it all before: the black trainers, the black jogging bottoms and a black jumper. He knew it signalled nocturnal activities, though his mistress Valérie could pull off the 'breaking and entering' look with greater elegance and aplomb. What the usually diffident chihuahua hadn't seen before was Richard's mask. Richard had searched high and low for a balaclava that he thought he owned, but had failed to locate. What he had found instead would do just as good a job, but had definite 'connotations'.

Years ago he and Clare had decided to throw a spur of the moment winter party to liven up the dark days of late January. The hastily arranged theme of the party was Superheroes and the worse the costume the better; it was all about lightening moods. Richard himself, the worse for wear after a few early *apéritifs*, had simply put his pants over his trousers and declared himself to be Superman. Clare had worn a revealing basque and gone as Wonder Woman and Gennie had painted her face green to represent She-Hulk. Richard had insisted she looked more like the Wicked Witch of the West from *The Wizard of Oz*, but she wouldn't have it. Needless to say Martin took the prize for the most risqué. He had simply worn a rather short silk dressing gown and called himself Flash Gordon. Richard remembered Martin's words with clarity every time the robe flapped open, which it did with alarming regularity. 'Oops,' he'd cackle, 'the chandeliers have popped out for a dusting.' The memory nearly made Richard retch. In a further effort at debauchery, however, Martin had also worn a leather gimp mask.

Why it was in his hat and scarf drawer he had no idea, but Richard was now wearing that leather gimp mask. He was going to do what he'd been calling all evening 'a Valérie' and break into the *mairie*. He wanted to find Turners, paints, evidence of forgery and anything else he could dig up and that, in his mind, was the place to look. So, necessity being the mother of invention and the imperative being that if he were seen he had better not be recognised, he had swallowed his pride and covered himself up. He had no idea why anyone would wear such a thing for titillation though; all he had was a sweaty head.

'One more time,' he repeated to the dogs. 'Keep your paws to yourselves, get it?'

He pulled the zip shut on the mask and turned to go, walking straight into Clare as he did so.

'Richard, what *are* you doing?' she asked, not unreasonably.

In return he mumbled something incoherent from inside the mask, then rolled his eyes and unzipped.

'Sorry,' he said confidently as he then strode past her. 'Glad you're here. Try and keep these dogs apart, will you? I'm popping out. Are they for me?' He pointed at a Marks and Spencer packet of Butter Thin biscuits.

'If you want.' Clare was understandably perplexed. 'What do you mean keep the dogs apart, why? How?'

'Because one of them's pregnant already and I'm getting the blame for it, that's why.'

'Do you want to re-phrase that?' she said sarcastically.

'Yes, very funny. Just make sure they don't get frisky, please. It shouldn't be too difficult, pretend you're married to one of them.' With a flourish he re-zipped his mask and closed the door behind him before she could come back with something equally devastating.

Besides the smoothness of the ride, there was another advantage to Valérie's car. While the inside was all beeps and various other electronic ejaculations, the outside was practically silent. The large black car moved through the shadows of the night like an underwater predator. If he had come in his 2CV he'd have woken half the town by now. He parked up behind the back wall to the *mairie* and sat still, making sure that there really was no one else around. It was completely silent and, with only a sliver of a moon, dark enough. He sat for a while, munching on a Butter Thin biscuit, which gave him comfort and steadied his nerves. Eventually, he decided to move and, for safe keeping, put the remnants of Valérie's car key in the biscuit box and left it in the central drinks holder. The last thing he needed to do was to drop the thing and lose it. Silently he left the car behind. There was no street lighting at the back of the *mairie*; in fact there wasn't much street lighting at all as the lights went out around midnight to conserve energy; *good for the planet, good for breaking and entering*, thought Richard.

Unfortunately, he had forgotten just how high the wall was. It was at least a good eight feet or so, and though he felt like he was dressed as an Amsterdam version of Spiderman, his wall-scaling skills weren't up to much. He found a wheelie-bin and, as quietly as he could, manoeuvred it into place, though even climbing on top of that proved a struggle and doubts began to creep in. *What am I doing?* he asked himself, before then telling himself to shut up. Finally reaching the top of the wall, he allowed himself a moment of rest before the sound of a car made him jump to the ground. What Richard imagined was the majesty of a leap into the unknown became a painful exercise in gravity as he crashed through a laurel bush, disturbing a cat, which howled and spat before realising that it was probably not wise to mess with a middle-aged man in a leather mask.

It turned and ran away.

Richard lay still in case the cat had roused anyone and also to make sure he had no injuries. When he realised with some surprise that neither had happened, and feeling fortified by it, he scurried across the courtyard to the back of the building.

There was a door at the back that he knew Mayor Planchet, when he made a rare public appearance, used often so he could nip out for a cigarette. It was also slightly set back into the wall giving Richard further cover. Not only had Valérie given up her car and dog, she had also left her bag of tricks in the car, which Richard now took off his back. There was a small torch and, most importantly, her skeleton key set. Richard had seen countless films where someone, usually a cop or a shamus, had broken into a place using a skeleton key and from his cinematic-minded point of view, it was simply a case of putting it in, wiggling it about and waiting for a click.

Ten minutes later and he was cursing how once again cinema had let him down. Once again, he'd been fooled into thinking there was some reality in what he'd been watching all these years and he swore heavily at the recalcitrant lock while he slumped in defeat with a sense of betrayal. The cat returned, meowing this time, looking for company and Richard told it to clear off, which surprisingly for a cat it did. It slinked its way along the back of the building and jumped on to a window ledge. It didn't jump down again and Richard decided to check if there might be another way of getting inside.

The large double window was wide open.

He looked to the dark heavens and thanked whoever it was for the lackadaisical attitude to security and climbed in after the cat. He stayed crouched on the floor, firstly to make sure the cat hadn't lured him into a trap and secondly to get his bearings. He knew that the entire top floor had been kitted out as a grace and favour apartment for the mayor and that's really where he wanted to start looking. There was a large central staircase in the building and that was the place to head to first, even if it left him exposed. *But then, exposed to whom?* he thought, not unreasonably. Still cautious he headed for the staircase. The advantage of a marble staircase is that there are no floorboards to creak and give out a warning, so he moved as quickly as he could up the stairs, the weak moonlight coming through the large windows unnervingly leaving a shadow of him against the wall.

It was a steeper climb than he had envisaged. He was aware that he wasn't exactly fit, but four floors of marble staircase, darting in between shadows, left him completely breathless by the time he reached the door to the mayor's apartment. There was also so much sweat under his mask it felt like he had his head in a water balloon. He undid the zip and took in some deep breaths. Then he heard a sound. What was it, the cat? His heart was beating so fast and hard it sounded to him like the bass drum on a marching band and certain to wake the neighbourhood. *You've come this far*, he told himself. *No turning back now.*

He turned the handle silently on Planchet's door, hoping it would be unlocked and was greatly relieved, if surprised, that it was. Opening it slowly, he stepped into the darkness and waited for his eyes to adjust again, not confident enough to use the torch. He preferred to go by what little moonlight there was, just to be on the safe side. Then he heard it again, that sound he'd heard just before. He recognised it now, it was a sneeze. Somebody *was* here further down the corridor. He hid in the recess of an open bedroom door, out of sight and listened carefully. There was some muffled talking and he dared to peer around the corner. He couldn't see anyone, but he did see a loft ladder hanging down from a previously concealed hatch in the ceiling. *That must have been Planchet's hidden studio,* Richard thought, *but who has beaten me to it?*

The voices were coming from up in the loft and from his vantage point Richard could also see the zigzagging of torchlight as whoever was there searched the secret room. He hid in the dark, as close as he dared to the ladder and sank back even further when he heard the voice come back to the hatch.

'They're not here, dammit. I thought they would be!' The voice was male and angry though Richard didn't recognise it at all. Feet came step by step down the ladder and he dared not look from his hiding spot in case he was spotted.

'It's dusty up there,' the man said, trying to avoid sneezing again. 'There's no point putting the ladder back though, I'll leave it how I found it. The police had finished here anyway; the council must be moving stuff out for whoever the next mayor is.' He waited as whoever was on the other end of his call said something in return. 'Maybe. I need to think. I'll speak to you later.'

Richard risked a quick glance and a champagne cork popped in his head! It was all he could do to bite his tongue and not cry out in triumph as a limp-less and eyepatch-less Edmond Masson stepped into view. He watched as Masson then moved off down the corridor and out of the door. Richard waited a good five minutes before moving, too excited to feel anything other than clumsy, but when he finally did move it was with a jig and his arms aloft.

Eventually turning on his torch he slowly climbed the ladder himself. Again, he was pleasantly surprised to find that he was right. It was an artist's studio, or at least the far end of the room was. There were easels and paints haphazardly disorganised, overalls, and brushes in jars. On one large trestle table there were an array of inks and pen nibs and some sheets of paper with what looked like Arabic symbols on them, some kind of press too. At the far end of the studio were stacks of paintings, arranged against each other like albums in a record shop. He flicked through them. They were all Turners; he even recognised the one from reception, so the others he guessed must be from the meeting hall. But someone surely must have put them here since Planchet had died?

Is this what Edmond, and whoever his accomplice was, had been looking for? Only they wanted the originals – that's what Edmond had said. Richard picked one from the pile and turned it over. It hadn't been mounted and the canvas was bare at the back except for some more calligraphy, which he couldn't quite make out. He shone his torch on the ink and nearly fell backwards in shock. Noel Mabit, it said, 2012.

Chapter Twenty-Six

Richard sat in the car outside his gate for a full ten minutes ostensibly to ruminate over what he had just witnessed and partly to get his story straight as he was certain Clare would be up waiting for him. Mainly though, it was to try and remove the damned mask that, via a combination of heat, moisture and assorted plastics, was refusing to budge. He'd have liked to imagine himself as Louis Hayward in the 1939 version of *The Man in the Iron Mask*, imprisoned by villains, his face hidden from public view. Only this was more humiliating, something that might be called *The Berk in the Gimp Suit*, and was far, far less appealing.

Eventually, he got it to budge a certain amount without ever finally getting the thing off and it sat on the top half of his head as though someone had picked him up with a plunger. He trudged in, not bothering to continue the fight with fetish rubber, consoling himself with his box of biscuits instead.

He was right, Clare was waiting for him. She sat on the sofa wearing a silk nightgown, a dog either side of her and a glass of white wine in her hand, a bemused look on her face.

'Good party was it?' She arched an eyebrow in mockery.

'Is there a glass of that for me?' he asked wearily.

'Of course, darling.' She got up and shimmied to the kitchen while Richard collapsed on the opposite sofa.

'I am exhausted!'

Clare returned with a cold glass of wine. 'It's hardly surprising, is it, dear? At your age? Running around half the night dressed as a sex slave, getting up to God knows what!' She sat next to him, leant her head back on the sofa and said, 'What are we going to do with you, Richard?'

This is exactly the kind of question that would normally have Richard's head clanging with warning sirens, but he was too tired and his headgear too tight.

'Can you help me off with this thing, please?'

After something of a struggle in which Clare repeatedly told him to stop whining, he was released, albeit with a thumping headache.

'Do you want to talk about it?' Clare asked, though in a way that left no doubt as to the fact that he would have no choice in the matter.

He sighed. 'It's a long story and to be honest, I'm not entirely sure what's going on. Why are you here anyway?' It seemed suddenly to occur to him that she wouldn't normally be there.

'I was wondering when you might ask!' Her tone was playful rather than admonishing. 'I saw that live Facebook thing. Firstly, you weren't there, and that had me worried. I'm very well aware that these things always end with oh, what do they call it?'

'*Un verre d'amitié*,' he said quietly, knowing exactly where this was heading.

'That's right, free wine. Well, that certainly struck me as odd, you not being there. Then I see Valérie, with a face like a slapped arse, and you're still not there. Odd thing number two. Then that policeman chap starts issuing *brocante* orders and before you know it, that other woman, what's her name?'

'Oriane Moulin.'

'Oriane Moulin, that's right. She declares that *she's* now your business partner and then rather drops you in it by telling everyone that you think a plainly invalided, decorated war hero is a double murderer.'

'And you thought…?'

'I thought you could probably do with some support.' Richard nodded slowly. It was clear that Clare was enjoying herself enormously, but he had to admit she was likely to be a more useful sounding board than his hens and he didn't feel that he could fully trust anyone else. 'Let's take it from the top.' She smiled at him encouragingly.

He took a deep breath. 'OK,' he said. 'Strap in. Firstly, Mayor Planchet is dead…'

'I don't think I ever saw him alive!'

He looked at her coldly. 'This isn't going to work if you interrupt with your flippant remarks.'

'Sorry.' She pretended to zip her mouth, which he chose wisely to ignore.

'Mayor Planchet is dead. I found him, well, I'd actually been trying to sell him all morning.'

'You'd been trying to sell a dead man?' She wasn't being flippant this time.

'Yes, but I didn't know he was dead and I didn't know I was trying to sell him.'

She put a hand on his knee. 'Richard, take another deep breath and start again.'

He did so. 'I was looking after Mayor Planchet's stall at the *brocante*. There was this big dresser that was for sale, along with a load of other tat as well, oh and a calligraphy set, but I'll come to that later.' He took a sip of wine. 'Anyway, Noel Mabit...'

'I knew he was involved.'

'Noel Mabit starts introducing the *boules* match.' He paused.

'Why have you stopped?' she asked, slightly worried.

'I was waiting for you to say *pétanque*.'

She shook her head. 'I have literally no idea of the difference, does it matter?'

'No, not really.'

'Then move on.'

'Noel Mabit introduces the *boules* match...'

'*Pétanque*.'

'Clare!'

'Sorry.'

He frowned at her. 'There's this *boules* match going on to mark twenty-five years of town-twinning between Saint-Sauver and Anglethorp Spa. A team from England and an all-star pro-team called the Avignon Arrivistes, possibly a local team too, but I doubt it now.'

Clare put her hand up. 'Sorry to interrupt again, but did you say professional *boules* team?'

'I know, right?' he nodded enthusiastically. 'That's what I thought. One of them is number three in France, though he'd probably be number one if he concentrated a bit less on Johnny Hallyday. Two are sort of committee, world *boules* organiser people, devoted to the sport certainly and to each other in a kind of mother–son way. And then there's the women's world champion! She's called Fatouma and she's from Mali.'

'Mali! How exotic.'

'Yes,' he replied gravely. 'Martin has rather taken a shine to her. He saw some documentary or other.'

'One of Martin's *documentaries*.' She raised her fingers to indicate sarcastic speech marks. 'I see. And the English team?'

'A duke who can't pronounce his Rs…'

'Lucky he's not a baron then.'

'Yes, you're not actually helping at the moment. Can I carry on?' She pulled a face at him. 'Thank you. So there's the Duke, then there's Angela, who was his nanny and I think to a certain extent still is. Her niece, who seems to be some kind of *boules* protégé and Derek Munro. Though he's dead.'

Clare puffed out her cheeks. 'OK, that's rather a lot to take in for now. Let's deal with the mayor's death before this other chap – Derek, was it? One at a time, I think. Noel was introducing the match.'

Richard nodded. 'That's right. Well I couldn't see, so I stood on the dresser to get a better view and I fell off.'

'Of course you did.'

Richard let that one go too. 'Well, as I fell, one of the doors on the dresser opened and the mayor just kind of flopped out.'

'And he was dead?'

'And he was dead.'

She considered this for a second. 'Obviously being in the dresser raises some questions, but first, how did he die?'

'Well, he died twice actually, sort of. He was poisoned by lily of the valley that caused a heart attack. Apparently he'd drunk the stuff from an old 1980s perfume bottle. Then someone stabbed him in the neck with a biro.'

Clare shook her head. 'I need another drink,' she said, standing up.

Richard gathered his thoughts while he watched the sleeping dogs and Clare returned with the bottle.

'So,' – she poured out two large measures – 'Mayor Planchet is dead. Twice. Why even once?'

Richard took a large sip. 'Right, Planchet and Mabit had apparently fought over the same girl in the late seventies. Planchet left to go to art school in Paris, leaving the door open for Mabit, which he took advantage of. So there's that. But René bought a calligraphy set at the *brocante*...'

'Oh, you mentioned that.'

'Right. Well that set my mind thinking.' He stood up and began to pace the room, thinking aloud. 'You see, two things. This Derek Munro, he told me he was a policeman investigating art smuggling. That's one connection there, the art school. Also, paintings have been taken down in the *mairie*!'

'What paintings?' Clare was now struggling to keep up.

'Very good copies of Turner watercolours.'

'Oh, the originals would fetch a fortune.'

'Quite. Well, Roddy's father...'

219

'Wait, who's Roddy?'

'He's the duke.'

'Who can't pronounce his Rs?'

'Yes.'

'How unfortunate.'

'Roddy's father gave a lot of Turner originals to the Tate.'

Clare nodded. 'I think I see where you're going with this. You think Planchet was copying the Turners.'

Richard lifted his hands, indicating for her to slow down. 'Hang on, I'll come to that. You see, Derek told me that his main suspect was Edmond Masson.'

It was Clare's turn to sigh. 'And who's Edmond Masson?'

'He's the invalided, highly decorated war veteran that Oriane Moulin says I have accused of double murder.'

'And have you?'

Richard took a moment. 'Yes,' he said eventually.

'OK, but who's the second victim?'

'Derek Munro.'

Clare looked at him in triumph. 'Well done, Richard. If this policeman Derek suspected Edmond Masson of being involved, then Edmond Masson must have killed him to keep him quiet. It seems pretty obvious to me. Well done, Richard,' she repeated. 'I'm very proud of you.'

He didn't return her smile. 'Only, it's not as straightforward as that.'

'Go on…'

'Derek Munro wasn't a policeman. He was just a fantasist.'

'Ah. And Edmond Masson?'

'Is Valérie's husband.'

Clare poured herself another glass. 'So, everybody really thinks that your accusations, via this Oriane Moulin, are based purely on jealousy?'

'Yes, they do. Particularly Valérie.'

'And Oriane? Is she trustworthy?'

Richard shook his head. 'She's currently in a police cell for violently trying to attack Passepartout and for kneeing the Duke in the groin.'

'She sounds a bit hot-headed, Richard.'

He sighed. 'She's having a difficult time,' he said quietly. 'She thinks Passepartout sexually assaulted her dog.' He pointed at Zsa Zsa.

Clare rubbed her temples. 'Are there any other suspects?'

'Just one,' Richard replied morosely. 'Me.'

'You!' She laughed, though not confidently.

'Valérie and Edmond tried to get me arrested for Derek's murder. And Edmond threatened me.'

'And how did you get off?' There was a slight note in her voice that suggested this had gone far enough and that, actually, she didn't believe a word of it.

'As Derek's replacement in the English *boules* team, I now have diplomatic immunity.'

It was a full minute before either of them spoke again. 'I really don't know where to start, Richard. When I lived here this was the dullest place on earth and it suited you, no offence. You've certainly changed, I must say.' Richard said nothing. 'So, what happened tonight then? Why the fetish gear?'

Richard suddenly looked up. 'Of course!' he cried enthusiastically. 'I went to the *mairie* tonight. I broke in…'

'You broke in?'

'Yes. I was looking for the missing Turners.'

'And who are the Turners?'

'Not who, what. Paintings.'

'Ah. And did you find them?' Clare's enthusiasm returned too.

'No.'

'How disappointing.'

'But then neither did the other people who broke in!'

'What other people?'

'Well, only one person really, the other was on the phone.'

'You can burgle by phone these days? Is it an app thing?' Richard gave her a cold look. 'Sorry. So who did you see?'

'Edmond Masson,' he said triumphantly, 'who was noticeably un-invalided!'

'Oh my God! Richard!' She clapped her hands. 'So you were right all along!'

Richard drained his glass and lifted it almost like a trophy.

'And that's not all,' – his voice was now like that of a showman, about to deliver the finale – 'all the Turners, the copies, are signed by Noel Mabit!'

Clare stood and shook her head in amazement, while an exhausted Richard fell on to the sofa in her place between the two dogs, who ignored him completely.

'I think you deserve another drink!' She laughed, taking his glass from his outstretched arm.

'Can I just have a glass of water?' he said with a yawn.

Clare padded off to the kitchen for the water. 'I must say, Richard, again, I am so proud of you! You really have changed,' she said over her shoulder before pausing as she turned on the tap. 'It makes me think, you know. Well, I have been thinking already actually, for some time… maybe you and I…' She walked back to the sofa, a glass of wine in one hand, water in the other. 'Maybe there's life in us yet, you know?'

Richard, an arm across either dog, head to one side, snored gently.

Chapter Twenty-Seven

The plain, honest truth of it, as Richard saw things the next morning, was that he'd rarely felt this good about himself. Over the last few years he had begun to live, not exactly live again, but to feel really alive for the first time. Now, thanks to his previous evening's activities, he could add solo breaking, entering, trespassing and, most satisfying of all, highly successful sleuthing to a previously fairly mundane existence. He knew who to thank for it too. Valérie d'Orçay. It wasn't all one way of course; in return she had gained a grasp of sarcasm and a regular dog-sitter, so it was an even trade. But she had taught him the skills, given him the confidence and now he had used those two things and proved that she was wrong; her husband, Edmond Masson, was indeed a crook. Unfortunately, something she hadn't yet imbued in him was the courage to share that kind of news.

He poured away the cold, stewed coffee and tried to work out the best way to take this next step. He decided to draw up a list of the available options first and, having made sure Passepartout and Zsa Zsa were in different beds, he secured a pen, paper and his box of biscuits and went to work. He divided the sheet of paper into three columns and wrote the words 'OPTIONS', 'PROS' and

'CONS' above each. The first and obvious option was to leave immediately, drive to Martin and Gennie's place and confront both Valérie and Edmond with his theory. The pros to this option were firstly, his current level of self-confidence, and secondly... well, perhaps he could flesh that out later. The cons were pretty obvious and involved him running for his life.

Another option would be to get Valérie on her own; the con here was exactly the same because she probably wouldn't believe him. He could of course get Edmond on his own, tell him what he'd seen and take it from there. Again, Edmond's limp was fake, so he would probably have to run. He sighed. The fourth option would be to go to Commissaire Lapierre with his findings, but this just felt wholly inadequate and something of an anti-climax. It would also involve admitting to illegally breaking into the *mairie*. He could email Valérie, which was pathetic on all counts, or he could keep the knowledge to himself and ride off into the sunset taking his moral victory with him. Again, a massive anti-climax and who the hell wants just a moral victory anyway?

Clare burst into the salon and disturbed his thinking. 'Richard,' she said, slightly out of breath. 'I've been out for a walk and given all this some thought. I think we need a plan!'

Richard didn't take long to think about this. 'I already have a plan,' he replied, a trifle tartly, hoping that would put her off asking him what his plan was.

'Oh, good! What is it?'

Even if he had had a definite plan of action in mind, Richard would not have been keen to share. This was nothing against Clare herself, but more for his own protection. His partners, sidekicks, immediate superiors, – call them what you will – were changing with alarming regularity, like it was some kind of speed-dating detective agency or a line-dancing hoedown. The nub of it was that he'd had his greater success, moved things on further, by going solo, acting alone or, as he now liked to think of himself, being the Lone Wolf.

Clare clicked her fingers. 'Don't go off on one of those 1940s dreams of yours, we haven't time.'

'What do you mean we?' He definitely wasn't keen on the idea.

'Richard, I told you last night. I'm here to help you.'

'But I don't want any help!' It wasn't the commanding voice he'd intended to use, it came out as more of a toddler whine really, but the sentiment was the same.

Clare pulled a chair out and sat down opposite him. 'Richard,' she said. 'You do. You always have and you always will. There's nothing wrong with that, but there it is. I should never have left you alone in the first place; if I hadn't, all of this would never have happened.'

He sat back and tried to imagine all of this 'never happening'. It was like a void, a life vacuum, a terrifying black hole of non-experience with him, Richard Ainsworth, lying at the centre of it, a speck of dust on a molecule of insignificance. It wouldn't do. He leant forward and put his hand on Clare's.

'Clare,' he smiled warmly. 'I...'

'Not another one!' Madame Tablier appeared as a sun-backed silhouette in the doorway where Clare had failed to close the door. 'I'm surprised you have the energy at your age.' She tutted loudly. 'More women than hens,' she moaned, shaking her head.

Clare turned her head slowly, though not without giving Richard a withering look beforehand. 'How nice to see you, Madame Tablier. Is that a new housecoat? My how it suits you.'

'Oh, it's you,' the old woman replied, clanking her bucket through the salon. 'I thought it was one of his women. How long you 'ere for this time, then?'

Clare turned back to Richard, placed her hand back on to his and looked into his eyes. 'Let's just say I haven't booked a return ticket.' Her voice was smoother than a velvet shoehorn and inside Richard's overly dramatic mind, the black hole closed in around his soul.

'Tuesday, then,' Madame Tablier snorted and went out the other door, slamming it behind her.

Clare raised an eyebrow. 'We may have to review that woman's position,' she said threateningly. 'Now, where were we? I think we should start with the Duke. Who was his father you talked about, into his art you said?'

While Richard was glad of the interruption and the subsequent change of subject, he was somewhat irked that Clare had come up with a better course of action than he had. 'Yes, that's what I thought too,' he said sulkily.

Clare got her iPad out from her handbag. 'What did you say his name was again?'

'Rodney Darius Rougemare, fourteenth Duke of Anglethorp Spa, Marquess Shireholme, the seventh Baron...'

'I'm sure that will do, Richard, thank you. Right, let's see. Who was the thirteenth Duke of Anglethorp Spa? Oh, well he died very recently.'

'Six months ago.' Richard was still feeling somewhat put out.

'Less than that, dear. It's nearer three months and there was some confusion over the succession it seems. He had only one son, this Rodney Darius as you say, but they'd been estranged for nearly twenty years and no one had seen the son in all that time.' She looked up to see Richard with his arms folded. 'Don't sulk, Richard, it's very unattractive. I'm sure we'll find a housekeeper just as efficient, but one that doesn't look like a, well…'

'A housekeeper?' he replied.

'That's right! Now, look at this picture of the thirteenth duke. He's quite good-looking in a rascally kind of way, don't you think? I am a sucker for long, dark hair.'

This information finally got Richard out of his slump. 'Let me see that.' Clare was right. In fact the thirteenth duke looked nothing like his son at all. He was, according to Wikipedia at least, five foot six and a former boxing champion in his regiment. This did not fit at all with the rather pasty, ginger-haired, rangy offspring. 'Who's the mother?' he asked.

'The mother was an Egyptian heiress, it says here, named Amunet. The poor woman died in a car crash.'

Richard took this in. 'Egyptian? I'm not surprised there was some confusion over the succession, the parents look nothing like the son. Presumably they had to do a DNA test, did they?'

Clare read on. 'Not according to this, no. It wasn't necessary. His former nanny, Angela Babcock, recognised him immediately from a birthmark and that was good enough for the solicitors and executors.'

'Perhaps if he was the only successor, it was more convenient to get it done quickly. Nobody contested it?'

'No.'

'Interesting. Anything else on the thirteenth duke?' Richard had to admit he was rather enjoying this now.

'He was a world-renowned expert on Muslim cultural heritage and history, and was a major part of the international committee to find artefacts looted from Mali in the civil war of 2012.'

'That's it!' Richard cried. 'That's the connection. This duke, the dad, what was his name?'

'Marmaduke Rougemare.'

'Fancy calling a duke Marmaduke? Anyway, Rougemare senior must have met Edmond Masson on one of these looted art shindigs. Masson has spent most of the last twenty years in Mali. He provides the original Turners, Mabit copies them and these two sell them off to private collectors as originals! Clever.' Clare stared at him in awe and part of Richard wanted to rein in his brilliance as she'd only get the wrong idea. 'And, I suspect,' he continued, punching a fist into the opposite palm, 'that his phone-in accomplice then was none other than Fatouma Dembele, women's world *boules* champion and from Mali!'

'Incredible,' she muttered, before eventually tearing her eyes away from him. 'The estranged son could have the titles and so on, but the financial assets of the estate, according to this, would go to charity if he contested the will in any way. Specifically, his bequeathment to the Tate of a dozen J.M.W. Turner miniatures. Richard, I actually think you're right, you know!'

He might have been hurt by the note of surprise in her voice if he wasn't actually quite shocked himself. Also, he knew the hard work was still to come. He had been determined to see this investigation through to the end in order to protect, even to save, Valérie, but what if Valérie was actually involved too? The thought was a depressing one and briefly knocked him back. It also occurred to him that though Roddy had got the titles and no doubt a ton of money, he'd still been quite resentful about Angela getting two Turner paintings. What if those paintings weren't copies? Surely the new duke, if he was a duke, would want those too. Especially as Roddy was such a Turner enthusiast. He took a biscuit from the box and bit it thoughtfully. He felt he was so close to solving the whole thing, tying up every loose end, but there were still questions hanging in the air. Valérie's involvement, Noel Mabit's involvement, why kill Planchet or even Derek for that matter?

'So, what next?' Clare asked. 'Where do you think the original Turners are?'

'I have some ideas,' he replied enigmatically.

'Aren't you going to tell Valérie about her husband?' Clare asked the question nervously and for the first time Richard sensed her jealousy in regard to Valérie. Up until now, she'd treated the subject as a rather amusing distraction but that was clearly no longer the case.

'I don't honestly know,' he answered truthfully, but didn't want to reveal yet the suspicion that she may even be involved.

Thankfully further explanation wasn't possible as his phone rang and he decided to take the call outside. It was the Commissaire and he didn't bother with any pleasantries.

'Where were you last night, monsieur?'

It caught Richard completely by surprise. Thus far he had been preening himself on his night-time success, having convinced himself that he had got away without being seen. Who could have spotted him then? Or had he left something incriminating behind?

'I was at home with my wife,' he said flatly.

The Commissaire was thrown completely. 'Your wife?' he asked weakly.

'Yes. My wife.' Richard decided to play it grand. 'I do have one, you know?'

'Yes, I know. Yes.' The Commissaire fell silent. 'How do you do it, monsieur? Is it some form of hypnotism?' Richard heard a commotion in the background of wherever it was the Commissaire was speaking from. 'Never mind!' he blustered. 'I want to talk to you here at René's bar now, monsieur, *d'accord*? Now!' The phone went silent.

What can it mean? he thought, the question bouncing around his head again like a pinball.

Clare was feeding the dogs when he went back into the salon. 'Sorry,' she was saying, 'that's it.' She tipped Richard's box of biscuits upside down to show that it was empty and Richard's heart sank. 'Oh, Clare,' he groaned, 'what *have* you done?'

Chapter Twenty-Eight

Richard drove carefully into town. Not his usual 'carefully' of strictly adhering to speed limits and annoying local French drivers by being polite, but carefully because he was trying to keep his temper in check. How long had his triumph lasted? An hour? Forty minutes? He had gone from believing that he had practically busted an international fake art smuggling ring and double murder to now being brusquely summoned by the chief of police. What was worse though, what really upset him, was that he couldn't arrive nonchalantly as he would have hoped, oh no. He had to arrive taking two amorous mini-dogs with him, both belonging to warring and erstwhile business partners, because his wife had fed one of them the remnants of a car key and the car remained obstinately silent without one of the guilty dogs in tow. Commissaire Lapierre had made it very clear that he wanted to see Richard immediately, and that did not mean waiting for the internal transit system of a small hound to take its natural course and provide the necessary car key technology.

Richard was fuming. That Clare thought it hilarious only confirmed Richard's decision to keep her at arm's length investigation-wise to be the correct one. He parked up opposite René's bar, put the dogs on leads and made his way towards the Commissaire who sat at a corner table and who looked like he'd had a fight with a *pain au chocolat*. The *patisserie* had inevitably won and the policeman's face was covered in crumbs and flakes. Nevertheless he eyed Richard sourly, taking a sip of coffee as he did so.

'You have brought dogs?' he observed, as if it were some kind of threat on Richard's part.

'It's a long story,' Richard replied, unwilling to go into any details.

Lapierre saw his way in. 'There is always a story with you, monsieur, is there not? *Une grande histoire.*' Richard didn't much care for the tone in the Commissaire's voice. 'You pretend to be this bumbling incompetent, this poor put-upon man hiding from the world. Poor Richard Ainsworth, they say. His wife left him, now Valérie has left him...'

'She was never with me!'

'Now, worse, Oriane Moulin has grabbed him and his wife comes back!'

Richard ordered a coffee from René who was trying to keep a discreet distance, what with angry law enforcement in his bar.

'Commissaire Lapierre,' Richard said eventually and with a touch of defeat. 'I don't pretend to be anything. I am all those things, there really is nothing more to it than that. Maybe that's the problem.' His coffee arrived and he stirred in some sugar.

'What do you mean, monsieur, "maybe that is the problem"?'

Richard thought about it; what *did* he mean? 'I mean, that I *am* boring, at least I was, and you know what? People think that's a bad thing. The idea is that if you're slightly dull then you're unhappy. Well, I'm not, I mean I wasn't. But a certain type of woman always seems to think that a boring man craves excitement, that he must feel he's missing out on something or other. I was perfectly happy until all this excitement came along, now look at me! I'm the town pariah; you suspect me of double murder, or at least of knowing more than I'm telling. My wife has come back thinking I'm a changed man all of a sudden, which is the last thing any marriage needs, especially an estranged one. My business partner has left me, my new business partner, who didn't bother to ask if I needed a new bloody business partner, is a lunatic and a public menace. I have two sexually rampant lapdogs controlling a hire car and somehow I've achieved diplomatic immunity while playing a game I know nothing about!' The Commissaire went to interrupt, but Richard rode over him. 'All the while you seem to have me down as some kind of international crime kingpin while thinking that my dull exterior is hiding a blazing criminal mind controlling a continent-wide web of lawlessness. You know what I am, really? I'm a ball in a game of polo, that's what. I sit there quite happily and then every few seconds someone will ride into my life on a snorting angry beast and hit me with a bloody mallet! No, Commissaire Henri Lapierre, do you know what this dull exterior of mine hides? It hides an even duller interior, one that isn't getting fed enough dullness right now. And,' – he stood up sharply, his upper lip wobbling slightly – 'I'm bloody knackered!'

The Commissaire stared at him while wiping the crumbs from his unkempt moustache. He silently indicated with a gentle hand gesture for Richard to sit back down, which he was happy to do having thoroughly worn himself out.

'I believe you,' the Commissaire said quietly, pouring Richard a glass of water. 'From experience I know that Valérie d'Orçay is a force of nature, a five foot seven hurricane that can be intoxicating and devastating but always exhausting. Your problem, monsieur, it seems, is that you currently have three Valéries to deal with. No man could manage that.'

Richard gratefully took the glass and sipped the cold water. Every so often he and the Commissaire shared a moment, not of bonding exactly, but of understanding. They weren't all that dissimilar, they both sought peace and quiet above all else, but equally they both craved the exotic as an occasional palate cleanser to their hermit tendencies.

'Why did you ask where I was last night?' Richard spoke up eventually. He was regretting his display of emotion, a moment of pure un-Englishness, but he was also hoping it might get him off the hook as to his actual whereabouts the night before.

The Commissaire again looked him in the eye for signs of mendacity and Richard felt he looked guilty as a result, but then he always thought he looked guilty. More often than not he felt guilty too, though he had no idea why or what for. Fortunately, Lapierre was distracted by the arrival of an ambulance taxi, that peculiarly French system whereby taxi firms are also used as official hospital transport, something

Richard could never imagine working back home. In his experience most black cab drivers in London didn't even like to transport fit people, let alone the injured and the sick. The French taxi driver got smartly out of the long white Peugeot and opened the back door. With some difficulty, Philippe Gratin emerged, helped by the driver. Gratin had a Band-Aid on his forehead and a small smattering of blood on the inevitable Johnny Hallyday T-shirt, but most strikingly of all, his arm was in plaster. The heavily insured *boule*-ing arm was heading for a pay-out.

Richard leant forward. 'What's happened?' he asked urgently.

The Commissaire, still slightly dubious of his innocence in the matter, explained anyway.

'In the early hours of this morning I received a phone call from your friend René here.'

Richard turned to look at René, who was busily cleaning glasses behind the bar. René pretended not to notice.

'And?'

'He had been woken in the middle of the night by the screams of Monsieur Philippe Gratin. René found Gratin in the doorway of his room, holding his wrist and crying in pain. He had been attacked.'

Richard was somewhat taken aback by this. All of his theories so far, everything he thought he'd worked out about smuggling, Turner forgeries, murder and potentially fake aristocrats had nothing to do whatsoever with the Johnny Hallyday obsessed, third best male *boule* player in France, Philippe Gratin. He didn't see where that fitted in at all. He shook his head in confusion.

'Why though?' he asked, slightly exasperated.

The Commissaire poured himself some water. 'He says that someone was after his Johnny Hallyday albums and that he disturbed them in the process.'

Richard shook his head and puffed out his cheeks. Art, he knew more than anyone, is subjective but not being French he'd never really got the whole Johnny Hallyday thing. He remembered the day the great rock star had died; the country had gone into national mourning on a scale that was unprecedented. It was like a cross between the demise of a Pope, the death of Princess Diana and the end of a communist general secretary when the airwaves of the old Soviet Union would be filled with sombre music. Only it wasn't sombre music in France, it was various iterations of the man himself belting out larynx-busting throw-the-kitchen-sink-at-it rock'n'roll instead. To some in France Johnny Hallyday was a demigod, to others he was much bigger than that. He was Elvis Presley with Cliff Richard's longevity, a constant through post-war France and, as such, part of the very fabric of the nation. Richard understood that much, though tellingly he also knew Johnny Hallyday lived his later years in America, a place he never remotely conquered; maybe because it was somewhere he could walk the streets unrecognised. Still though, was there really a market in second-hand Johnny Hallyday LPs to the extent that it warranted extreme violence? Go to any *brocante* in France and you would see thousands of the things. They were about as rare as James Last albums in an English charity shop.

Philippe Gratin shuffled into the bar and slumped on to a bench seat next to the Commissaire and Richard. 'So,' he began with a painful flourish, 'here you are, having your breakfast and a nice coffee. Me? I spend all night in a dreary hospital, my career in ruins!' With some difficulty he held his plaster-cast arm aloft. 'Have you caught my attacker? No. Have you even looked? I doubt that too.'

'Monsieur,' Lapierre said with heavy patience, used to dealing with a taxpayer's complaints. 'Why do you think someone was after your record collection?'

The man's jaw dropped as if an old rock star's vinyl was akin to Marie Antoinette's jewels. 'Also,' Richard couldn't but help ask, 'why do you carry your collection around with you?'

'I do not carry my collection around with me! Don't be absurd! I have many thousands of Johnny's recordings.'

'He made that many?'

The man rolled his eyes. 'I buy up everything I can find. I have many copies of the same recording. I am the number one collector in France!' He tried to raise his finger to indicate as much but winced as he remembered his injury.

'And the third best *boule* player in France,' Richard said, trying to placate the man.

'Not anymore,' Gratin wailed, disconsolate. 'How will I ever be able to recreate my triple forty-five-degree backspin shot now? My arm, my wrist, it will never be the same.'

The Commissaire and Richard glanced briefly at each other.

'Monsieur, do you have any particular recording in your room that would warrant such an attack on your person?'

Gratin looked about him, making sure that they weren't overheard, then he lowered his head and his voice in conspiratorial fashion. 'Vogue LD five, four, three.' He sat back, a look of immense pleasure on his face.

'I am so sorry, monsieur, but…' the Commissaire began.

'Nineteen sixty, *Hello Johnny*. A rare pressing in Israel, different songs, different cover to the French pressing.' He shook with glee.

'Is that rare?' Richard asked, knowing as an expert himself, though not in Johnny Hallyday, that the man would be disappointed in his ignorance.

'One of these sold for nine hundred and twenty-seven euros only a month ago! I already have three.' He giggled in a particularly unappealing way.

Once again the Commissaire and Richard exchanged a quick glance. Nine hundred and twenty-seven euros didn't seem like the kind of earth-shattering, life-changing amount of money that warranted a personal, potentially career-ending assault, nor did it, on the face of things seem to be connected with two murders.

'And has it been taken?' Richard asked, unable to hide his scepticism.

'No!' the man replied, then tapped his nose with his good hand. 'I hid it well.'

He got up from his table, his confidence momentarily restored, leaving Richard and the Commissaire wondering where it left them exactly. Richard was building himself up to confide to Lapierre everything that he thought he knew. He'd much rather have confided in Valérie, but still felt she might be in danger and didn't want to make that situation worse.

Richard, however, never got the chance to do so. As the ambulance taxi pulled out of its parking space, Valérie's vintage Renault Alpine, restored to its roaring glory, came skidding into the vacant spot, finishing halfway up the kerb. The two men watched as she jumped out of the vehicle and come running into the bar. She spotted them immediately.

'It's Edmond,' she panted, and in some distress. 'He's vanished!'

Chapter Twenty-Nine

It was difficult to tell from Valérie's demeanour whether she was upset, confused or really quite cheesed off, but the first thing Richard had to do was ignore the temptation to say, 'Don't worry, I'm sure he'll pop back in another twenty years.' It was clear that Commissaire Lapierre, in briefly catching Richard's eye, felt much the same way. Edmond Masson may indeed have vanished but he most certainly had previous in this regard.

'When did this happen, madame?' a noticeably weary Commissaire asked.

'Well, obviously, I don't know when exactly, but he was not at breakfast this morning and he was not in his room either. I checked.'

Obviously this statement asked certain questions of the married couple's actual relationship and again Richard caught Lapierre's eye as Valérie picked up Passepartout and hugged the little dog so hard it looked like his eyes might pop out. It was then that she noticed Zsa Zsa.

'Let me explain,' Richard said hurriedly, but it was too late. Valérie was in a state of extreme vexation and the effect for those in attendance was like watching microwave popcorn. A perfect storm of volatility, known personality traits and environment.

'Richard Ainsworth,' she began, making it clear that if she had known his middle name, she'd have used that too. He was certainly grateful that she didn't, however, as her imminent eruption was already attracting a crowd. Philippe Gratin decided to sit back down and was joined by teammates Alphonse and Agathe, who crept in like latecomers at the theatre. Richard braced himself while Lapierre moved his chair back slightly from the table. Often Richard had been caught in storms while driving and it was always his policy never to fight them, never to risk anything with confrontation, but to simply turn into the next lay-by and wait for the tempest to either blow itself out or move on. He decided that was the best course of action here too, so mentally he indicated off the road, put his brain in neutral and pulled on the handbrake.

Valérie, eschewing a slow run-up and starting at a point most people might consider their peak, looked like she was setting herself in for the long haul. 'Richard Ainsworth!' she repeated, presumably feeling she hadn't yet got his full attention. 'I trusted you! First you accuse my husband, a decorated war hero of murder, two murders no less and now, worse, you allow this, this *hussy*, this Jezebel, this *dévergondée* to parade my poor, sweet innocent Passepartout like some milquetoast, some pantywaist...' Passepartout's ears pricked up at the mention of his name. 'Yes, my sweet. I know. What did the nasty man do to you?' She stared hard at Richard who puffed his cheeks out. He'd be the first to admit that he was far from perfect but the accusation that he was some kind of dog pimp was pushing it somewhat. Still, he stayed quiet.

'Madame.' It was a brave Commissaire Lapierre who attempted a diversion and Richard appreciated it no end, but it was a futile gesture and only opened the policeman up as collateral damage.

'And you!' Valérie turned on him now. 'I have absolutely no doubt whatsoever that you are involved in this. You made sure that Oriane Moulin was behind bars just so that this, this *souteneur*,' – she pointed at Richard – 'could indulge in puppy farming and animal slavery.'

Richard sensed that Valérie was beginning to lose the crowd. They would have had every sympathy with the suggestion that Richard was slandering France's gallant military personnel, indeed they still did, but the idea he was running some kind of canine brothel seemed, even for the usually ambivalent, somewhat far-fetched. Richard was also surprised that the Commissaire, who had quite a few years on him in terms of Valérie-experience, would rise to the bait quite so easily. Perhaps it was the fisherman in him? Whatever it was, it was easy to see why their marriage had been, in Lapierre's own words, brief.

'Madame d'Orçay, get control of yourself and remember who you are talking to!'

'Why?' she demanded immediately, which wasn't as unreasonable as it sounded. She may as well have been talking to God himself; if the object of her ire needed a dressing-down, they got a dressing-down. Rank didn't come into it. 'What will you do?' Her lip curled; it was clear she was rather enjoying herself now and was feeling much better for blowing off some steam. 'Put me in the same cell as Oriane Moulin?'

'No!' the Commissaire reacted. 'Oriane Moulin was released this morning, as the English aristocrat decided not to press charges!'

This brought some gossip from the watching Greek chorus and had the effect of slowing Valérie down too. She turned slowly towards Richard.

'I have no doubt that she will want to retrieve her harlot of a dog and discuss matters with her *business partner*.'

He wasn't keen on how she'd stressed those words, but then he wasn't keen that they were even in use.

It was an unfortunate moment for Zsa Zsa, hitherto not overly affectionate towards Richard, to jump on to his lap. He assumed she'd done this so as to be at the same level as Passepartout on Valérie's adjacent lap but it hinted at a deeper relationship and was awkward at best. Valérie gave him a filthy look. A look which quickly turned to hurtful astonishment when Passepartout leapt on to Richard's lap too.

'Madame, Valérie.' The Commissaire was brave enough to try and get back on track. 'You say your husband, Edmond Masson, has vanished. What evidence do you have for this? Why would he run?'

Valérie took a deep breath without taking her eyes off a seemingly unrepentant Passepartout. 'I do not know,' she said quietly, though without emotion. 'He cannot have gone far, but I do not know why.'

'And what makes you think that he has not gone far?' Lapierre pushed.

'Because he took Monsieur Ainsworth's car.'

There was so much for Richard to unpack in that simple statement. The formal use of title and surname, the fact that his beloved 2CV had been stolen and the seemingly calculated insult that said beloved 2CV wasn't up to long distances. He decided to just snort derisively instead, while holding the dogs visibly closer as a comeback.

'And you first noticed him gone this morning?'

They were interrupted by Philippe Gratin who stood up quickly for such a large man, knocking over Agathe's walking frame as he did so. 'Are you talking about the man with the eyepatch?' he demanded, ignoring his clumsiness.

Agathe's frame had fallen at Richard's feet and he reached down awkwardly, trying not to disturb the dogs as he did so. He regretted trying to do anything at all, expecting to pull a muscle while trying to balance, but the walking frame was helpfully light and he righted it with some relief.

'Yes, we are talking about Edmond Masson, monsieur, why do you ask?' Lapierre now stood, sensing something important.

'Because that was the man I disturbed in my room last night! It was Edmond Masson!'

There was a brief moment of hush before everybody started talking at once.

'Impossible!' Valérie argued, insulted by the suggestion.

'Can you be sure?' Lapierre asked.

'What has happened to your arm?' Alphonse asked, noticing Philippe's cast for the first time.

'Oh, Philippe!' Agathe cried. 'Will you not be able to play?'

'Why is it impossible, madame?' An equally insulted Philippe demanded of Valérie.

'Yes, madame.' Lapierre took a step back, just in case. 'Why is that so impossible? Were you with your husband last night?'

'Philippe, answer me!' Agathe was almost distraught at the idea Philippe might be ruled out.

A pained expression came over Philippe's face as, with his good hand, he reached across and took Agathe's very thin, bordering on arthritic fingers in his. 'My dear Agathe,' he said. 'I am so sorry.' Then he lifted his cast high for everyone to see. 'I have been struck down!' he wailed, hyping up the drama.

At first Richard expected Agathe Deschanel to crumble at the news and it was clear Alphonse Berlioz felt the same. A worried look crossed his face and he put a comforting arm around the old woman's shoulders. They were both wrong. Agathe angrily shrugged off his attentions and concentrated instead on Valérie. 'Saboteur!' she screamed. 'Terrorist! *Agitateur!*'

Her wrath was uncontrollable; even Valérie was momentarily taken aback by it which was hardly surprising. First, she wasn't used to being outdone in the angry overreaction stakes and second, Philippe Gratin was, by his own admission, only the third best men's *boules* player in France. Was he really that much of a loss?

In response Valérie managed some kind of half-gargle, half-nasal riposte and a Gallic shrug so hard most people would have dislocated a shoulder. 'Your silly games!' she barked, not really helping the situation. 'If you need an extra player, I will take his place!'

'You play *pétanque*, madame?' The deep, calming voice of Fatouma Dembele cut through the charged atmosphere as she appeared from the same door as Alphonse and Agathe. As usual she was resplendent in the most magnificent costume, a riot of colour and vibrant jewellery; her dark eyes looked warm and friendly despite what would have been clear to anyone was a fraught situation.

'I do!' Valérie seemed slightly affronted that her abilities were open to question. 'I was twice the winner of the inter-service individual *pétanque* championship.'

Richard looked at Lapierre for confirmation, who just shrugged his ignorance of the fact in reply. It was of course perfectly feasible that Valérie was telling the truth but she had never mentioned it before, never shown the slightest interest in competitive sport and it seemed unlikely to Richard that the French secret service would even have an inter-discipline *boules* tournament. On the other hand, it would be an incredibly and wholly appropriately French thing to do, especially within their spy agencies.

There was a moment's silence before Agathe, who was naturally taking the whole thing with a pinch of salt, eventually said, 'Right then, let's see what you can do!' and began, with Alphonse's help, to get up from the table.

The Commissaire hadn't finished though. 'Madame,' he managed to sigh, as close as any man in history to complete exasperation. 'I have not finished, please sit down for a few more minutes yet.' The old woman wasn't happy, but did as she was told anyway, waving away the fussy attention of Alphonse in the process.

'I want to know where everyone was last night.' Richard remembered that that was exactly why he had been summoned to René's bar in the first place. In the tense atmosphere he had completely forgotten and was hastily thinking up his own story while almost everybody else trotted out the 'I was asleep' routine as if the Commissaire were an idiot for asking.

'I spent a very pleasant evening with Martin and Gennie Thompson,' Fatouma said quietly, looking the Commissaire confidently in the eye.

'How late?' Lapierre asked.

'I do not know for sure. But I was very tired after a most stimulating evening and I went straight to bed.'

Richard's mind literally boggled at the thought of what a 'stimulating' evening in the company of Martin and Gennie entailed and hoped the Commissaire wouldn't pursue it, at least in public. He also had to consider whether this ruled out Fatouma as Edmond's accomplice.

Alphonse Berlioz's story also strayed slightly from the majority. 'I was trying to sleep,' he said, a touch of guilt in his voice, wary that he might drop someone in it, 'but there were voices coming from another room.'

'So you were awake then?' Lapierre asked needlessly. 'And who is in the room next door to yours?'

'I am in between Philippe and Fatouma,' he replied. 'But I could not say which room.'

'You must have heard me being violently attacked!' Philippe Gratin held up his damaged arm once more, but there was noticeably less sympathy from Agathe now she had a full team again.

Finally, Commissaire Lapierre turned to Richard. In fact everyone turned to Richard and even the dogs on his lap seemed to go rigid with the tension.

'Me?' he stuttered. 'You mean where was I last night? During the night you mean?'

The Commissaire had had a stressful morning thus far, but he was well aware when someone was stalling. 'Yes, Monsieur Ainsworth, where were you last night at… what time did you say you were attacked, monsieur?' He turned to Philippe for the answer, but the man was opening his record, the black vinyl glinting in the light when he slipped off the cover and the sleeve.

It was an answer that was destined not to be given anyway, however, just as in the Caribbean during the hurricane season, one storm was about to follow another.

'There you are!' cried an emotional Oriane Moulin from the doorway, her face a grimace of anger and relief, but mostly anger. Richard put both dogs carefully on the floor, and in the ensuing uproar, took the opportunity to sneak out while he could.

Chapter Thirty

Richard was feeling very pleased with his surreptitious exit until he got to the hire car and realised that without the key-swallowing dogs he couldn't even get in, let alone drive away. Instead, after a five-minute circuit of the market square, he decided to go and hide in the church just in case Lapierre also felt compelled to escape the madding crowd and come looking for him.

It wasn't unusual for Richard to feel intimidated, most of life's trials left him feeling slightly under the cosh, but churches were a whole different level. Not being a religious man, his gods and goddesses lived only on celluloid; the sheer enormity of French churches even in the humblest of towns always made him feel guilty. Guilty of what, he wasn't altogether sure, probably of not being religious. He felt a fraud, and the pain and torment that were on show from the cracked paintings and immaculate stained glass windows were made with that specific intention in mind; he knew that and they were doing their job well. He was supposed to forget his earthly suffering and instead reflect on the sacrifice that had apparently been made on his behalf. He couldn't help himself though; one day he might have time to reflect on the smallness of his own problems in comparison to the son of God, but right now he had a high-level policeman asking his whereabouts, two very angry women with lovelorn dogs, one of whom had eaten his car key, two murders of which he was still suspected, an estranged wife who had moved back in, a seriously complex international art smuggling ring to deal with and a *boules* tournament to practise for.

He slumped into a pew and, for the first time since he was thirteen years old and had asked God to give him the courage to kiss Alison Steele in the playground, he silently prayed for a helping hand.

When a hand actually grabbed his shoulder he nearly jumped out of his skin. 'I was coming in here myself,' the Commissaire said with respectful, hushed tones. 'I am guessing for the same reason as you, monsieur. Some peace and quiet, some time for reflection.' His face was about as hangdog as a human face can be without actually qualifying for Crufts. His eyes were tired but wide open with excess fatigue and his jowls rolled down his face almost like Roman blinds. Even his moustache drooped more than usual, probably with the pressure of it all. He took a place next to Richard, genuflecting before he did so but, instead of bowing his head in penitence, rolling his eyes in the direction of the altar as if to say, 'Here we are again.'

'I'm not a religious man,' Richard began, by way of an apology. 'But I do enjoy the silence.'

The Commissaire leant on the back of the pew in front. 'Silence is a very rare thing these days,' he said, still fixing what was now a glare in the direction of a large particularly detailed crucifix. 'Now, monsieur.' Lapierre sighed and it was like air escaping from the opening of a thousand-year-old crypt. 'I will ask you again. Please tell me where you were last night?'

Richard could have made up a dozen stories on the spot, all pulled from fake movie alibis. Nobody could have proved or disproved them right away. Indeed he had planned to do so, if only the Commissaire hadn't gone and asked the question in a church. By rights, being a lapsed agnostic, it should have made no difference to Richard at all that he was in a house of God; in many ways it might even have worked for him. The Commissaire could never believe that Richard Ainsworth would lie to him *in a church*. The Commissaire would have been right though, Richard couldn't. Whether he believed in him or not wasn't the point, it was what the place stood for. You wouldn't go to a wine-tasting as a teetotaller. No, Richard was compelled to tell the truth *because* he was agnostic. It would be just his luck to tell a falsehood under the shadow of a dying Christ and then find out it was all real.

'I didn't break into Philippe Gratin's room,' he ventured first.

'I would expect you to deny it,' Lapierre replied, slightly bored at the answer. 'Anyway, I checked this record of his, this rare Johnny Hallyday.'

'And?'

'It is just a rare Johnny Hallyday record, that is all. It is hiding nothing.'

'Shame.'

'So, I ask again. Where were you?'

'I broke into the *mairie*.' Richard's own eyes were looking straight in front, but he was aware that the Commissaire had turned his head very slowly towards him and that his eyes were searching his face for signs of guilt. He had the feeling that Lapierre simply didn't believe that he'd trespassed government property and that instead Richard had invented something so un-Richard-like to hide the truth, which was already pretty un-Richard-like, but was at least slightly more credible.

'You broke into the *mairie*?' He sounded deeply sceptical.

'Yes.'

'Were you missing some forms to fill in, perhaps? Looking to see if bin collection day has changed?'

'Well, really!' Richard was quite put out and had inadvertently raised his voice. He carried on in a harsh whisper and – even more inadvertently – sounded liked Valérie. 'Has it occurred to you that I am trying to do your job, Commissaire? There have been two murders, why? What do you think the motive is? Art smuggling, that's what. I think someone – let's for now assume it's Mayor Planchet – was a forger, a copyist. His clients would bring him the originals, say a J.M.W. Turner from some stately home in England, and the crooks, the murderers, would sell the copies as real to private collectors. Only I think the murderers, the crooks, have got greedy and want the originals too.'

Lapierre's expression didn't change, almost like he was now immune to any emotion or even thought. 'And these murderers, these crooks you speak of...?'

'Well, I know Edmond Masson is behind...'

Now the Commissaire broke. 'Oh, Monsieur Ainsworth, Richard! Again with the jealousy... and this art smuggling theory, that is the Derek Munro theory, no? The *Detective Inspector* he called himself? A fantasist!'

'I agree. Derek Munro was a fantasist.'

'*Bon, c'est ça.*' He threw his hands up in frustration, then muttered an apology to the church itself.

'Commissaire, even a stopped clock is right twice a day.'

'Meaning what precisely?'

'Meaning that Derek Munro was, as you say, a fantasist, a liar maybe, more of a Walter Mitty.'

'What is a Walter Mitty?'

Richard, for the umpteenth time, couldn't hide his dismay. 'You've never heard of Walter Mitty?' The Commissaire shook his head. 'Danny Kaye?'

'No. Are they involved?'

Richard closed his eyes and reset himself. 'Never mind, what I'm saying is, is that Derek Munro lived a fantasy life because his own life was so dull. He made things up for the excitement. I think this time though he made something up and it was actually close to someone else's truth.'

'This art smuggling.'

'Yes.'

'And so this murderer couldn't have even an obvious fantasist talking like that.'

'I think so, yes.'

The Commissaire sighed heavily. 'Do you have any proof at all? Because the terracotta piece you hid in your hen feed is not antique at all.'

'That's what I'm trying to tell you, I do have proof. And I found it last night when I broke into the *mairie*!' Richard stood up. 'Come on, I'll show you.'

The Commissaire took one last look at the figure of Christ and wondered aloud if this Walter Mitty thing wasn't contagious.

Richard didn't wait for the Commissaire as he strode with unusual determination across the road to the *mairie*. He had come to a decision. He had done the leg work for the Commissaire; he had identified motive, opportunity and the culprits. Well, his pace slowed slightly, he had identified the motive for the murder of Derek Munro at least. The murder of Mayor Planchet still rankled when it was becoming increasingly clear and – as he was about to prove – it was Noel Mabit who was the forger, hiding behind Planchet. The culprits *plural* was a bit hazy as yet, but he knew Masson was the ringleader. He just hoped Valérie wasn't involved in the same way.

He stood at the large double entrance doors and waited for Lapierre to catch up; the man was practically dawdling in Richard's opinion, dragging his heels because he couldn't bear the idea of Richard cracking this case on his own. Richard took a long, deep breath. He had to admit it to himself again, he had never felt more alive. They walked through the door together rather taking Madame Mabit, who was on reception duties, by surprise.

'If you're looking for the mayor presumptive,' she said loftily, 'he is busy with civic duties and must not be disturbed.'

A toilet flushed in the public WC in the corner of the reception and Noel emerged still wrestling with his fly. When eventually he looked up, he didn't look pleased to see them at all. Richard and Lapierre turned back to Madame Mabit to see if there was any sign at all of embarrassment that her little white lie had been rumbled. There was none.

'Gentlemen,' Noel said, holding out his hand to be shaken. An offer that was not taken up. 'To what do I owe this pleasure?'

It seemed to Richard that Noel Mabit had grown a couple of inches since the demise of Mayor Planchet. He had emerged from the bureaucratic shadows and it suited him; he was his own man now fulfilling his administrative destiny. And the way that his wife looked at him was different to before as well; there was something there that Richard had never seen between the two, it was admiration. Richard couldn't help but feel very pleased for them both; being at heart a romantic, it was a heart-warming thing to observe. Slightly nauseating, of course, but heart-warming nonetheless. Then the thought occurred to him that Mabit, being a forger and a cog in a smuggling ring, might also be an accessory to murder and had possibly committed this litany of crimes just to win the heart of his own wife.

'It is our wedding anniversary today.' Madame Mabit beamed as she came from behind the reception desk and put her hand gently on her husband's arm. 'Forty-seven years!' she added proudly while Noel blushed.

'You married in 1978, madame, *mes félicitations.*' The Commissaire bowed his head in salute at their achievement.

'Yes, congratulations,' Richard added, knowing something of the history. 'You must have been very young.'

'We were barely eighteen,' she replied, giggling almost. 'But it was love at first sight for me; there was never another man in my life.'

This didn't fit with Richard's knowledge at all, but he had no idea how to diplomatically dig any further. 'You must have been at school together,' he tried, while his mind searched for a more prodding question.

'Oh, yes.' She smiled again. It wasn't a warm smile, Richard noted.

'And poor Mayor Planchet was with you at school as well?' Richard felt Lapierre's questioning gaze fall on him.

'He was,' Noel replied a trifle stiffly.

'Then he went to Paris.' Madame Mabit's reply was wistful. 'My Noel had a scholarship at an art school there, but he gave it up to stay behind with me.' She held his arm tighter and Richard got the impression that now her husband was on the brink of recognisable civic supremacy, as opposed to being the power behind the throne, she wasn't letting go of him.

'I thought it was Mayor Planchet who had the scholarship?' Richard pushed.

'Oh, yes! They both had scholarships. Both were talented. Noel I think more so. But he gave it up for me.'

For his part Noel looked decidedly uncomfortable, shifting his weight from one foot to the other and avoiding eye contact. That could of course be put down to a very public display of affection, which he wasn't used to at all. Hitherto, in Richard's experience, Madame Mabit had been pretty caustic about her husband and didn't care who heard it. It could also be guilt though. Noel Mabit, the ace talented forger with his signature on some pretty damning Turner copies upstairs.

'We would like to have another look at the apartment of the late mayor,' the Commissaire interrupted, not keen to get stuck on romantic history.

There was no sign of nerves from the Mabits as he asked, but Richard hadn't really expected any. This supposedly loved-up sexagenarian couple were cold, but then one of them was used to dealing with international smuggling rings, organised crime cartels. They weren't going to be easily shaken.

'Of course,' Noel said. 'Though since you gave us permission, Commissaire, we have begun to move the mayor's belongings out. My wife wants to add a woman's touch.' Richard had assumed that Noel Mabit's accession to high office was to be a mere formality but even so, he thought, the mayor presumptive was being very presumptuous.

The three men climbed the stairs in silence, while Madame Mabit went back to the reception. Noel unlocked the door and was about to cross the threshold when the Commissaire gently but firmly held him back. 'If you don't mind, monsieur, I will ask you to wait downstairs. I will call you if I need anything.'

Noel looked surprised but didn't argue the point, his small eyes giving nothing away. He simply nodded his head like a butler backing out of a room and walked slowly back down the marble staircase. Richard and the Commissaire went in through the door and Richard was relieved to see that the loft ladder was still in place. If the Commissaire had trouble believing Richard had broken into the place, then Richard felt the same. It was an act so out of character that it felt almost like a dream.

They both stood at the bottom of the ladder. 'Up there, Commissaire, at the far end, you will find a studio, an artist's studio. Paints, easels and so on, some other stuff presumably for ageing a canvas, some kind of press thing. And copies of Turner paintings signed by Noel Mabit.'

He lowered his voice in case Noel had doubled back and was listening in the outside corridor. 'This is where I saw Edmond Masson last night. He was searching for the originals.'

'He was alone?' the policeman asked.

'Yes, but he was talking to someone via a phone link or something like that. I couldn't hear who though, he had an earpiece in.'

The Commissaire didn't say anything more but began to climb the ladder, while Richard held it for him. He stayed standing on the top rung, shining the torch from his phone. Richard saw him nod gravely and sigh almost in triumph.

'Monsieur,' the Commissaire began, 'you have excelled yourself!' Richard puffed his chest out. 'I should of course arrest you for wasting police time, but I think you may get off on a plea of insanity.'

Richard couldn't believe what he was hearing as Lapierre's heavy tread came back down the ladder. Silently he invited Richard to take a look. Reaching the top, he shone his own torch around the loft. It was completely empty. At the far wall where all of the forging and art materials had been stored, there was nothing but bare brick.

Richard slumped on the opening of the loft. 'They must have noticed that somebody had been here and cleared the place out,' he called down, but in a way not exactly brimming with confidence. Commissaire Henri Lapierre didn't respond; he had already left.

Chapter Thirty-One

Richard staggered out into the blinding sunlight, ignoring the half-hearted *au revoirs* from the Mabits. Or, as he was now thinking of them, the sinister Mabits. The same question reverberated around his confused mind: *What the hell is going on?* The Mabits surely couldn't have moved all of that paraphernalia out on their own? And what had they done with everything? And why move it anyway? Had someone seen him or Edmond skulking about? Every time he thought he had a handle on the whole thing, a solid theory, evidence even, the rug was pulled from underneath him leaving him more bewildered and with less idea of what was going on than before.

His eyes slowly adjusted to the harsh light and his heart sank even further when he saw Valérie and Oriane walking their dogs around the square, chatting warmly as they did so. He shook his head and was overcome by a mixture of bafflement and fatigue. *It's a conspiracy*, he concluded. *Everybody's in on it except me and with the sole intention of driving me bonkers.* He turned in the opposite direction of the dog-walking assassins and headed for the river to clear his head in what he hoped would be a cooling breeze.

The breeze was indeed cooling but as for clearing his head, that would have needed a hurricane of immense power and he sat heavily on a bench in the shadow of the old bridge. Ducks and swans were milling about in the shallow waters, a pastoral scene that was lost on Richard who was making a mental list of everything he had seen, or at least thought he had seen, the night before.

Firstly, Edmond Masson had been up to no good, breaking into the *mairie* in search of the highly valuable original Turner artworks. But then against this was that Richard had also broken into the *mairie* looking for the highly valuable original Turner artworks and he wasn't up to no good; far from it, he was up to good. But who had Edmond been in communication with? Initially Richard's money was on Fatouma Dembele. She had told the Commissaire that she'd been with Martin and Gennie talking 'documentaries', something Richard didn't want to dwell on, but she hadn't specified at what time she had been dropped back. He made a note to check that with the Thompsons. There was also the possibility though, and it was something else he wasn't keen to dwell on, that Edmond had been talking to Valérie. Valérie, who was at that very moment enjoying a convivial walk around town with her supposed arch enemy. Then there was the attack on Philippe Gratin. Surely that can't have happened just so someone could get their hands on a rare Johnny Hallyday record?

Then there was the actual physical stuff he had found too, wherever that now was. All of that equipment, paints and easels and brushes; presses too, different nibs, presumably to make up the frames and the signatures. Mabit's signature. *What a racket!* he thought. Noel the power behind the admittedly low-wattage civic throne but also the real forger. Whoever had killed Planchet must have thought that the old mayor was the copyist. So Noel must now be terrified. Unless, and Richard still found this barely believable, Noel Mabit wasn't just a cog in an international art forgery empire, he really did defend that position with murder. The evidence certainly pointed in that direction. But then why had Edmond Masson run away? Had he run away even? And without finding the originals?

He threw his head back and looked to the skies. It was all so complicated, even more so without Valérie at his side. Though it was true to say that, deep down, he was enjoying himself, it was also incredibly frustrating. People he thought he knew just weren't what they seemed anymore. He heard an old car misfire across the bridge, taking the one route out of town and towards the big city of Tours and he felt a pang of nostalgia that he might never see his 2CV again. Everybody said it was the perfect car for Richard; it symbolised all that he represented: slightly battered, incapable and largely unwilling to rush anywhere, misfiring on a regular basis. He shot to his feet and watched as his 2CV was driven over the bridge and out of Saint-Sauver.

'Right!' he said to himself, slightly angry but also very determined. 'I am not letting you get away.'

He turned and ran back towards the hire car a couple of hundred metres away in town. Puffing heavily as he approached the thing, he was grateful to see Valérie and Oriane still in conference nearby. Passepartout was sniffing about at Valérie's feet while Oriane was hugging Zsa Zsa to her chest. They didn't see him coming, which was to his advantage as he brushed swiftly past a startled Valérie sweeping up an even more surprised Passepartout in one motion and holding him in the crook of his arm like a rugby ball. Without breaking stride and with surprising deftness, he managed to steal Zsa Zsa from Oriane's grasp as well and now had a dog under each arm, racing towards the hire car. He banged the door button with his knee, threw the dogs in and got into the driver's seat, quickly shutting and locking the door behind him.

He preferred not to look at the angry, startled faces of the two women banging on his window shouting imprecations along the lines of 'dognapper!' and sped off, knowing for sure that, as Valérie had pointed out, Edmond couldn't have gone far.

Richard couldn't remember if he had ever had to drive fast. He had certainly never chased anyone in an actual car and it wasn't in his nature to be late, he planned too far ahead for that and always took into consideration traffic snarl-ups and acts of God if he was planning a route. He therefore had no idea what he was doing as he sped at an illegal forty-seven kilometres per hour over the bridge, a strict thirty kilometre zone. He was in a quandary; he didn't want to be stopped by the police or even draw attention to himself, but he still wanted to get on Edmond's tail as quickly as possible. On the outskirts of town, he came to a fork in the road. Having convinced himself that Edmond was heading for Tours, he now had a decision to make. Would Edmond have taken the motorway route or the scenic route? He stopped the car briefly and gave it some thought, before indicating left. Again, he wasn't altogether sure that indicators were a necessary part of high-speed car chases, but he chose the scenic route banking on Edmond having more places to stop and hide should he feel the need to do so. Richard gritted his teeth, gripped the steering wheel hard and reached a hundred kilometres per hour in an eighty zone, knowing that his 2CV barely managed fifty going downhill and with a following wind.

Within five minutes he spotted his car on the brow of an incline some two hundred metres ahead and slowed to a legal pace while considering his options. He even took the opportunity to adjust his rear-view mirror to check on the dogs, who were curled up on the backseat oblivious to the drama unfolding around them. If Richard had had a plan, then everything was going fine, so far. He readjusted the mirror and his heart sank. Roaring up behind him was a yellow 1979 Renault Alpine V6. The top was down, and Valérie and Oriane, no doubt intent on rescuing their dogs, were having their hair blown about as they sped up behind him. They looked like a pair of wild-eyed Medusas, terrifying and hell-bent on canine rescue at all costs.

Richard again decided to do something very un-Richard-like and put his foot down hard, to which the car's powerful engine responded despite the admonishments from its computer conscience. The gap opened quickly before Valérie, undoubtedly more experienced at these things, closed the distance with ease. Richard gulped. If he were to get any more out of his depth he'd drown, but he wasn't going to pull over. Edmond was the key to the whole mystery and he was determined to rein him in and prove that was the case. He was now right behind the 2CV and Valérie was right behind him, so again Richard considered his options. Without thinking he pressed the accelerator intending to swing out and overtake his 2CV, hoping to sandwich Edmond and bring him to a stop. As he did so, Valérie and Oriane appeared at his side, blocking his way, both glaring at him. He could sense the dogs stirring on the backseat, that sixth sense dogs have knowing that their beloved owners are close by. Both dogs jumped up at the rear passenger door, a look of doleful innocence etched on to their faces, then they started howling in unison, giving the strong impression that not only had they been kidnapped but were being treated appallingly as well.

Valérie was shouting something at Richard which – and it was probably for the best – he couldn't make out. A large lorry blared its own horn as it appeared suddenly around a corner from the opposite direction, forcing Valérie to pull back and settle behind him once more, giving him some brief respite. The dogs, however, continued their baleful whine in a heart-rending duet of canine loss. Richard, sweat dripping from his forehead, didn't know what to do other than keep going. He had to get Edmond; that was the only thing he could do, get Edmond, and get some answers.

He swung the car out recklessly just as another car was coming from the opposite direction. He pulled further to the left and on to a grass verge as the oncoming vehicle went between him and Edmond who, he noticed, was wearing his eyepatch, which if it wasn't against the French highway code surely should be. Valérie, with the skill and opportunism of a Formula One champion, took this brief window to place her car between Richard and Edmond, the three of them now in a row across the highway. Her husband, apparently oblivious because he was effectively wearing a left-sided blinker, continued steadily forward while Richard, crashing through the bushes on the grass verge, was howling along with the dogs in blind panic, the car itself a digital symphony of rude beeps and exasperated electronic babble hurling abuse at the human driver. Out of the corner of his eye he saw Valérie indicating for him to stop, something he had no intention of doing, so he found more speed and got in front of her, swerving back to the right side of the road and in front of Edmond and the 2CV. Now Edmond seemed to realise what was going on and he leant on the small car's horn, a pathetic sound at the best of times; it sounded like a kazoo player on helium. Valérie, in a typically aggressive move, pulled across Richard slowing down dangerously as she did so, forcing Richard to slow down too or go into the back of her. Edmond, rather than risk the brakes, pulled off and on to a dirt track into a roadside forest. Now Richard braked to a stop, carefully put his hazard warning lights on and began to perform a laborious three-point turn to follow Edmond. Fifty metres down the road he saw the Renault Alpine spin round in a perfect handbrake turn bringing Steve McQueen pleasingly to mind in *Bullitt*. Now realising that Richard was going to pursue Edmond into the woods, Valérie sped past him and angled the car through the trees chasing her husband. Richard, opting to keep his warning lights blinking, followed at a slower pace but was roughly thrown about anyway on the uneven track. The car swore at him as it bounced unhappily along.

By now Valérie was clearly worried about the detrimental effect the track was having on her own car and had also slowed. Some way in front, Edmond was probably being brained by the 2CV's roof. Then Valérie braked sharply, forcing Richard to do the same. She and Oriane leapt out of the car and came running at him. Richard made sure the doors were locked as the dogs howled, Valérie and Oriane howled too and Richard tried to sink into the soft leather seat. He opened his window slightly.

'Yes?' he said, affecting some sort of bravado.

'What do you mean yes?' Valérie was white with fury.

Before Richard could answer, however, they all turned as they heard the metallic crunch of metal hitting centuries-old wood. Edmond had careered Richard's car headfirst into a large oak tree. Richard, no longer concerned for his own safety, but more for the state of his cherished old car, unlocked the doors and emerged. He was ignored by Valérie and Oriane who were frantically grabbing at their pooches, cuddling and cooing. Slowly he began to walk towards the crash site. 'Maybe it won't be that bad?' he muttered to himself. 'Purely superficial, a bit of spray here and some panel beating there.' He even managed a faint smile at the thought of driving the old girl again in the not-so-distant future.

The explosion took him completely by surprise then and he hit the ground in fright as he saw the 2CV burst violently into flames. A wing mirror landed at his side and he grabbed at it before ducking his head down again as a second explosion ripped through what was left of his car. He didn't know how long he remained in that foetal position clinging on to the mirror part like a baby to a comfort blanket; he just knew it wasn't long enough.

Chapter Thirty-Two

There was silence in the car as Richard drove Valérie back to Martin and Gennie's place. Even the hire car was being less belligerent than usual, recognising the mood within. Oriane was driving Valérie's car and fortunately it was discovered that Passepartout was the car key eating miscreant or things might have been even more awkward. The police and the fire services had arrived quickly and doused the flames before they could spread and there would now be a wait for the forensic team to examine in detail what was left. The Commissaire had arrived on the scene after the others and though clearly exasperated by the situation knew to wisely back off questioning Valérie or Richard for now. Even Lapierre, not hitherto known for his subtlety and tact, could see that Valérie, and Richard in his own way, were in mourning.

For his part, Richard was trying not to equate the loss of a beaten-up vintage car with Valérie's widowhood. Trying but failing. On the one hand he was absolutely furious, he had loved that car. He was fully aware that it was seen as a symbol of his own life, chugging along while being frayed at the edges, but that only made the loss more poignant. He was also aware that its end should not be compared to the loss of a human life, but seeing as, for one, he had Edmond Masson down as a possible art trafficking murderer and for two, the man had already been dead at least once, his sympathy was somewhat limited. This naturally meant that he hadn't said much to Valérie; just standing stoically by her seemed to be doing the trick, while he privately seethed.

They turned into Martin and Gennie's gravelled drive-way, where the couple were waiting, Richard having briefly called ahead. He turned the engine off and sighed. Valérie placed her hand gently on his knee.

'Thank you,' she said softly, her face as white as a yacht's sail.

'Thank you?' he replied. 'What for?'

'For being English and not knowing what to say, so you said nothing.'

He smiled at her, really and truly not knowing what to say. He had never seen her like this before. Normally so full of energy and verve, Valérie now looked small and frail. All those years she had mourned Edmond Masson; to then briefly have him back before being taken away again was obviously a cruel blow that had hit her hard and Richard felt a wave of guilt at his preoccupation with the fate of the 2CV.

'Oh, Valérie, you poor thing!' Gennie hugged her close as she stepped out of the car, while Martin hovered awkwardly, occasionally patting her shoulder. He came around to Richard's side of the car.

'Bad luck, old man,' he said with a low voice. 'That's going to be quite the loss.'

'Yes,' Richard replied, concentrating on Valérie and her ghost-like fragility. 'I'll probably buy another one when the insurance pays out.'

Angela, Olivia and Roddy wandered slowly over from the *boules* piste, nervously preparing their condolences.

'I suppose they'll definitely have to cancel the tournament now?' Roddy's freckled face, his eyes squinting in the bright sunshine, couldn't quite hide a note of hope in the question.

'Absolutely not!' Angela retorted. 'I didn't know Monsieur Masson very well, but carrying on is what he would have wanted, I'm almost certain of that!' She did indeed look very certain on the point, her cheeks flushed at the very idea of a cancellation.

'I think we must go ahead as planned,' Valérie said weakly. 'I do not think Edmond was acting alone.' She left this enigmatic adjunct hanging in the air like fine drizzle as everyone pondered what she meant. Richard knew that Edmond had had an accomplice; he just hoped still that it wasn't Valérie. But if not Valérie, then who? Oriane skidded on to the driveway, her timing perfect in Richard's mind; after all it was Oriane who had brought Edmond back into Valérie's life in the first place. Richard had always thought that was out of sheer mischief, but maybe there was far more to it than that. Closely following Oriane, the Mabits arrived, too, and mob-handed with both Madame Gondard and Madame Filbert squashed into the back of their small sensible car, which Noel slotted neatly between Richard's hearse-like behemoth and Valérie's exotic roadster. They looked prim and official and Richard didn't like what he saw; the two elderly ladies had angrily furrowed brows too but with a nervous twitch or two. Oddly, Noel Mabit didn't look nervous, he even looked puffed up with civic pride, but Richard knew that Noel had been the forger all along and not Mayor Planchet at all, who was simply used as Noel's beard.

Clare then pulled into the driveway in her large SUV, taking Richard by surprise as he'd completely forgotten that she was even in France. Another surprise was that she had the Avignon Arrivistes with her: Fatouma in the front passenger seat with Philippe, Alphonse and Agathe lined up in the back.

'This lot were in the café when Noel told everyone the news,' Clare said breathlessly, clearly enjoying the excitement of it all and with difficulty lifting Agathe's walking frame out of the boot. 'I said I'd bring them over; they're worried the tournament might be called off.'

Gennie looked troubled at the unexpected arrival of so many people. 'I don't think we have enough biscuits,' she said wanly, before snapping into action. 'Martin! Get out the good china!'

Clare, after giving Valérie and Gennie a warm hug, though cleverly avoiding Martin, followed Gennie indoors while the others gravitated towards the *boules* piste and the attendant dining furniture. Valérie kept herself apart from the group and Richard joined her.

'Is there anything I can get for you?' His shadow fell upon her and she looked up at him from the low stone wall she was sitting on.

'Your forgiveness, Richard, would you give me that?' Her voice was quiet, but determined all the same. There was little doubt that she was in shock, but she was angry too. She had been taken in and wasn't used to having to admit to that kind of weakness.

'Maybe you wanted to be taken in by the man.' His own voice matched her quiet tone. She looked at him in confusion.

'He *was* Edmond, Richard. There is no doubt of that, but he was not the Edmond I remember. The honourable, honest man that I married.'

'I see,' he replied uselessly.

'Maybe he changed after thinking we had abandoned him. I do not know. Now, I never will.' She stood, a slight hint of the old Valérie returning in her proud posture. 'You were right all along and I didn't believe you, Richard, I am sorry for that.'

'You really don't have to apologise for anything.' He blushed.

'I think I do.' She took a deep breath, flashed a smile and appeared to be on the verge of saying more. Whatever it was, she changed her mind mid-thought. 'Well,' – she shrugged – 'that is that.' She walked towards the *boules* piste leaving behind a confused Richard, who sat down slowly. He could almost understand how cold one would have to be in the secret service, not to get too emotional over the loss of a colleague even in the most violent fashion. But Edmond was her husband after all and she had just brushed his death aside like the crumbs of a baguette on her lap.

Richard would like to have given this theme some more thought, though he'd probably have concluded that if anyone could get over the loss of a husband then

Valérie d'Orçay had certainly had the practice. This was even, of course, the second time with Edmond himself. His thoughts were interrupted by an angry voice that he immediately recognised.

'I know it's earlier than we planned…' The voice was just around the corner from where he sat, trying to keep its temper and didn't like being interrupted. 'Look, I know! But we don't have a choice, do we? Just get them back where they were mate, asap, all right?' He was interrupted again, and Richard heard the footsteps crunch away a few metres. He knew exactly who it was, but felt compelled to have his eyes confirm what his ears had heard. He dared to peek around the corner. 'Listen, sunshine, if you don't put them back today, and I mean today, I lose everything. And you know what? If I lose everything, you'll lose even more!' An angry hand slammed into the wall. 'Am I making myself clear? Put them back, and do it now, right?'

Richard ducked back quickly before he was seen while the current Duke of Anglethorp Spa, Marquess Shireholme, seventh Baron of wherever marched back to the *boules* piste. Just what did he want put back? Surely the answer to that had to be a couple of Turners?

Richard sat down again. This was all getting very confusing. It seemed like he was surrounded by a whole gang and that Edmond's demise had only hurried things up.

'Monsieur Ainsworth.' Madames Gondard and Filbert now stood above him, interrupting his thoughts. It was the formidable Madame Gondard who spoke after what she thought was a surreptitious nip from a small bottle hidden in her bag. 'Monsieur Ainsworth,' she repeated, making sure she had his full attention. 'It seems that we might owe you an apology.'

Despite being somewhat distracted, Richard had strong opinions on apologies and the ones that contained the words 'seems' or 'if' were non-apologies in his book. They weren't an actual admission of error at all but instead just claiming some sort of misunderstanding. Even so, he had to concede that for a French woman of advancing years to offer up even a non-apology apology was surely something of a first. No wonder Madame Gondard needed some Dutch courage.

'Yes, we may have been wrong about you,' she said, her words ever so slightly slurred.

'Well,' Madame Filbert interrupted. 'Wrong may be taking it too far. We weren't in full possession of the facts at the time.'

'Ah, yes, quite. Apparently though, it looks like you were correct, monsieur.'

'Was I?' Richard, his mind a muddle, had no idea what they were referring to.

'Yes. We have just been informed that Commissaire Lapierre has closed the case.' Madame Gondard took another nip.

'Edmond Masson was indeed the murderer,' her friend stated.

'As you suggested.'

They paused. 'We're very sorry,' they said in unison.

'Most unfortunate,' Madame Gondard concluded.

'We all make mistakes.' Richard was back to thinking about Roddy. The Commissaire had acted a little too quickly. Richard was convinced that Edmond was guilty, why else run? But he certainly had an accomplice and Roddy looked favourite for that title now, though it was becoming a crowded field.

'You just cannot trust anyone these days.' It was Madame Gondard who seemed to be thinking aloud.

'I know!' Madame Filbert agreed. 'A war hero too! If you hadn't chased him away like that, Monsieur Ainsworth, well... I dread to think.'

'He might have murdered us in our beds!' The look on Madame Gondard's face made it quite clear that she might have enjoyed at least part of that experience.

'Saint-Sauver needs people like you, Monsieur Ainsworth.' Madame Filbert looked like she'd been on the homemade hooch as well and was now in speech-making mode.

Richard, however, wasn't really listening. Instead he was now watching Roddy and Oriane in the distance, their body language awkward, almost coy; flirting had its rituals and traditions though and they were definitely in teenage mode. Again the thought came to him: *was she in on it too?* He was vaguely aware of the two women still babbling at him and he tried to re-focus.

'So, Monsieur Ainsworth, would you do us the honour?'

Richard stood up and smiled warmly. 'Of course,' he said, 'I'd be delighted, now if you'll excuse me, *mesdames*.'

'Thank you!' Madame Gondard clapped her hands in childish delight. 'It is about time our little town had a mayor that is actually visible and does the job.'

Richard stopped in his tracks. 'Sorry, what did you say?'

Chapter Thirty-Three

'Richard, I am afraid we are needed.' A downcast Valérie had appeared at Richard's shoulder. Previously 'we are needed' might have been because together they could solve a puzzle or a murder, be a team at least. Unfortunately though, she was holding two sets of *boules* in leather sacks that looked like tubular pencil cases, the prospect of the 'silly' game compounding her grief. Richard, however, had his own problems and though he turned towards her he was momentarily unable to speak.

'Leave it with us, monsieur. I was the former mayor's *femme de ménage*. I know some tricks of the trade.' Madame Gondard tried to tap her nose in conspiratorial fashion, but somehow missed. The drink was taking its merry toll.

'Are you OK, Richard, you look like you have seen a ghost?' Valérie briefly forgot her own problems and showed genuine concern for her ex-business partner.

'Those women want me to be mayor!' he wailed, unable to remove the sense of injustice from his voice.

'But that is an important position of responsibility, no?'

'Exactly. Who in their right mind wants that?' Richard could feel the colour draining from his face just at the thought of it.

'Well.' Valérie put on her most comforting voice. 'It is a vote, so you are not likely to win that.'

While on the one hand grateful for the reality check that becoming mayor of Saint-Sauver was unlikely due to the electoral process and probably his sozzled backers, it was still vaguely insulting that his winning such a vote was considered a remote possibility. He decided to shove the small town bureaucratic call to arms to the back of his mind and concentrate on the now instead. And the now was this. Edmond Masson may have indeed been a forger of nineteenth-century art, may also probably have been a murderer and had certainly been Valérie's husband – but he didn't act alone. No one was safe then until the accomplice was discovered and dealt with. The number of suspects, however, was growing by the hour.

'You throw first, Monsieur Ainsworth,' Angela hectored. 'We've decided to lighten the mood a little and have some fun. We're playing mixed doubles.'

Richard caught Roddy's eye, which rolled at the prospect. *Yes*, thought Richard, *no doubt you have more pressing matters.*

'I will partner Richard,' Valérie said quickly, even putting her arm through his, staking the claim. A claim not lost on Clare who was serving tea with Gennie and over-pouring it while she watched.

'I will sit this one out.' Agathe Deschanel sounded exhausted as she heaved herself and her frame to the table and a grateful seat.

'In that case I will take your place,' Oriane declared and grabbed a startled, though not unwelcoming Roddy.

'And I will partner you, madame.' Fatouma approached Angela, a warm smile spreading across her face, though

Richard wondered if that was more because Angela's Turners were actually originals. He remembered Fatouma's face at the town hall when she noticed the missing paintings.

'Well, that's hardly mixed doubles, is it?' Angela seemed rather put out. 'But I suppose we are rather women heavy, what with the men dying off or injured.' Philippe Gratin gave a dramatic wail at his position now as mere observer. 'That leaves Olivia and… Alphonse, is it?' Alphonse stood from the table wearily, unhappy not to be staying at the side of the fatigued Agathe.

'Martin could play,' Clare declared. 'Then it would be boy, girl, boy, girl.'

'He's not available,' a rather demure Gennie said, appearing quietly at Richard's side and leaving him wondering if she had left her husband trussed up somewhere. 'He's sulking,' she added in a whisper.

'Is he all right?' Richard asked, never having seen Martin anything other than irritatingly jaunty.

Gennie shook her head. 'The truth is,' she began, 'this is all getting a bit much for him. All these people here, all the time and well,' she looked about, to see if she was being overheard, 'not *our* kind of people, if you see what I mean.'

Richard did see what she meant, Martin was quite simply frustrated. 'Gennie, can I ask, did you and Martin spend the evening with Fatouma last night?'

'Oh, yes!' Gennie smiled widely. 'She loves a good documentary does Fatouma.'

Richard wasn't keen on pressing that particular point. 'And you dropped her back late at René's?'

'Very late. She and Martin were talking all hours. He even carried on as he walked her to the door. He's such a gentleman!'

'And did you see anyone else around at that hour?'

Gennie thought about it. 'Come to think about it, there was someone.'

'Really?' Richard sensed a breakthrough. 'Do you know who?'

Again, she paused to think. 'He looked like that man, you know, who was in that thing.' Richard's shoulders slumped. 'Sorry, Richard, I'm not much help, am I?'

'Never mind,' he replied, knowing it was futile to push it. 'So where is Martin then, is he here?' he asked, though immediately regretted opening himself up to the possibility of some horrifying sulk details.

'He's in that bedroom up there.' She pointed at Derek Munro's former bedroom. 'He closes the curtains and imagines himself in the centre of Amsterdam. It cheers him up.'

Richard tried hard to suppress his laughter. 'And they're that realistic?' he asked instead, remembering the curtains and the explicit street scene.

'Oh, yes!' Gennie's enthusiasm returned. 'We bought them at an auction of film backdrops and made curtains out of them. You should see our room; our curtains were used for the orgy scene in *Caligula*.' Gennie wandered off leaving Richard trying to get the image of her and Martin's private boudoir out of his head. Then suddenly a thought struck him and he sidled quickly up to Valérie who was looking disapprovingly at her set of *boules*.

'It is a silly game,' she said with typical force.

Richard ignored her though. 'Can I borrow Passepartout?' he asked, affecting an air of nonchalance. He wasn't altogether keen on the look she returned.

'Why?' she asked suspiciously.

'Oh, you know. Er, I need to get yoghurts for tomorrow's breakfast. I completely forgot!' Overdoing it by a mile, he slapped his forehead indicating forgetfulness.

'Richard, I think that you are up to something. You want Passepartout because you need the car. Where are you really going?'

'Well, I'd rather not say actually.' He avoided her eye. 'I mean, what with you in mourning and anyway, it's not as if we're partners anymore, is it?'

She put down her *boules* and picked up Passepartout, who wasn't too keen on being separated from Zsa Zsa. 'From now on,' she said quietly with only the slightest hint of threat, 'I go where he goes.'

The car made some equally threatening statement via a series of buzzes and pings, while Richard drove the three of them out of the driveway and towards Saint-Sauver, leaving behind some frustrated players. 'Right,' he said, sounding as in charge as he could, 'when we get where we're going, you two stay in the car, got it? I work alone, unlike your husband.'

He was very pleased with that last line. It was the economy of dialogue, the control and it said two things. I am a Lone Wolf, and this isn't over yet.

'It is obvious now that Edmond was guilty,' Valérie began in reply. 'I have you to thank for that, Richard, but, as you say, it is also clear that he was not working alone.

When we get to where we're going,' she repeated his line, in a tone that only increased his worry, 'Passepartout will stay in the car and I will come with you.' She turned towards him and held out her hand for a handshake. 'Is that OK with you, partner?' She didn't smile, she was perfectly serious and if pushed, he'd have admitted to liking her dialogue even more. It was pure nineteen forties noir dialogue, both his and hers. Shamus and client, man and woman, sap and femme fatale. That, it struck him with a slight depression in his mood, was exactly the problem. There was an accomplice missing, and Valérie d'Orçay, his partner in one sense, his saviour in another, was still on that list.

He pulled to a stop outside the *mairie*, the car sighing to a standstill as if resting, but feeling the need to leave some parting electronic remark before finally lapsing into silence.

'The *mairie*?' Valérie asked, a pleasing element of surprise in her voice.

'The *mairie*,' he replied confidently. 'Amsterdam taught me how to break down a wall.' There, he'd said it out loud, he only hoped that his hunch would prove correct now or he was going to look very foolish indeed, which was the main reason he'd wanted to come alone.

'But it is Wednesday afternoon, Richard. The *mairie* is closed on a Wednesday afternoon, is it not?'

The apparent innocence with which she asked the question; the implication that they would have to come back another time, was the kind of thing he would once have asked. Until he'd met Valérie d'Orçay that is.

'You're more than welcome to stay here,' he answered with the vocal equivalent of a slight swagger. She smiled at him and her eyes lit up. *Just like old times*, he thought. *Well, very recent old times anyway.*

They made their way to the back wall which Richard had scaled just a couple of nights before and where the wheelie bin still remained in its position.

'Ladies first.' He gave a slight bow as he ushered her forward, and watched in awe as, in one swift movement akin to artistic gymnastics, she scaled the wall and dropped silently on the other side. He was grateful therefore that, having gone and being out of sight, she couldn't see him struggle to get on top of the bin and then nearly fall back as he scrambled on to the coping. He landed, to his great surprise, right way up and on his feet, standing completely still as he did so.

'What is it, Richard?' Valérie whispered next to him. 'Do you think someone is here?'

'No,' he replied slowly. 'I'm just waiting to see if anything starts to hurt or fall off.'

From their vantage position behind the bushes, they could see that the *mairie* was as quiet on a Wednesday afternoon as it had been around midnight when Richard had last used the back entrance. They scuttled across the courtyard to the door, which was shuttered. Valérie reached into her bag looking for tools.

'No need,' Richard said quietly, putting his hand on hers. 'Follow me.' He led her down the back of the building towards the window, which he knew would still be open to allow the cat to come and go. '*Voilà!*' he said with a flourish and indicated for her to climb in.

Moments later they silently climbed the marble stairs towards Planchet's apartment and the vindication Richard hoped would be his. Valérie easily picked the door lock and this time showed Richard in first, who stepped cautiously over the threshold. The only thing different from his last two visits was that the ladder was no longer in place to access the loft.

'What are you looking for here?' Valérie asked, no longer bothering to keep her voice low.

'Well, firstly,' he replied, 'we need to find the ladder so we can get into the loft space.'

'And what is in the loft space?'

Richard still wasn't one hundred per cent certain of her innocence in events, but she was certainly playing her role to perfection if she wasn't. He opened what looked like a cupboard, but just found the electricity fuse box instead.

'I hope,' he replied, closing the cupboard, 'that we will find the forger's studio.'

Valérie looked at him doubtfully. 'But Henri told me that you had both searched the place and there was nothing here.'

'Ah!' He managed to inject a note of confidence, again hoping it wasn't completely misplaced. 'I think it was hidden behind a fake wall.'

He opened another cupboard door and this time found what he was looking for. Tidied behind buckets, cloths, an ironing board and various other bits of cleaning equipment was the extendable ladder. He placed it under the loft hatch and climbed, pushing the hatch cover to one side and sticking his head through.

Valérie handed him a torch. 'Well?' she asked impatiently, unhappy at not being in the lead.

'Well, I can see the wall.' Richard's voice no longer had any conviction in it as he climbed into the loft itself. It was true, he could see a wall. Red brick, perfectly pointed, impeccable in fact and therefore, he sincerely hoped, not the kind of wall usually found in a loft space. Valérie climbed smoothly in after him and stood at his shoulder, also looking at the wall.

'It does not look very fake to me,' she uttered, unable to hide her lack of faith in the project.

Richard stepped forward nervously. There was a lot riding on this now, more than just the evidence he longed to find hidden: namely, a belief and a self-confidence in his own abilities which was now make or break. He put his hands forward while turning his head towards Valérie and running his fingers along the brick. In one swift movement he grabbed a brick and tore the wall down. The curtain fell silently to the floor revealing everything that Richard had seen the last time he'd broken into the apartment.

'Ta da!' His voice couldn't hide the relief he felt that he, Richard Ainsworth, amateur sleuth, shamus, PI, had been right. He allowed himself a fist pump.

'Richard!' Valérie returned his joy. 'Brilliant!'

'Well, you know...' He allowed a boast too.

'So this is where the counterfeits are made.' She set to work looking at the tools, picking things up and examining them.

'Yep,' he acknowledged proudly. 'This is where I thought Planchet was knocking out the fake Turners, but

I was wrong.' He picked up one of the stacked paintings, and showed her the back where the signature was written.

She wasn't looking, however. 'What is this?' she asked, picking up what looked like a vice or press.

'I think that's used to attach the canvas to the mounting. Anyway, look!'

She turned and read the signature that he was pointing at. 'Mabit?' She looked at him in disbelief. 'Noel Mabit?'

'The very same!' he replied, affecting disappointment. 'I mean, what a racket!'

'So, whoever killed Planchet was meaning to kill Noel.'

'I think so, yes. Noel hid himself and used poor Planchet as a cover. So, when the murderers came looking for the original Turners and confronted Planchet, he obviously knew nothing about the whole business.' His voice dropped. 'So they, Edmond and his accomplice, killed the wrong man.'

'And all for the original of one of these paintings?' She shook her head sadly and held up the copy.

'Technically,' Richard began, 'I've been looking this up. It's not even a painting, it's an etching. Worth a fortune though.'

Valérie handed it back to him. 'It's not very big, is it?'

'No,' he agreed. 'I suppose that helps to hide them; you could slip one in a book, or even a…' He grabbed her arm in excitement. 'Hang on! I think I've got an idea!'

Chapter Thirty-Four

Once again the small Follet Valley town of Saint-Sauver gave over its eclectic mix of medieval, Renaissance and nineteen sixties breeze block streets to the usually annual *brocante*. Only this time there was even more excitement in the air than the previous Thursday. It was another bank holiday for one, Victory in Europe Day; the promised *pétanque* showdown would finally get under way, barring the appearance of municipally linked corpses, and the sun shone magnificently. There was another added edge too. There had been three deaths, at least one break-in, a violent attack, gossip, backbiting, familial support and recrimination. The atmosphere then was at fever pitch for what was essentially a large-scale crime reconstruction, and far from keeping people away as had been feared, the place was even busier as word had got around that Saint-Sauver was effectively putting itself on trial.

Richard had been there since dawn, along with the other stallholders. He had set up Planchet's stall almost exactly as it had been the week before, minus the original *buffet* dresser, however, as that was considered a macabre step too far, even for the Commissaire who had only reluctantly allowed its omission. He had insisted on a replacement though, a cheaper, more modern *buffet* different in every way from Planchet's final resting place, but with a small sign on it informing the more prurient that this was most definitely not the original murder scene dresser. Richard understood too that this was probably for the best, but he also reckoned he could have made a killing selling the original. Wisely, he kept the joke to himself.

The idea was that, exactly as the week before, Noel Mabit would again be in charge of the stall for the first hour or so. Inevitably, however, with his deep-seated need for fussy bureaucracy, he was roaming his domain issuing orders such as, 'You were at least a metre to the right last week, madame!' or 'You definitely wore a different hat, monsieur!' Eventually, the de facto mayor – Richard didn't want to contemplate any alternative – and forger kingpin was persuaded to take his position at Planchet's stall. A freed Richard then decided to break the rules and, rather than go into René's bar and have an early pastis as he had done the Thursday before, to have a wander about and check out the lie of the land. He gave 'Operative number one', as he called her – or Clare to be more specific – precise instructions on what to keep an eye on regarding Noel and began his reconnaissance.

There was a time, before Richard and Clare had moved to France, when a French *brocante* was considered to be the equivalent of just finding money in the street. He knew this because numerous expats had told him so. But not anymore, they all said, invariably shaking their head at the demise of civilisation. The locals had quite rightly cottoned on to the fact that their old rubbish, which for generations they had happily exchanged for their neighbours' old rubbish, was actually considered a gold mine by the English, steeped as they were in lifestyle television shows, high on 'shabby chic'. Bargains then, in the modern *brocante*, were a rarity, but that didn't dull the ambience; there was always hope in the air and Richard was a fan.

Briefly he allowed his mind to wander, recognising that each stall had a different story to tell. There were a number that spoke of grief, or at least a change in circumstances. One elderly lady sat behind a large trestle table which had a collection of exotically covered spy novels, a monogrammed grooming kit and men's silk pyjamas. Their owner perhaps had passed on, or maybe even run off to lead the life he clearly hankered for. Either way, the woman he'd left behind looked almost delighted by the change and was swapping lewd stories with her neighbour, a plump lady selling off an entire library's worth of po-faced dieting books and a clearly brand new with tags on juicer. She looked happier for the decision as well, laughing along while chomping on a croissant. There was a sour-faced old man across the street who was selling a variety of animal cages, all of them slightly grubby and badly repaired. On the stand next to him a youngish family had arranged a large set of young children's clothing by month, then year and also, somewhat bizarrely had a pair of adult shoes that, though shiny and in good order, were quite clearly very different sizes. An ex-hunter had a grisly collection of glassy-eyed animal trophy heads; a fox bared its teeth, some of which were missing. One sinister individual was selling an array of Samurai swords at extortionate prices and attracting only children who were rudely shooed away. The atmosphere was jolly, however, even if some stallholders were trying to sell prosthetic limbs at knock-down prices; there was a sense of anticipation hanging in the air. Something was going to happen, and Richard, possibly for the first time in his adult life, was the ringmaster.

He gulped nervously. It was time to go back to his own stall and get to work.

'You are late,' Noel Mabit complained as Richard arrived. The little man was his usual bumptious self, but he didn't know yet that he was about to be unmasked so Richard decided to let it pass without comment. Clare sidled up to him with a report on the stall's morning so far.

'No sales,' she whispered with disappointment. 'Do I have to stick around still?'

'Not at all,' he replied.

'You don't think he might do a runner?' she asked sarcastically. 'Skip town?'

Noel hadn't actually gone anywhere; in fact he was talking rather nervously into his phone. 'Of course I didn't book him!' he was saying. 'Is he here now?' His body seemed to sag with the stressful duty of it all and he put his phone back in his pocket.

'Problems, Noel?' Richard asked, affecting a friendly air.

'Apparently, before he died, Mayor Planchet actually did some work.' Richard had never heard Noel talk like that before. He sounded like he had the weight of the world on his shoulders and gave a deep sigh. 'Our late mayor booked some entertainment for our May the eighth bank holiday and failed to tell me about it.'

'Oh, how exciting,' Clare said in a voice that failed to register that excitement at all.

'A Johnny Hallyday tribute act,' Noel continued, making it sound like the town was about to be invaded by the Four Horsemen of the Apocalypse instead.

Richard thought about this and wondered if the unexpected turn of events would help or hinder his plans. It did, however, remind him to uncover the box of old records that he had put aside when he set up. The same box that he had hidden from the sun the week before, but with one new addition. He watched as Noel wandered off with Clare following comically close behind, then he waited for his baited trap to spring.

Forty minutes later he was still waiting for the trap to spring and was seriously beginning to doubt if it would spring at all. He had brusquely fended off a number of semi-interested parties, sold a wooden door handle without fittings and been hassled repeatedly by a group of children who wanted to see inside the dresser. His mood wasn't helped much by Noel Mabit constantly haranguing everyone over the town hall microphone. Go there, see this, the *tournoi de pétanque* will begin shortly and so on. What was worse than Noel, however, was the Johnny Hallyday tribute act whose voice was terrifyingly close to the real thing, so much so that Richard thought his ears might bleed.

Close to giving up the entire thing as a bad job and nipping off for a drink, he was eventually approached by Madame Tablier who was wearing her favourite Johnny Hallyday T-shirt.

'Where have you been?' he asked, trying not to sound anxious.

She looked at him as though he were an idiot. 'Watching Johnny!' she replied. 'I don't know who that bloke is, but he's very good, has the mannerisms down to a tee.'

Abstractedly she began to flip through the box of vinyl, tutting at the usual *brocante* selection of Mantovani and Nana Mouskouri records. She was joined by a similarly clad Philippe Gratin, who stood close looking over her shoulder as she flicked through the selection.

Madame Tablier sensed his proximity and turned to give him a warning growl, but on seeing his latest Johnny T-shirt she relented and they nodded curtly to each other. It was an odd gesture, Richard thought, an acknowledge-ment of mutual interest like VW camper van drivers who pass each other on the motorway.

The redoubtable Madame Tablier turned back to the records, flicking through slowly before stopping with a gasp. She snatched at the record facing her and pulled it out with a girlish squeal.

'Oh my!' she said in a most un-Madame Tablier way. 'Johnny's rock opera *Hamlet*, picture disc edition!' She held it aloft in triumph, like a hard-won trophy. Unfortunately, it gave her rival collector a chance to snatch the thing rudely out of her hands.

'Eh!' the old woman cried. 'I saw it first.'

'And I saw it second!' Gratin sneered. 'How much, monsieur?'

Richard looked at his housekeeper apologetically and said, 'Ten euros.'

It was Gratin's turn to squeal with delight as he dismissively threw a ten euro note on to the table before stealing off into the crowd.

Madame Tablier turned on Richard and growled. 'I want that back.'

Richard didn't get a chance to respond as he was collared by Angela Babcock. 'I've been looking for you, Mr Ainsworth!' she said breathlessly. 'Are you ready to do battle?'

Richard took a deep, deep breath and stood slightly taller. 'I'm ready,' he replied seriously. 'I'm ready for my close-up, Mr DeMille.'

Chapter Thirty-Five

The not-insubstantial crowd cheered loudly as the *cochonnet* hit the ground signalling the start of the match. Then, almost as one, they all grabbed on to the person sitting next to them as the makeshift stand worryingly began to shake under their raucous weight. Nonetheless, it was quite a sight. Despite there being no team officially representing Saint-Sauver – at the last minute it was deemed disrespectful – the town had turned out for the Anglethorp Spartans and their *pétanque* showdown against the favourites, the Avignon Arrivistes.

Richard hadn't considered that there might be such a big crowd and once again he swallowed nervously. Each team had their own bench, placed like football dugouts in front of the bleachers, though Agathe had chosen to lean on her walking frame as Fatouma and Valérie sat either side of Alphonse. Philippe sat just behind them, presumably to offer advice, though he was also clutching his new Johnny Hallyday record to his chest, aware that a glowering and not best pleased Madame Tablier was sat immediately behind him. The English team, aside from Richard, were also sitting down with Angela in between Olivia and Roddy. Roddy was directly in front of Oriane and dotted about in the crowd were the Mabits, Madames Gondard and Filbert, René and Jeanine, the Sharifi brothers and Clare, Martin and Gennie, who were joined by a flustered, late-running Commissaire Lapierre. 'Johnny Hallyday' was also present, even having the temerity to be signing autographs, something he was clearly enjoying. His blond 'Johnny' wig was so outrageous it looked like it might get up and leave at any moment and his enormous sunglasses reflected the match in front of him.

At the right point Richard would address all of them, the throng. He would present his evidence, filibuster any gaps in his theory and await the fall-out. At the moment, however, his palms were sweaty and his grip was off. He tossed his first *boule* and barely managed to land it on the piste at all, eliciting a synchronised groan from the audience and a stinging rebuke from Angela.

'Mr Ainsworth, if you could try and keep your mind on the task at hand, we should all very grateful.'

Richard would have normally looked to Roddy for support at this point but he was being kept busy in conversation by Oriane. His playing partner, Olivia, didn't look too impressed either though, in fact she tutted rather loudly. Clearly this was not the confident start he'd been hoping for, but he had to bear in mind that the outcome of the *pétanque* match was just about the least important thing that would happen over the course of the afternoon.

Not that you would know that from the cagey opening end that ensued. Each throw, hit and near miss was greeted with the oohs and aahs of an over-invested pantomime audience, the stress that Saint-Sauver had collectively been under for the past week finding its release in a traditional French recreation. Richard's final throw of the first end was precisely and fortunately the confidence booster he needed, nudging Agathe's *boule* to one side. A gasp of surprise went up from the audience as one of their own, well Richard anyway, was showing the pros some wrist-flicking expertise. Agathe wasn't impressed, however, and with some difficulty dragged herself and her frame away from the action. As things stood, Richard's *boule* was the closest to the *cochonnet*, potentially giving the Anglethorp Spartans an early lead. There was one throw to come and it was to be Valérie, replacing the injured Philippe for the Arrivistes. She stood in her circle, a picture of concentration and intense competitiveness and bent to throw as the crowd hushed.

A mobile phone went off momentarily puncturing the tense atmosphere and the Commissaire apologised as he took the call. Valérie crouched again and threw, but her *boule* was slightly off and Richard won the end for his team, much to everyone's astonishment.

'Your silly phone put me off, Henri!' Valérie shouted above the ensuing din; clearly she was more interested in the outcome of the match than she had previously let on.

'It was very important news!' he replied a touch defensively.

Meanwhile the crowd ignored their spat and were chanting Richard's name making him, in a brief daydream, feel like Spartacus. It was time and he raised his hands calling for silence.

'Friends, Saint-Sauverians, countrymen,' he said, not only mixing his Roman epics but behaving with an absurd level of grandeur too. He knew he was doing it though, and it wasn't entirely accidental. *When*, he thought, *would he get the opportunity to impress on this scale again?*

'He's definitely mayor material,' Madame Gondard said loudly, receiving a filthy look from Madame Mabit as a result.

'We have all been under some pressure this past week,' Richard continued, 'and it is time to put this behind us. I know the identity of the murderer of Mayor Planchet and of Derek Munro. I know the motives and I have the evidence to prove it!'

The crowd cheered wildly at this potential pressure valve release; even Valérie slowly re-took her seat on the bench. The audience noise coolly died down and was replaced by an eager silence as rapt, captivated faces stared back at Richard in anticipation. He felt like an all-powerful orchestra conductor. The one fly in the ointment from his perspective was Clare. He didn't like the look on her face at all. It was a mixture of pride and ownership. Surely she could see that this Richard, this masterful man of action, this man of the people orator and investigator was a one-off and not remotely sustainable? Even if he had it in him to do this on a regular basis, he simply didn't have the stamina. He was exhausted as it was and he'd only got the crowd to quieten down; he hadn't even started yet.

'Monsieur Ainsworth,' the Commissaire interrupted. 'Before you begin your story, may I have a quiet word?'

It was a power struggle, right there in front of an eager crowd and Richard had to shut it down like a stand-up comedian dealing with a drunken heckler. Whatever the Commissaire had to say, it could wait.

'Not just now, Commissaire,' he said swiftly. It wasn't exactly a biting censure, but it worked, and Richard decided now was the moment to begin. 'It all began in nineteen seventy-eight,' he said grandly, though he heard some sections of the crowd groan at this beginning. No doubt they feared a long story ahead and the very possibility that they would still be hearing it at the next bank holiday. 'In nineteen seventy-eight,' Richard continued undeterred, 'two young men from this town won scholarships to a prestigious art school in Paris. One was Narcisse Planchet, the other was Noel Mabit. Only Narcisse Planchet took up the scholarship, however; Noel stayed behind and married his sweetheart Monique Lafarge.'

The throng, whose hearts were melted at the romance and sacrifice of it all, cooed and ahhed in the couple's direction. The couple themselves went bright red, though Noel managed a rather weak *merci*.

'At least, that's what we were led to believe!' Richard punched a fist into the opposite palm for emphasis, something which he felt sure he'd seen lawyer James Stewart do in *Anatomy of a Murder*. 'In fact, Monique Lafarge was the sweetheart of Narcisse Planchet and when he returned after just a few months, he was heartbroken to see that Noel Mabit had taken his place. And so began a lifetime of cross and double-cross, pretend servitude and ruination!'

If pushed he had no idea where these words were coming from, nor if they were even entirely on the money, but they roughly fitted the facts as he knew them and he was building the tension in classic, courtroom drama style. He decided to continue before someone asked a question.

'Saint-Sauver has been at the centre of an art forgery and smuggling operation for decades,' he explained, now pacing as he did so. He expected a few grumbles at this apparent stain on the town's reputation, but instead it received a polite smattering of applause and even one hearty cheer. Civic pride is civic pride even if that pride is based on illegal activity. 'The original town-twinning between Saint-Sauver and Anglethorp Spa was set up by the thirteenth Duke of Anglethorp, the current duke's father – though we'll come to that later – and the late mayor. They both had an artistic background,' he carried on quickly before Angela or Roddy could interrupt. 'In fact, specifically, they both loved the work of J.M.W. Turner.' He paused while some people had it explained to them who J.M.W. Turner was. That's when he noticed the look on Valérie's face. There was the same kind of pride that Clare was showing, which quickened his heart to almost dangerous levels, but there was something else too. It was worry and he could see also that her brain was working overtime on what might be the fall-out from these revelations. Well, he concluded, he'd deal with that when it came.

'J.M.W. Turner, though, was more than a mutual enthu-siasm,' he carried on, raising his voice a little to re-focus the crowd. 'The Duke had original Turners and our mayor, the artist, had the skills to reproduce them. Several copies would be made of each painting or etching before the original would be donated to galleries. The copies would then be sold to secretive buyers who were told that they now owned an original Turner and that the galleries had the copies.' He looked into the eyes of his hooked spectators. 'It was foolproof,' he intoned dramatically. 'The authenticity could not be questioned nor could they be sold on without risk of being found out.'

The Commissaire now stood up and made it clear he wanted to say something. Whatever it was, Richard talked over him. 'How did they smuggle the art around the world? I'm glad you asked that, Commissaire!' Lapierre shook his head and sat back down. 'With the help of none other than Johnny Hallyday!' The fake Johnny Hallyday seemed to take this rather personally and threw up his hands in disgust. He wasn't the only one either. Just a few days ago much of this crowd had believed Richard to have defamed an invalided war hero; that was bad enough. But to suggest now that the late and beloved icon of the French nation, Johnny Hallyday himself, had been involved in art forgery, multi-million euro scams and smuggling was too much for some and they reacted angrily, shouting their displeasure. Predictably it was Philippe Gratin who led the calls for Richard to be publicly flogged.

It was exactly as Richard planned. He approached the standing Gratin who, with his one un-plastered fist, was gesturing violently while under the other arm he loosely held his new record. Richard grabbed it off him, took out the sleeve and slowly revealed a Turner etching hidden inside.

The crowd went silent as Gratin, white-faced, sat heavily back down.

'Can I have my record back now?' asked a concerned Madame Tablier.

'I have nearly finished,' Richard said quietly, overcome with a wave of fatigue.

'Richard, this is just marvellous!' Clare couldn't help herself.

'You're on fire, old man!' Martin joined in, before Gennie led a thunderous round of applause.

Richard signalled that there was more to come. 'We know that Edmond Masson travelled the world, and we know that the Avignon Arrivistes travelled the world also. They were part of a wider network, but they were overcome with greed. It wasn't enough for them to simply handle the copies, they wanted the originals as well.' He sighed. 'They pursued Narcisse Planchet who they *believed* to be the forger, and when he would not, or *could* not tell them where the originals were kept, they killed him. A tragedy.' The crowd bowed their heads. 'Poor Derek Munro was similarly fated,' he said, holding his jacket lapels like Charles Laughton in *Witness for the Prosecution*. 'Derek was a fantasist. He believed he was an undercover policeman and made up stories about the people around him. Unfortunately, one of his fantasies was too close to the truth and he couldn't be allowed to spread it any further.' He bowed his head and the audience, en masse, did the same. 'And so,' he began solemnly, 'the late Edmond Masson was a murderer, turned insane by torture and what he believed to be injustice at his treatment. Gennie, it was Edmond who smashed your terracotta pots; they reminded him of his time in Africa where he was forced to work in a quarry. It kind of stuck with him.'

'Poor man!' Gennie cried. 'Apart from the murdering bit obviously.'

'And the Turners aren't even here,' – Richard paused, raising and pointing his finger – 'are they, Roddy?'

There was a gasp from the crowd. 'No,' a contrite Roddy said quietly. 'Sorry, old girl.' He turned to Angela. 'I wanted to get them cleaned up for your birthday. I know a chap, you see?'

'Ha!' Richard wasn't to be put off. 'A likely story. They were removed from the *mairie* only recently, right under the nose of the real forger! By Philippe Gratin, who smuggled etchings via his record collection and then deliberately broke his own arm to give himself an alibi!'

'It is not true!' Gratin wailed. 'Someone attacked me!'

Again, Richard raised his finger in accusation and was about to deliver his charge with a final flourish when Valérie sprang from her bench, grabbed Richard in a tight bear hug, which even if he'd wanted to he couldn't have freed himself from, and loudly shouted, 'Brilliant, Richard!' She continued in a whisper. 'It's too dangerous, not yet.' Then, as a confused Richard pondered her words, she shouted 'Brilliant!' again and the whole crowd erupted in a thunderous ovation.

Chapter Thirty-Six

Richard had always been of the opinion that control, whether of emotion, future, fate or situation, was much like a bar of soap in the shower. The minute you think you have everything in hand is the exact same moment the thing shoots out of your grasp, making you look clumsy and inefficient. His current predicament was doing nothing to dissuade him of that viewpoint. If recently he'd had some semblance of control over proceedings then that baton had now passed to Valérie, who was addressing the bleachers directly, and he wasn't too keen on what she was saying. It was a mixture of citation and eulogy and he felt distinctly uncomfortable.

'Ladies and gentlemen,' she said, 'we owe this man an enormous debt of thanks!' The crowd cheered in response, but he couldn't help feeling it was all a bit premature. He hadn't yet revealed Noel Mabit as the real forger, nor wrung a confession from Philippe Gratin or hinted at the involvement of Fatouma Dembele or unmasked Roddy as a fake duke. The thought struck him that the infernal woman may even be jealous and wanted to cut short these revelations as it took the spotlight away from her. What she was saying, however, didn't fit that particular theory at all, and the audience were lapping it up. Even 'Johnny Hallyday', despite earlier concerns, was leading them in a chorus of '*Car C'est un Bon Camarade*', the French equivalent of 'For He's a Jolly Good Fellow'.

It would have been churlish then to dampen the atmosphere, but there were questions that needed to be asked. 'What's going on?' he said to Valérie through a politician's rictus smile.

'Let me explain,' Valérie replied, but not as a whisper, rather as a call to the crowd who quietened back down allowing her to speak. It was clear from their faces that they would hang on her every word too, as would Richard who, while secretly revelling in the attention, had pretty much no idea what was now going on. 'Monsieur Ainsworth,' she began, 'the nations of France and Mali owe you a significant debt!' Again the crowd cheered and he noticed also that the expressions on the faces of Clare and Madame Gondard looked uncomfortably similar, in that they both appeared to have designs on his future. Valérie continued her story. 'This man,' she pointed at him, almost accusatorially, 'deliberately put himself in the firing line, acting as a lightning rod for your anger, guiding your eyes to a false suspect so that the authorities of both France and Mali could lure the real culprits into a trap!'

The cheering was now so loud he half-expected a marching band to come trooping past and complete the scene.

'I did?' he asked her quietly.

'Yes, you did, Richard. You were brilliant!'

He waved regally. He had no idea why, but then he had no idea he'd been a vital cog in an internationally cooperative gang bust either, so he might as well enjoy the moment.

Fatouma approached him from the team bench, her arms wide and for a moment he thought she might attack him, as he'd nearly revealed her as one of the smugglers. She hugged him instead. 'Our nation thanks you,' she said emotionally.

'Oh, you know…' he stammered in reply.

Fatouma turned to the crowd. 'Some of you may know the story,' she began, the audience once again on the edge of their seats. 'In two thousand and thirteen, the priceless libraries of Timbuktu were ransacked by fleeing Jihadi forces, before the Malian and French armies liberated the city. Many of these ancient manuscripts have been scattered around the world by smugglers and collectors. Many more have been copied, before being handed back as the real thing.' The crowd began to talk among themselves, telling each other what they thought they already knew of the situation.

'There's a famous documentary!' It was Martin who spoke the loudest and he stood up to add his tuppence. 'Absolutely fascinating stuff about how UNESCO is trying to repatriate the libraries. The best one was called *The Bad-Ass Librarians of Timbuktu*.' He sat down before standing straight back up again. 'I just stumbled across it on a quite different Google search,' he added, getting a round of applause before retaking his seat and receiving a kiss on the cheek from Gennie.

'So it wasn't Turners, then?' Richard again asked Valérie quietly as Fatouma continued her historical explanations to the audience.

'No, Richard, it was not the Turners.'

He shook his head. 'But there are definitely Turner copies in the loft, signed by Mabit, and I heard Roddy saying the originals must be put back!'

She smiled at him like a teacher to a pupil who was putting in a level-par solid effort. 'I think this Roddy actually was having the original paintings cleaned as a surprise for Angela. They are very close.'

'But he's not even the real duke! He looks nothing like his parents.'

Richard nodded theatrically towards Roddy and Angela who looked wildly confused by what was happening around them.

'I think he looks a little like his mother, no?' Valérie asked suggestively.

'Well, no. I mean his mother...' He stopped. He saw it now. 'Yes,' he agreed. 'The eyes and a little of the hair colour.' He was momentarily deflated before remembering the Turners.

'So, why *are* there forged paintings in the loft and why are they signed by Mabit?'

'I think that was the mayor's hobby, the Turners, but because they are not really very good, he signed them as Noel Mabit. He hated Noel, I think. He loved Monique Lafarge and Noel had stolen her from him.'

'And Noel felt guilty enough to work for him as he did?' She nodded. 'You just never know, do you?' He scratched his head. 'I found a letter that old Planchet must have written pretending to be Noel, an apology for marrying Monique.'

She looked at him. 'Where did you find it?' she asked seriously.

'It was in a calligraphy set that René bought at the first *brocante*. René said it reminded him of a set that belonged to an old money forger he knew in Paris years ago. Hang on...'

'Yes, Richard. Planchet was a forger of the Timbuktu scripts. The late duke, Roddy's father, supplied the original texts while pretending to authenticate them.'

'Are you sure it wasn't Turners?'

She looked at him with some sympathy, but carried on. 'Mayor Planchet also copied the design of ancient gold coins. Listen.'

They turned their ears towards Fatouma. 'Mansa Musa was the wealthiest man in the world in the fourteenth century, but he gave away millions and millions in gold before the Malian Empire finally collapsed. It is rumoured that some of this gold still exists today.'

'So why kill Planchet if he was needed for his skill? That doesn't make sense to me,' Richard whispered to Valérie, looking for an explanation.

'Because he had become a liability, Richard. That's how Edmond came to know of him.'

'So I got something right then!' he said morosely, before apologising for his tactlessness.

She shrugged and carried on. 'There were rumours that some coins had surfaced with the famous Catalan Atlas of the world on it. The map shows this Mansa Musa holding a gold coin.' Valérie held one up as an example.

Richard took it from her and picked out one exactly the same from his own pocket. 'I don't want to say you've been had,' he said, 'but these have been flooding out of Jeanine's *boulangerie* for a few weeks now.'

Valérie smiled. 'I know. Monsieur Planchet was working on these coins for a criminal organisation, but as you know he was a heavy drinker. I think his *femme de ménage* found the coins to buy his groceries when he wasn't able…'

'Madame Gondard!' He had difficulty keeping the name quiet.

'She looked after him in his apartment while Noel Mabit looked after him in the office. All the man could do was forge, he could do nothing else.'

Fatouma was still explaining about the scripts and the gold, so Richard pushed for more information. 'So, this gang gets wind that some of the coins are out and they send Edmond to put a stop to it?'

'It certainly brought Edmond here, from Mali, yes, and others. Someone threatened the mayor at the dinner when both teams arrived. Planchet then did what he always did when he wanted to hide from the world. He took Madame Gondard's homemade alcohol and went to sleep in the dresser.'

'She poisoned him too!' Richard was feeling like he was literally dodging a bullet by not allowing her to put him up for mayor.

'No, Richard, she did not poison him. In his panic, he drank the wrong bottle and died of a heart attack.'

Richard shook his head. 'And this got Edmond so riled he stabbed the poor man in the neck with a pen.'

'Edmond stabbed Mayor Planchet in the neck with a pen,' she confirmed coldly.

'Well, with all due respect to your dead ex-husband, that wasn't very smart was it? That got the police involved and meant he couldn't leave without raising suspicion. Without the pen theatrics, it would have been put down to misadventure and everyone would have gone home.'

She smiled at him and nodded.

'Listen, I am very sorry to interrupt.' By the tone in her voice Agathe Deschanel was anything but sorry and she heaved her walking frame with difficulty across the piste. 'Are we playing *pétanque* or aren't we,' she began, 'because whatever Philippe Gratin and Fatouma were up to in their spare time has absolutely nothing to do with either myself or Alphonse?'

Commissaire Lapierre stood and walked down from the stand; in his hand was a bag and he brandished its contents: a wide selection of Johnny Hallyday records.

'Why have you taken my Johnny records?' An outraged Philippe Gratin stood and angrily addressed the policeman. Lapierre took one of the LPs and removed the disc and sleeve. But it wasn't a sleeve at all. It was an ancient-looking sheaf of paper covered in ornate symbols and Arabic script.

'The ancient documents of Timbuktu!' Martin shouted.

'I hope they haven't scratched my records,' Gratin wailed, 'some of those are worth upwards of seventy euros!'

'What is going on now?' Agathe Deschanel looked like she had had quite enough of this nonsense and briefly let go off her frame. It was Fatouma who grabbed her just in time before she fell. 'Thank you, my dear,' the old woman said gratefully. Fatouma smiled and sat Agathe back down next to Alphonse who held her hand. Then the Malian *pétanque* ladies' world champion and undercover UNESCO operative removed a rubber stop from one of the walking frame legs and, before an astonished crowd, watched as gold coins came tumbling out of the hollow frame.

Once again the audience gasped, then cheered, then applauded really quite politely, not noticing that Alphonse Berlioz had stood up and dragged Agathe with him. 'Nobody do anything silly,' he shouted, 'or the old woman gets hurt!' His eyes were aflame with anger and, Richard suspected, fear but he also had a gun, produced suddenly from his *boules* pouch. 'We're going and no one's going to follow, understand?'

'Alphonse?' Agathe cried. 'What are you doing?'

'Shut up!' he said. 'Do you really think I like this silly game, being your secretary? Do you?'

'But, but you have made us, it, into a world sport,' she wailed. 'I don't understand.'

'I made an international network.' He smiled cruelly. '*Pétanque* was just the vehicle I needed.'

'Leave the old woman,' the Commissaire said calmly. 'You can go, but alone.'

'She's coming with me! And I'll take that car there!' The crazed man pointed at Valérie's replacement car.

'That'll be a bit awkward, I'm afraid.' Richard was hoping his interruption would buy some time for at least one of the agents, policemen and bounty hunters to get involved physically and stop Alphonse. 'You see the dog ate the key and it hasn't actually emerged just yet.'

A brief look of confusion and disgust came across Alphonse Berlioz's face and it was just the opportunity someone needed. That that someone happened to be fake Johnny Hallyday who knocked Alphonse to the ground with his microphone pretty much summed up the morning and in doing so, his ridiculous hairpiece fell off, stunning the crowd into silence, and then they all roared in applause once more.

Chapter Thirty-Seven

'How very clever of you, Richard!' Clare was in her element handing out cocktails back at the *chambre d'hôte*. 'Fancy you being brave enough to put a target on your own back just for some old books and coins. You really are not the man I married at all.' She meant this last sentence as a compliment, which also meant that it was a partial insult too. For his part, Richard was sitting on the outdoor lounger in between Valérie and the Commissaire, while Fatouma looked through her haul of Timbuktu manuscripts. He had a scowl on his face that he felt would probably never leave him.

'Was there no other way of pretending to disappear without blowing up my bloody car?' He'd been a mass of frustrations and grievances since an unrepentant Alphonse Berlioz had finally been taken away. Now, sitting opposite an eyepatch-less and limp-less Edmond Masson, who was casually sipping on a cocktail of his own, his frustration got the better of him. And in what he considered to be a fairly full list of affronts including stabbing an admittedly already dead mayor with a ballpoint pen, the car was right up there. If the state was willing to overlook the one, Richard certainly wanted justice for the other at the very least.

'It was Valérie's idea,' Edmond replied breezily, not realising that this wasn't going to do anything for Richard's deep, possibly terminal, sense of persecution.

'I tried to tell you, but you would not let me speak.' The Commissaire seemed genuinely put out on Richard's behalf. 'Just as you were starting, I had a call from forensics; there was no body in the car.'

'No physical body maybe,' Richard retorted, 'but that car had a soul!'

'Oh, Richard! Never mind that nasty old thing!' Clare interrupted, placing a drink down for Valérie. 'We'll get something brand new with all the whistles and bells.'

Richard caught Valérie's eye and his mood darkened even further. As far as he was concerned, things hadn't turned out terribly well. 'So, let me get this straight.' He put his glass down slowly, deliberately edging up the drama, then looked from Edmond to Valérie. 'You two used me almost as some kind of bait, so while I was breaking, entering and being generally shunned by the community, you two could just carry on regardless.'

They all looked at him – Clare, Valérie, Fatouma, the Commissaire, Edmond, still in his Johnny Hallyday denims, and even Passepartout. They understood precisely what he meant, but not why he was so upset by it.

'Richard.' Valérie put on her softest voice. 'We really could not have done it without you.'

'But you might have told me!'

'If we had told you, you would not have played the role so convincingly.' Valérie was pouring on the charm. 'You are too honest, Richard, too genuine a human being.'

He shuffled uncomfortably in his seat. 'Yes, well.' Frankly he hadn't finished being hurt yet, and the compliment rather took the wind out of his sails.

'She's right, darling,' Clare strategically intervened. 'Look at you, you can't even take a compliment without turning red.'

Everybody laughed except Richard, who eventually joined in with a false chuckle, which nobody was fooled by and therefore proved the point.

'So who knocked me out then?' he asked, putting a swift end to the jollity.

There was a pause. 'That was I, Richard,' Edmond said, with a hint of genuine apology. 'I really was worried about you, putting yourself in danger like that searching Derek Munro's room.'

'So you hit me to keep me out of danger?' He made a point of rubbing the back of his head. 'You couldn't have just said, "Excuse me, Richard, but you might be in danger?" Not your style I suppose?' There was an awkward silence. 'It strikes me, no pun intended, that you were the danger and by putting me in the position of town pariah, you rather hung me out to dry.'

'Which is why I sent Oriane to keep an eye on you!' It was clear Valérie had had quite enough of Richard's woe-is-me attitude to things.

'And what a terrific job she did, getting banged up for assaulting a police officer.'

'It's true,' Edmond admitted. 'She can be impulsive.'

'I'll say! Where is she by the way? I thought she'd be here giving Passepartout an earful.'

'Oh, that was all made up!' Valérie giggled nearly sending Richard's dudgeon so high it could count as a satellite.

'Madame Moulin is moving to Anglethorp Spa.' The Commissaire at least seemed relieved at the news. 'She is to become a duchess.'

Richard shook his head in disbelief. 'Well, God help the British aristocracy is all I can say.'

Everybody took a drink at the same time, trying not to say anything that would set Richard off again.

It was Fatouma who spoke next. 'We really are so very grateful, monsieur,' she said, raising her glass. 'These scripts are priceless, not just to our nation, but to the world.'

This had a soothing effect on Richard's wounds and for the first time since returning home, his scowl softened. 'It was nothing,' he said, turning red again.

'Literally,' Clare pointed out archly.

Richard ignored her. 'So neither Agathe, with her increasingly heavy walking frame, nor Philippe Gratin had any idea he was smuggling these things, then?'

'That is right.' Edmond nodded. 'Everywhere the team went, Alphonse Berlioz would suggest a *brocante*; sometimes he would say it raises funds and interest. Really, he knew that Philippe would always, always buy up any Johnny Hallyday records he found. Then later, Berlioz would add his copies to the record sleeves.'

'You see,' Valérie said, 'why else have the number three men's player. He was Alphonse Berlioz's cover.'

'So who broke his arm, then?' Richard was glad Clare had asked, but he hadn't a clue.

Fatouma smiled. 'It wasn't really broken, he bribed a nurse at the hospital. The rearranged *pétanque* game was to be played during the *brocante*; the original fixture was to be on a different day.'

'And he was so obsessed with his collection, he faked breaking his own arm?' Clare wasn't the only one who found this difficult to swallow.

'He did say it was you, Edmond,' Richard stated quietly.

'Oh no! That is not my style at all.' He didn't wait for any response. 'Valérie, could you take me back to Martin and Gennie's, please? We need to collect our things.' He stood up, not taking no for an answer, and the Commissaire and Fatouma, who offered another awkward onslaught of gratitude, left with them.

Richard watched them all go, trying to hide his low spirits. Would he even see Valérie again now that she was properly reunited her with her husband? He'd even miss Passepartout, who had finally returned the car key and didn't look to be pining for the temptress poodle, Zsa Zsa. He hoped they would both come and say goodbye at least.

'Poor Richard,' Clare said, sitting down next to him. 'I think you should be very proud of yourself though. You solved *a* case, just not *the* case. You sort of showed your workings in the margin, so to speak.'

He thought about this. Any decent detective, investigator, sleuth, whatever he was in this instance, would probably have seen through the terracotta nonsense immediately. It was true what Clare said, he had solved what was laid out for him to solve, but Valérie and Edmond hadn't had to work too hard to deceive him.

'Never mind,' he said, reaching deep into his English set of platitudes.

'That's the old Richard,' Clare reacted. 'I prefer the new Richard, the man of action.' She moved closer on the garden lounger. 'I think it's time I moved back in, don't you? I rather like this exciting life of danger you lead.' She leant in close to his ear. 'It's intoxicating,' she breathed.

Richard edged away. He didn't want to hurt Clare's feelings, but he knew, and not very deep down, that he could never be the man she wanted him to be. He also knew it would be a terrible idea for her to move back in. The hurt and dissatisfaction would all resurface, whereas for now, they had found some happy equilibrium, hovering as they were just above divorce. The thing was, in his mind, how to tell her.

'I don't think it's a very good idea, Clare,' he found himself saying. 'I mean, obviously, it's your house as much as it is mine but, honestly,' – he sighed deeply – 'I'm not really that man. I'm not a man of action. I don't even want to be one. You're looking for something that I'm not.'

'You see?' she replied quietly. 'The old Richard would never have had the courage to say that! Maybe you are that man.'

'We both should have had the courage to say these things a long time ago.' He smiled at her and she smiled back. 'I would just disappoint you,' he said. 'I know I'd try to anyway!'

She stood and laughed hard. 'Richard Ainsworth! Did you just quote Grace Kelly at me?'

'I did.' He shook his head. 'Just to prove a point.'

'*High Society*?'

'That's the one.'

Clare left shortly after and they both made vague promises to each other about cracking on with the divorce, but they both knew there was no hurry.

Madame Tablier appeared as if she'd been hiding and began tidying up. 'There's no guests tonight, then? No extra women you've got hidden away?'

He smiled at her own unsmiling face. 'No, madame, just us two now. I think that'll do.'

'You're staying too, then, are you?' There was a nervous edge to her voice.

Richard looked surprised. 'Of course,' he replied. 'Where else would I go?'

'Well, when you're mayor, you'll have the apartment in the *mairie*.'

Richard's heart sank. 'But even if I were to stand, I'd never win the election.' Five minutes he'd had. Five minutes without a blot on the horizon.

'From what I heard, you already put your name forward and after this afternoon's showing-off, they're calling you Mayor Landslide.'

She moved back into the salon, leaving him to his groans and with his head in his hands.

'Are you feeling all right, Richard?' Valérie had appeared from nowhere. She had Passepartout on a lead and had changed into a comfortable travelling outfit of red capri pants, a Breton shirt and red brogue-style court shoes. She had been wearing something similar, he thought, when he had first met her.

'I've been better,' he said, standing up. 'Are you two off, then?'

'Off?'

'Yes, you and Edmond. Are you going back to Paris, or Mali, or somewhere?' He really hadn't the stomach for this conversation right now.

'Well, Edmond is going back to Mali, yes. But I cannot go back to Paris because the apartment is finally sold.'

'Right. That must be a relief.' Neither of them liked or was any good at small talk.

'Not really. It is sad to see it go, you know. It was our childhood home, we grew up there.'

'Right,' he said again, 'so you share the money with your siblings, do you? I see. I didn't know you had any.'

She looked at him oddly and then eye-rolled realising her mistake. 'Just one brother,' she said. 'Edmond. Edmond is my brother.' Richard honestly felt he had been hit with a shovel. 'I am positive that I told you this!'

'Madame d'Orçay! I think I'd have remembered something like that!' Richard was utterly stunned. 'You and Oriane Moulin knew this all along? I can't believe it. I think you're carrying your work secrets just a little too far, don't you? I distinctly remember you telling me Edmond was your husband.' He threw his arms up in frustration and disgust. 'Whither trust? Whither cooperation?'

Valérie shrugged. 'Oh well, now you know.' It was possibly the most inadequate thing he had ever heard, but when he heard her next sentence he couldn't have cared less. 'This is the only home I have now, Richard.'

He shook his head as she bent down and let Passepartout off his lead. 'And there's no place like home, is there?' he said, under his breath. 'There's no place like home.'

Also available

Death and Croissants
(A Follet Valley Mystery 1)

Richard is a middle-aged Englishman who runs a B&B in the fictional Val de Follet in the Loire Valley. Nothing ever happens to Richard, and really that's the way he likes it.

One day, however, one of his older guests disappears, leaving behind a bloody handprint on the wallpaper. Another guest, the exotic Valérie, persuades a reluctant Richard to join her in investigating the disappearance.

Richard remains a dazed passenger in the case until things become really serious and someone murders Ava Gardner, one of his beloved hens... and you don't mess with a fellow's hens!

OUT NOW

Also available

Death and Fromage
(A Follet Valley Mystery 2)

Richard is a middle-aged Englishman who runs a B&B in the Val de Follet. Nothing ever happens to Richard, and really that's the way he likes it.

Until scandal erupts in the nearby town of Saint-Sauver when its famous restaurant is downgraded from three 'Michelin' stars to two. The restaurant is shamed, the town is in shock and the leading goat's cheese supplier drowns himself in one of his own pasteurisation tanks. Or does he?

Valérie d'Orçay, who is staying at the B&B while house-hunting in the area, isn't convinced that it's a suicide. Despite his misgivings, Richard is drawn into Valérie's investigation, and finds himself becoming a major player.

OUT NOW

Also available

Death at the Chateau
(A Follet Valley Mystery 3)

Richard Ainsworth's French B&B has been taken over by a production company shooting a historical film at the Château de Valençay. But everything grinds to a halt with the sudden passing of an actor under suspicious circumstances.

To get to the bottom of things, Valérie d'Orçay and Richard offer catering services to the hastily resumed production. There they discover that the vanity, duplicity and murder of an eighteenth-century French court is nothing compared to that of a twenty-first-century film set, with more heads yet to roll.

OUT NOW

Also available

Death in le Jardin
(A Follet Valley Mystery 4)

On the surface, Richard Ainsworth has life where he wants it. Middle-aged navel gazing and Olympic levels of procrastination are exactly what rural life in France should be about.

Then crisis hits his posh B&B when redoubtable housekeeper Madame Tablier is accused of murder. Even more surprisingly, it's the murder of a former fiancé, turned brother-in-law. None of which the stubborn old woman denies.

Valérie d'Orçay is having none of it and their investigation leads them to a strange tourist garden village, where backbiting, recriminations and even former colleagues provide a deadly scenario more tangled than knotweed.

OUT NOW

About the Author

Ian Moore is a leading stand-up comedian, known for his sharp, entertaining storytelling and observations. He has performed all over the world: in luxury, in war zones, to royalty, to the Russian mafia and, on one occasion, to nobody at all. A TV/radio regular, he won four out of five days on Richard Osman's *House of Games* but having failed to win the prized dartboard is still shunned by his three children.

Ian lives in rural France with his wife, children and a menagerie of animals that do as they please.

He is also the author of the critically acclaimed Juge Lombard series which began with *The Man Who Didn't Burn*, and two memoirs on life in France contrasting with life on the road as a comic, *Vive le Chaos* and *C'est la Vie*.

Acknowledgements

There was a brief fashion, in the mid-nineties, for countryside pubs in the UK to fence off a bit of the beer garden as a *boules* piste and give it over to Sunday drinkers who didn't want to go home. Bowls was considered a retirement game whereas *boules*, or *pétanque*, had a whiff of the cosmopolitan about it and became popular on a sunny afternoon. That's largely where it stayed in my head until good friends of ours, Paul and Krys, invited us to their regular Friday *pétanque* sessions, and it was definitely *pétanque*, in the French *département* of the Deux-Sèvres. It was a serious business, wonderful fun and exactly the kind of fertile ground for a cosy mystery.

As always, first thanks go to my wife, Natalie, for putting up with my moody creativity, the inevitable Diva-esque highs and lows that come with that, and for always believing in me and us.

There is a wonderful team who make this all possible too. Huge thanks to my agent Bill Goodall and all at Farrago Books: Pete Duncan, Rob Wilding, Matt Casbourne, Josie Cassaglia, Daniela Ferrante and the sales team out there getting books on shelves. It's also about time I gave some credit to booksellers everywhere, your dedication and enthusiasm are vital, not just for authors but for the world at large. Bookshops and libraries are civilised oases in a turbulent world and should be cherished. A special thanks to Abbie Headon, my friend and superb editor, who knows more about Richard and Valérie than I do!

And a big thank you to you too, dear reader. The feedback I get from people who enjoy this series means more to me than you could ever imagine.

Note from the Publisher

To receive background material and updates on further humorous titles by Ian Moore, sign up at farragobooks.com/ian-moore-signup